Worth the Wait

ALSO BY KARELIA STETZ-WATERS

Something True
For Good

Worth the Wait

Karelia Stetz-Waters

**FOREVER
YOURS**

New York   Boston

Copyright © 2018 by Karelia Stetz-Waters
Excerpt from *Something True* copyright © 2015 by Karelia Stetz-Waters

Cover design by Brian Lemus. Cover images © Shutterstock.
Cover copyright © 2018 by Hachette Book Group, Inc.

Forever Yours
Hachette Book Group
1290 Avenue of the Americas
New York, NY 10104
forever-romance.com
twitter.com/foreverromance

First published as an ebook and as a print on demand: June 2018

Forever Yours is an imprint of Grand Central Publishing.
The Forever Yours name and logo are trademarks of Hachette Book Group, Inc.

The Hachette Speakers Bureau provides a wide range of authors for speaking events. To find out more, go to www.hachettespeakersbureau.com or call (866) 376-6591

ISBNs: 978-1-5387-2703-4 (print on demand); 978-1-5387-2704-1 (ebook)

To the crazy friends who keep us sane and,
always, to my beautiful wife, Fay

Worth
the Wait

Chapter 1

Avery Crown stood on the veranda of the Vale Academy Alumni House, looking out over the Hawthorne District. Nestled under its canopy of heritage oaks, it was not nearly as beautiful as Catalina Island, where she had just spent a month in a rented villa with ostriches (at no extra charge!). And yet this familiar view filled her with a feeling she hadn't experienced in years: homesickness.

Beside her, her costar, Alistair King, lifted a flute of chardonnay to his lips. "You know," he said, "part of going to your high school reunion is *going* to your high school reunion. Get out there. Talk to them."

"I can't." Avery fingered her Bellito Bellatoni Gemstone Moments charm bracelet.

One of the reunioners hurried over, her young daughter in tow.

"This is Avery Crown," the mother said. "She's on TV."

The girl looked up with large blue eyes. "Television is make-believe," she whispered.

Her mother corrected her. "This is reality TV."

Avery knelt before the girl. "You're right," she said. "Alistair and I are real, but we're a little make-believe too." She slipped a charm off her bracelet. The little silver pony had sapphire eyes, just like the girl. Avery handed to it her. "For good luck."

The Bellito Bellatoni representative would be pissed, but that was the price of product placement. Things got lost.

"They love you," Alistair said when the woman and her daughter moved away.

Really, the Vale Academy alumni were not the *King & Crown* set. They were more Oregon Public Broadcasting. But a recent Sentinel Survey suggested that every single human being in America had at least

    a.   seen a *King & Crown* product line advertisement

    b.   bought a *King & Crown* Decorate the World travel guide

    c.   used a *King & Crown* Real-Feel Decorating Solutions product.

In trailers in Appalachia, women stored buttons in old *King & Crown* paint cans. The problem, which was becoming clear to the executives at TKO, was that more people had used *King & Crown* paint than watched the show. And another survey said that 29 percent of viewers thought the show was a spin-off of the products.

"I can't believe I'm back here," Avery said.

"We've been everywhere twice," Alistair said.

They'd been to the O'Hare Airport so many times they had the terminals memorized, and they were back in L.A. every three months to meet with TKO network's latest producers. But Portland was different. She'd been a normal teenager in Portland. It was in Portland that she'd last seen tough, beautiful Merritt Lessing—the girl she had loved in high school. Fifteen years ago. On this veranda. She remembered Merritt sweeping her short dark hair out of her eyes, shy and cocky at the same time. Merritt had been so beautiful it had taken her breath away.

"What do I do if she's here?" she asked.

"Say hello."

"And if she's not?"

"Say hello to someone else."

They had been over the possibilities so many times Alistair's eyes had glazed over, and he had propped his chin on his hand the way he did in their L.A. meetings. *This is my listening-to-you face.* But he *had* listened. He was that good.

"I was crazy about her."

Avery had spent the last month imagining their reunion: how surprised she'd act when she saw Merritt, how they'd run into each other's arms for a friendly hug, how Merritt would whisper, *I missed you, Avery.* She had spent three hours blotting and reapplying her makeup, not that it had helped. *Every woman's face:* that's what she had, the kind of face that made plain housewives think, *Oh, look, even I could be on TV.* But in her fantasy Merritt told her she looked beautiful.

Then again, maybe Merritt was still angry. The reality of how she had left Merritt had been sinking in ever since her mother and agent, Marlene Crown, had suggested Avery attend the high school reunion. Merritt had been so young and so alone, so happy to have someone in her life after all the boarding schools she had been shuffled through. The more Avery thought about it, the worse it seemed. She wanted to race back in time, fling her arms around Merritt, and tell her, *I'm sorry. I didn't mean it.*

"She hates me."

Alistair sighed. "You stood her up at prom."

"It was more than that."

"Aves, you stood her up at prom *fifteen years ago.* If she's still thinking about that, it's not your fault. She's regressed or something. You know what you're supposed to remember about prom? The first five beers."

"It's just so real being back here." Avery leaned into Alistair's massive chest. He towered over her. "Don't you think people remember things like that? That they make a mark on you?"

Alistair put his enormous (albeit beautifully proportioned) arms around her.

"What if she gets here and she rages at me? I was cruel to her. *I* would rage at me."

"If she rages, she's got more problems, and we'll get Bunter to eighty-six her before she can get two words in."

Alistair hugged her closer. She could feel the reunioners watching them. The perfect couple. All those women wished they had what plain Avery Crown and the dashing, blond

Alistair King had, not realizing that what they were looking at wasn't a romance; it was friendship.

"You've never been cruel to anyone in your life," Alistair said. "And we get a pass on everything we do in high school. Your brain hadn't grown in yet."

A squeal of "It's King and Crown!" startled Avery.

Alistair released her. He waved to a group of women by the wine bar. Avery lifted her hand reflexively.

"You didn't sleep with her." Alistair's smile was fixed in place like a ventriloquist. He knew how to whisper so that only Avery heard him, and she knew how to listen.

"I wish."

"You didn't date her."

"No."

"You were just friends who had a falling out."

"I guess."

"And you haven't seen her in the last fifteen years. She hasn't called the show? She hasn't stalked you on Twitter? Why would some woman show up at your high school re-union and try to mess with you? You're fine."

"I guess."

Avery fiddled with her charm bracelet.

"Sweetie," Alistair said, "you're the best friend I've ever had and the only costar I ever want to work with. But you are not *so* fabulous that you break people's hearts fifteen years in the past. She's fine. You're fine. And now"—Alistair turned Avery around, his hands on her shoulders—"you've got a high school reunion speech to give, and you're going to be fantastic."

A ray of sunlight cut between puffy clouds, illuminating the distant hills like a Hudson River School painting, all beautiful, unblemished Westernness. Avery took Alistair's hand and walked across the courtyard and into the school. Like a scene from some Portland indie movie—the kind she had secretly always wanted to star in and which her mother not-so-secretly thought she didn't have the talent for—she was back at Vale, once again holding Alistair King's hand, once again scanning the crowd for Merritt's dark eyes and her dark hair threaded with strands of mahogany, once again realizing it was too late.

Chapter 2

Merritt Lessing stared at her reflection in an antique French Victorian gold trumeau mirror, the patinaed glass reflecting the face of a woman who would soon be holding a plastic flute of white wine and fake-hugging women she did not remember. She turned to her friend Iliana Koslov, who was lounging in a wicker chair, her girlfriend curled up in her lap.

"I am the best friend you have ever had," Merritt said. "I was not going to go to this thing, except for you."

Merritt could be in her apartment, sipping a Sadfire Reserve whiskey and watching traffic on Burnside, but Iliana's girlfriend, Lei-Ling Wu, was desperate to meet Alistair King and Avery Crown, the honored guests of the Vale reunion. No, it was more than that. Lei-Ling wanted Merritt to talk Avery into giving Lei-Ling and her food truck a cameo on *King & Crown*. It would be an awkward request even if Avery had not been the long-lost love who had broken Merritt's heart into a million little pieces of adolescent misery.

"You"—Merritt nodded to Lei-Ling—"had better appreciate this."

"You are the best!" Lei-Ling exclaimed. "You're going to get me on King and Crown."

Merritt turned back to the mirror. Behind her, the labyrinthine aisles of Hellenic Hardware rested in the glow of the skylights. In the center of the ten-thousand-square-foot warehouse, Merritt had installed a fountain. A Grecian woman poured water into a pool. Beside it a wrought-iron gazebo sheltered a pair of white wicker chairs. The white-painted gazebo had come from a Colonial house on Cape Cod. Together the chairs, gazebo, and fountain made their own landscape. For a second Merritt imagined sitting on a bluff or in an English garden with Avery by her side. She pushed the thought out of her mind. Beyond the gazebo was ephemera, windows and doors, tubs and sinks, kitchen, and the Land of Lamps, so named by her interns from the youth shelter. Perfect, uncomplicated hardware.

"But you'll miss it if you don't hurry." Lei-Ling had been bouncing around the hardware store all day. "You have to go. You have to see Avery Crown. You have to tell her how much you missed her, even if you didn't. Tell her I am in love with her and Alistair, and they have to put me on the show. Even if it's just for two seconds. She won't regret it. They want to film Portland, and nothing says Portland like my dumpling truck."

Merritt couldn't deny that. Lei-Ling's bike-powered, Slipstream RV covered in papier-mâché dumplings kept Portland weird.

"You've been hot for Avery Crown for fifteen years," Iliana drawled. "She's a big star, and you know her in real life. Who wouldn't go to the reunion? Go already."

"I've not been anything for Avery Crown. I once said, 'Avery Crown and I should have fingered each other in high school to get it out of our systems.'"

Of course, if that were true, she wouldn't have been thinking about Avery every day for the last month, tidying the shelves of her hardware store and putting everything in the wrong place because she couldn't shake the longing she thought she'd killed years ago.

"Did you do anything with her?" Lei-Ling's eyes got big with delight. "Of course you did. She's adorable."

Lei-Ling and Iliana were adorable. They could not have made a more unlikely couple. Tall, muscular Iliana, still in her aikido gi, and tiny Lei-Ling with a rainbow stripe dyed in her hair and every single color on the RBG pallet (and gold lamé) represented in her dress and graffiti-printed jacket.

"She's straight," Merritt said. "That's the show. She and Alistair King run around the country decorating houses to capture the spirit of the city they're in and fixing dry rot."

"You'll seduce her!" Lei-Ling said, as though she had just won at Clue. *It's Miss Scarlet!*

"Straight," Merritt said again. "In love with Alistair King."

"You'd just do that thing you do at the Mirage." Iliana tossed her blond braid over her shoulder, a gesture that had always meant, *You can't fight this one.*

"I play pool at the Mirage."

"Oh, the thing." Lei-Ling nodded. "Everyone knows your thing."

"You lean up against the wall," Iliana said. "You say, 'Hey, how's it going?'" Iliana imitated a deep alto. "Then you date her for two months, ghost, and repeat."

She didn't. She wasn't the one who left, but no one seemed to notice. The last girl she had dated had text-dumped *her.* Merritt had called the girl, pushing down the lump in her throat. *You couldn't at least tell me over coffee?* The girl hadn't hesitated. *You don't care,* she'd said. *You're fucking gorgeous, Merritt. And you use it to hook people. And you're so goddamn cold.* It was like being savaged by a puppy. The girl had pigtails. She knit socks for her nieces. She'd seen *Frozen* twenty-three times. And her niceness drove the words in deeper. *You'll always be alone.* As if Merritt hadn't already known that. She wanted to stand in front of Iliana and Lei-Ling and demand, *Don't you think I want what you have?*

Merritt had thought she had it with Avery, not romantic love but a friendship so deep it erased all those nights Merritt had lain awake at yet one more boarding school, gazing out of the window above her bed, trying not to cry. And then Avery had left. Without warning. Without apology. Without one word to say that just a moment of that friendship had been important. Avery hadn't been the first to leave or the last, but her leaving threw everything in sharp relief, like the security spotlight Merritt turned on in the hardware store when she heard a strange sound. Suddenly all the familiar shapes were cold and bright and lonely. Avery was why she hadn't cried over the girl with pigtails even though she'd wanted to. Avery was the reason she knew if she started crying over lost loves, she'd never stop.

"You have a fear of commitment," Iliana added. "It's because of your parents."

"Your inner child," Lei-Ling said knowledgeably.

If someone's happy inner child sprang to life, it would be Lei-Ling's. Her parents loved her. Her siblings were kind. And she had met the perfect girlfriend long before she could get jaded about love. It was annoying, but it made Merritt want to follow her around, moving sharp objects out of her way.

"This is closure," Iliana added. "She's going to have fake breasts, plastic surgery, that kind of hair that's real but it's not real. You're going to get that body snatchers feeling, and then it'll all be over. You can stop lusting after her."

"I have never lusted after her." The lie was big enough to bring a flush to her neck.

She had lusted after Avery. She had lain awake in her dorm room bed and touched herself for luxurious minutes she could never stretch out long enough, dreaming of Avery. Then she'd felt bad for fantasizing about sweet, straight, oblivious Avery. It was probably a form of sexual harassment. When the government invented mind readers, she'd be charged with something. She could still remember the details of each fantasy. And later, when her uncle learned she was at Vale and took custody of her and whisked her from the dorm into his spare bedroom, she had hung a framed photo of Avery beside her bed and gazed at the picture for hours. Yeah, she had lusted after Avery.

"Lust can be a substitute for intimacy," Iliana said.

Iliana seemed to think dating a twenty-two-year-old waitress had given her insight into the human heart. Merritt missed the old Iliana. The old Iliana would have said, *Hit that or not. Why are you telling me about it?* Then Iliana would have pulled her baseball cap down over her eyes and sucked down a Montucky Cold Snack beer, and in her silence, Merritt would have felt Iliana's sympathy because they both knew about wanting things and not getting them. Now Iliana had Lei-Ling and throw pillows that read, LIVE, LOVE, LAUGH.

"Emotional intelligence just isn't your thing. That's why you've got us," Iliana added. "And I say if you still like her, that's the longest relationship you've ever been in."

It was a joke. Merritt the ghoster. The determined bachelor. She played along.

"Fine. I'm going." Merritt adjusted her shirt one more time, opening one extra button, a little nod to lost hope. "I'll go to the reunion, seduce Avery away from Alistair, dump her, get Lei-Ling on the show, and overcome my fear of intimacy through lust." She checked her pocket watch. "That should take an hour. You want to get pizza afterward?"

Lei-Ling giggled. She and Iliana were going to make out on Merritt's wicker chaise lounge under her gazebo, neither of which was intended for romantic purposes. The chaises were there so that customers could take selfies and tag Hellenic Hardware, so their historic-home-owning friends would come buy lintels.

"You two," Merritt said, "are disgustingly cute."

Chapter 3

The reunion organizers had set up a stage and chairs in the glass atrium that opened onto the three main hallways of the Vale Academy. Avery sat up front, like a valedictorian, rereading her speech on her phone. The class president, a woman named Olive, welcomed the group, gave a public service award, and turned to Avery.

"Next I'd like to welcome our distinguished alumni speaker."

The crowd murmured.

"Avery Crown is the star of *King and Crown*. She and Alistair travel the country fixing houses and decorating them in local style. But that's not all," the class president went on. "The *Hollywood Insider* writes, 'King and Crown sparkle on-and off-screen, their real-life romance reminding us that love isn't just in fairy tales.'" The class president smiled at Avery. "What some of you may not know is that Avery and Alistair's fairy-tale romance started right here at the Vale Academy."

The class president delivered the story almost exactly as it was published in the press kit. Avery had been living with her father in Portland but frequently visited her mother in L.A. She had met Alistair King at a Save the Children fundraiser. Although the press was clamoring for photographs of Alistair, he was mesmerized by the bubbly brunette in the blue dress. It was love at first sight. Avery was eighteen. Alistair was twenty-five. But Alistair knew he had to see her again. He took her to her prom, and they knew it was true love.

In reality, Avery had first met Alistair in the bar at the Four Seasons, Los Angeles. Like a first date for an arranged marriage, they made small talk under the watchful eye of Avery's mother and one of the executive producers at TKO. *If they offer, we'll say yes*, Avery's mother had said on the drive over. *You're not A-list. No shame. Fact.* No one expected *King & Crown* to last past the first season, but it had, perhaps because it *was* true love. It just wasn't prom-queen love.

Now Avery rose, offering a wide smile to the audience. She cradled her phone in one hand, her speech glowing on the screen.

"I love to travel," she began. "There is nothing I like more than being on the go. You know what Alistair and I say. 'Never the same port twice.'"

Speeches didn't make her nervous. She had spoken at more award ceremonies and fundraisers than her Google calendar could remember. Half the time she didn't write a speech. But she had worked on this speech for days because Merritt might hear it.

"But that doesn't mean that the places I go aren't important to me. Vale has always been so special to me. You are special."

The publicists liked it. She was supposed to look directly at the crowd while she spoke, cementing the audience connection. She wanted to speak the words to Merritt. She had imagined the moment as she practiced her speech, how their eyes would meet, how everyone else would disappear. Even if Merritt were furious, there'd be that connection. But Merritt wasn't there, and the publicity department had also decided on a .5-second quote they wanted to use for a craft adhesive commercial. Avery glanced at her phone. Here it was.

"When I think about Vale, I think about the friends I made, bonded together by memories and united by the magic glue of dreams."

Gould, the cameraman, twirled his finger to indicate *go again.* He hadn't gotten the right angle.

"I think about the friends I made, bonded together by memories and united by the magic glue of—"

Detroit MagiGlue. That was the name of the product.

Gould nodded, but another movement caught her eye. The tinted glass doors to the atrium opened. Evening light flashed across the linoleum. The door eased shut. And Avery Crown, who had chatted cheerfully while she tripped over two-by-fours and knocked over garden sheds, found she was speechless. The latecomer stood backlit by the windows. Avery knew that graceful, sullen slouch. The head bowed slightly, hands in pockets. Then Merritt stepped into a beam of light from one of the skylights in the atrium, and Avery was sixteen again, staring across the biology lab at the transfer girl sitting alone, wondering if she could work up the nerve to sit next to her. She had looked around at all the other Vale girls. They were all cool pansexuals who wore Doc Martens and snuck into shows. Avery wasn't cool then. Merritt's wry, disapproving smile said Avery wasn't cool now.

The moment lingered. The crowd shifted in their seats. Avery realized, too late, that her pause read as disapproval. *How dare you arrive late to my touching speech about glue and friendship?* She hurried through the last lines. Everyone clapped. The class president concluded, "And even more exciting news! *King and Crown* is filming their next season in Portland, right here in the Rose City!"

When Avery sat down next to Alistair, he asked, "Is that her?" his lips moving so little it might as well have been a telepathic message.

"Yeah." The word caught in her throat. After all these years, that was her.

* * *

Avery walked slowly across the courtyard, past the people enjoying the wine bar and the perfect, eighty-degree twilight. Merritt leaned against a concrete pedestal. Her short, silky black hair fell over her eyes just as it had when she was eighteen. Her dark eyes and dark hair made a striking contrast with her pale skin. She was wearing tuxedo pants, suspenders, and a crisp white shirt that revealed the lace edge of her black bra. She looked at ease in the flock of women in pastel linen suits. Just like always. A half smile played on her lips, saying, *I'm better than this, but I don't care.*

Olive, the class president, appeared at Avery's side, leading her toward Merritt.

"Do you two remember each other? Merritt transferred in our junior year." Olive fluttered a hand over her frizzy hair. "Merritt Lessing was our alumni speaker two years ago."

Merritt had always made the Vale girls nervous, and even the straight girls had looked at her at least once and thought, *Maybe.*

"The famous Avery Crown," Merritt said, leaning back a little and pushing her hands farther into her pockets. "Fifteen years." She eased off her pedestal. "It's been so long. I thought maybe you were in jail."

"Avery is the star of *King and Crown*," Olive exclaimed. "That travel decorating show. You've got to have seen it."

"Oh, I know Avery Crown," Merritt said.

She moved toward Avery. Her cologne smelled of fresh cedar.

Avery felt her heart stop. She had imagined this moment. She'd whisper, *I want you.* Merritt would brush past her ear, *I know.* The thoughts raced through her mind. Merritt stepped toward her, her arms open. One hand held her wineglass away from their embrace. The other hand touched Avery's back. Was it a caress? An inch too low, too intimate, pressing down the ruffles of Avery's dress. Merritt's cheek brushed Avery's. Her breath caressed Avery's ear. They were pressed, shoulder to shoulder. Avery was aware of Merritt's strong frame and soft breasts. Merritt had always been a study in contrasts: that runway beauty, that androgynous style, her unyielding strength, her hidden vulnerability. The touch echoed through Avery's whole body. She wanted Merritt to pull her closer. She wanted to run her hands through Merritt's hair. Fantasy-Merritt whispered, *Darling.*

Real-Merritt kissed the air beside Avery's cheek and said, "Avery and Alistair, the dream team. You look just like you do on TV. I thought all that stuff was fake."

"You watch the show?"

Avery couldn't tear her gaze away from Merritt's eyes—such a dark brown they were almost black—or from her perfectly chiseled lips, a dusky red although she appeared to wear no makeup. If she had changed as she aged, it had just made her more beautiful. Avery could look at her for hours. She had when they were teenagers.

"I saw it at the gym," Merritt said.

"What are you up to these days?" Avery asked, surprised that her voice sounded normal. A life in unscripted television had taught her not to flinch.

"I run a hardware store."

One of the women in linen cooed, "Merritt's *amazing.* My husband and I bought this *beautiful* Neoclassical house, and she oversaw the *entire* renovation. She even did some of the work for us. You can't trust a regular contractor to install Versailles floors."

You have a crush on her, Avery thought. Straight, married, probably 2.5 kids, and Versailles floors and the woman was touching Merritt's arm with every word.

"I do a little construction for special customers." Merritt shot the woman a toothsome grin that said, *I will ravage you on your Versailles floors.*

"I love hardware stores," Avery said.

"It's more than hardware," the class president said. "Everything is vintage. She was featured in *Sunset* magazine."

The president asked Avery how long she was in town. Did her father still live in Portland? Avery managed a few questions about Merritt's work. Finally, the group dispersed, and they were alone. Merritt glanced at the heavy watch on her wrist...her beautiful, slender wrist.

"Well, I'm out." Merritt gestured toward the minglers by the wine bar. "These things, right?"

"Are you going to the after-party?"

"I can only drink so much cheap chardonnay."

The moment was over. Merritt was leaving. Like a camera that pulled back to show the crew drinking coffee as they waited to do their union-approved jobs, Avery saw reality for what it was. This meant nothing to Merritt. She had been worried for nothing, excited for nothing. Merritt hadn't been pining for her for fifteen years. She was the one who was *regressed*, as Alistair put it. She was the one who had made a whole soap opera out of a hug. She looked around for Alistair's comforting smile, but his back was turned. It struck her that she might not see Merritt again after this night. She felt a wave of embarrassment, but more than that, she felt a stab of sadness, like that strange homesickness that had hit her as she had walked onto the Vale campus.

"I'm sorry I didn't Facebook you," Avery blurted. "Please come to the bar tonight."

Merritt gave her that familiar, close-lipped smile: bemused, confident. Merritt might not be in Hollywood, but she had always been on the A-list, and Avery had been a fool to think Merritt would have spent all this time (or even just a little bit of time) thinking about her.

"Only old people do Facebook," Merritt said. "It's good to see you. I knew you'd be famous. You wanted that. I'm happy for you."

And then she was walking away. Everything about Merritt's receding swagger said, *Really? You thought this was something?*

"Wait," Avery called out. "We're filming in Portland. Let's get a drink sometime."

Merritt touched two fingers to her lips, half kiss, half peace sign, then lifted the plastic wineglass. "We just did."

Chapter 4

Merritt Lessing swung up into the cab of her pickup and rolled down the window to let in the summer breeze. From the vantage of the Vale Academy parking lot, she could see all the way down to the city glowing in the twilight. She pulled out her phone. There were the usual texts. Her contact at the Western Oregon Grange Association knew a farmer who was selling barnwood. Her Realtor had scheduled an inspection for the twelve-unit apartment building Merritt was buying.

Iliana had texted, *So?*

Done, Merritt texted back.

And Lei-Ling?

Shit. The story of her life: disappointing nice women. She could disappoint her vendors occasionally, very occasionally a customer. But you couldn't disappoint the Inner Child. The karmic ramifications of coming so close to Lei-Ling's dream, and forgetting it, were huge, even if it wasn't really fair of Lei-Ling and Iliana to ask. How could Merritt stand in front of the woman who had broken her heart while she scanned the crowd for Alistair and remember to lobby for Lei-Ling's food cart with the words DUMPLING HAPPINESS Is Now emblazed across the side? Of course, she hadn't told Iliana the truth. *Should have fingered each other in high school!* She had wanted to lay her heart down at Avery's feet.

Merritt was trying to figure out a dumpling-failure excuse that wasn't quite a lie when she noticed Avery meandering through the parking lot, not really looking for a car. When she reached the far end, she paused, looking out over the city. Reluctantly, Merritt got out of her truck. Merritt did not feel the dumpling-happiness promised by Lei-Ling's food cart, but she was a good friend, even though Iliana often told her she was *emotionally reticent.*

"Avery," Merritt called out when she was close enough for Avery to hear.

Avery turned. She didn't look like the body snatchers had gotten her. Her chestnut hair flowed over her shoulders, reaching almost to her waist but without looking eccentric. Sometimes long hair said, *When I was twelve I decided I'd never cut it because I'm an elven princess.* Avery's gold-streaked hair said, *Why would I deprive the world of light?* Her brown eyes sparkled with flecks of the same gold. A sheen of iridescent glitter sparkled on her round cheeks. Who even wore body glitter at their age? But it was subtle and caught the shimmer of twilight. Merritt felt defeat wash over her. Fifteen years and she couldn't tear her eyes away from Avery.

Avery took a step toward her, looking earnest. This was going to be the awkward apology, Merritt predicted. *I'm sorry I invited you to prom, stood you up, and showed up with Alistair.* If she were shameless, she'd add, *We were just going as friends. I hope you realize that.*

Merritt stopped her before she started.

"I am going to be that person," she said. "Sorry. I am doing this for a friend. My best friend's girlfriend is in love with your show. She wants you to feature her on *King and Crown*, just like every other person in Portland. She's very cute. She wears a lot of metallic jackets. And her dumpling truck is a Slipstream RV that she's turned into something that looks like...if you could put it on a string and dangle it on camera, it would look like a really bad science fiction movie. It's quintessential Portland. There. I've made my pitch. You can say no. I promised I'd ask."

"Our field producer does all the casting," Avery said. "He pretty much runs the show."

"No problem. I have assuaged my guilt. You have a good night."

She turned to go, feeling Avery's presence behind her.

"Wait," Avery said. "Don't go."

Merritt had to turn around. Not turning around said, *I still care.* But turning around meant looking at Avery's beautiful expressive face, her rosebud lips. She looked like the silent movie stars Merritt loved. The classic picture of Mary Pickford with a kitten on her shoulders, her smile mischievous and smart. Merritt turned a second too late.

"Come out with me," Avery said. "There are people back there who hated each other. Tanya Grish and Sal Morrison? Trent and that guy who played hockey. They're hugging each other and saying how much they missed each other."

"Did we miss each other?" Merritt asked.

"I missed you."

Please don't, Merritt thought.

Avery seemed to have resolved something. She straightened her shoulders. "I'll put your friend on my show. I never ask for anything. I never push. I'll push this time. Greg will say yes. Just walk down to Hawthorne and get a cup of coffee with me. Walk down the path."

* * *

At the far end of the campus, beyond the reflecting pool and the tennis courts, was a long stone staircase that led down to Hawthorne Boulevard. They had always called it the path (like it led to enlightenment, which it didn't. Merritt was proof.) It was still there, a little overgrown but so familiar.

"Have you been back?" Avery asked.

"Once to give a speech," Merritt said.

"Why not more? It's so beautiful, and—" Avery stopped, as though remembering a few reasons why Merritt might not want to relive their high school days. "But, of course, who thinks about high school anymore? You're not hanging out at Vale."

Merritt glanced down at the crumbling steps. On the veranda, the twilight was bright, but on the staircase surrounded by tightly grown blackberries and vine maples it was nighttime.

"So, tell me about your shop." Avery touched Merritt's arm the way she had when they were kids, a gentle pat that lingered a moment too long, the kind of gesture that lesbians had to remember meant *nothing* when coming from straight girls.

"It's all vintage. We sell everything from salvaged beams to curios. And your show? How's that?"

"I love it! Alistair. Me. The crew is great. Greg is a total sweetheart, and believe me, that is not normal." Avery sounded like a nervous interviewee. "We all want to do it forever. You don't get what we have. Television's full of assholes, but not on *King and Crown*. You know, Al and I don't even have a house. We just rent in between shooting. Someplace fun. We were just on Catalina Island, and we rented this place with real ostriches!"

"Ostriches. I knew there was a reason to get famous. But don't you want a home to go back to and your own ostriches?"

"Oh, the show is home. They're my family. Sometimes I think we're a little ship floating around the country. I don't want to buy a house in L.A. and be tied down, be stuck. If I've got Alistair, we're at home."

Avery spoke quickly, as though trying to prove how easy this all was. *Look! We're, like, totally friends now!* Or maybe Avery had sensed Merritt's teenaged attraction and was trying to remind Merritt that Merritt had been the only one. Maybe, despite Iliana's accusation that Merritt hid her feelings (if she even had any), Avery could feel Merritt's attraction now, the attraction that made it impossible to look at Avery without looking too closely. Avery shouldn't have gone walking with a lonely lesbian in the lavender twilight if she didn't want to be noticed, Merritt thought.

"If I lived in L.A., I'd have to have lunch with my mother." Avery pulled a honeysuckle bloom off a passing vine, smelled it, and tossed it at Merritt. "I never want to be stuck. I love everywhere we go, but I feel free when we leave. If I could move every day, that'd be perfect. There's something about looking at everything when you know you'll probably never come back. Do you like to travel?"

Merritt remembered sitting in a coffee shop telling Avery how her mother had been single and they'd lived in a studio apartment with yellow spider plants, yellow walls, and a yellow cat. Then there was the yacht. In her memory, her mother and stepfather never courted. Her mother simply led her out of the apartment and onto the deck of the *Astral Reveler*. They set sail, and in her memory—which couldn't possibly be true—she spent days alone: just white deck and blue sky. Then she turned seven, her mother put her in boarding school, and never came back.

"Traveling just gives you more places to miss."

Merritt hadn't meant to be honest. The right answer was, *Yeah, of course, but you know . . . too busy.* It had always been easy to tell Avery the truth. She had to remember Avery had just been one of those girls who had project-friends, and everyone got sick of their project-friend. That still hurt. Merritt had had so few friends.

"Is Alistair King just as charming as they make him out to be on TV?" Merritt asked.

"Yes! I shouldn't tell you this, but Alistair's not really from

L.A. He's totally down to earth. He's from Stone, Wyoming. His dad and all his brothers were miners...are miners. He's so cute. He says we're going to do *King and Crown* until he's visited one city for every person who never got out of Stone. He cares about everyone, everything, and me too. I can count on him for anything."

"I'm happy for you." She wasn't, but it was the right thing to say. "He sounds like a wonderful boyfriend."

"Boyfriend—"

Avery's heel caught in a crack in the steps. She grabbed for a railing, but there was no railing because the stairs had been installed in 1950, when people still believed in natural selection. But Merritt had spent hours practicing aikido with Iliana. Even in the dark, she knew the exact trajectory of Avery's fall. Without thinking, she caught Avery. For a second, Merritt held her. Avery's body felt warm, her curves a perfect match for Merritt's angles. Merritt's mind went still. Her body relaxed as though she had been holding her breath for fifteen years and finally released it. Iliana would say that was supposed to happen while meditating, but meditating felt nothing like holding Avery, who was still trembling with surprise. Merritt hadn't come on this walk for Lei-Ling, she admitted. She had come so the girl she had once been could hold Avery for the moment they had never had.

And then Merritt had stood there too long. Avery's feet were back on solid ground and she was pulling away, pushing her hair over her shoulder and, saying, "I...um...so clumsy. Wow. You're strong. Do you do ballet barre?"

Avery sat down and took of her shoes. "These'll kill you." She held up the heels. "Shoes just tie you down."

* * *

At the bottom of the hill, they turned down a street lined with tall oaks and stately bungalows. Avery put her shoes back on.

"I love walking in a city, just walking and walking," Avery said.

"Don't you get accosted by fans?"

"Sure. They all recognize my hair. It's signature hair. My mother's idea. But our fans are so sweet. I get letters all the time. *Paper* letters and pictures of people's kids. It's like we're part of their lives. They watch *King and Crown* when they're sad or to get ideas for their daughter's wedding. I'm not saving the world like Alistair and his charity foundation, but I'm making people happy. There's not enough of that."

Wasn't that the truth.

They walked another block in silence. Then Avery spoke thoughtfully.

"How's your uncle?" she asked.

"He died," Merritt said quickly.

"When?"

"After we graduated."

After you left.

"Oh, you were a just a kid. I'm so sorry. How did you make it by yourself?"

"Same way I always did." *Alone.* "Uncle Oli willed me the hardware shop. I worked construction until I could make enough money to keep it in the black. Oli had let it slide. My friend Iliana moved her dojo into the back building. She works at Hellenic Hardware for free rent, and we practice together, but she says I'm undisciplined."

"I'm sorry, Merritt. I really am."

It wasn't fair for Avery to come back after fifteen years of dead silence and feel sorry for her.

Merritt changed the subject. Now that Iliana had read *The Open Communicator* she told Merritt it was a way of *deflecting pain.*

"Remember sneaking into the Vale auditorium?"

"You were such a delinquent," Avery said affectionately.

"I was a model student and an athlete."

"Lacrosse..." Avery trailed off.

"Lacrosse is a beautiful sport."

"And you were a lovely player."

"I still am." Merritt shot Avery a smile that would have melted the girls at the Mirage, not that that meant anything. "Or so they say."

"Are you dating?" Avery asked.

"Depends on the night."

"That's not *dating.* I bet there are a hundred girls sexting you right now."

Merritt shoved her hands in her pockets.

"I bet you don't even text them back," Avery added.

In the shadows of old oaks, Avery didn't look much older than she had at eighteen.

"Nobody is sexting *me*," Merritt said. "I don't give them my real number."

It wasn't true. She would never do that to a woman, although everyone joked that she did.

"So some little old lady is getting your messages? I bet her grandkids got her a smartphone so she could do Facebook and now ... lucky old lady. Do the girls take your photo while you're sleeping?"

"Creepy. I'll give them *your* number next time."

Children had drawn a messy hopscotch in chalk on the sidewalk, and Avery skipped down it.

"Remember how we used to crash the country club pool?" she asked. "You had that black swimsuit that looked like it was made out of a wool overcoat. So modest! Porn sites around the world shut down when you put that thing on. It had global ramifications."

"It was a man's suit from 1915. They didn't just go around in Speedos with their junk hanging out."

Avery had worn a cream-colored bikini. It was like she was naked, except not quite naked enough. Merritt had swum down to the bottom of the pool, looking up through the water at Avery's pale, beautiful body. She'd had to put six feet of water between them because otherwise the sight of Avery swimming in the moonlight would have broken her heart.

The street widened. They were nearing the building Merritt was in the process of buying. The Elysium. Merritt hadn't meant to walk past it, but she hadn't meant *not* to.

"This is my new project," Merritt said. "I'm closing in a week or two."

She stopped in front of the Elysium, motioning for Avery to follow her into the alcove that housed the front gate. The wrought iron revealed a central courtyard. Inside the walls shone with green lichen. Avery peered through the gate.

"A place like this shouldn't go empty. It's the deal of a lifetime," Merritt said. "Short sale. Way under market value. I had to sell my house to buy it, but it's worth it."

"Oh, Merritt. It's where your uncle lived."

It was the only place that had ever felt like home.

"Whatever. It's a building. It's a great investment. I knew about it because I lived here. That's all."

They took a few steps into the courtyard. Avery gently wrapped her hands around Merritt's biceps. "Are you trying to get me alone?"

Did Avery purse her lips? Almost? Like a kiss that turned into a smile? That was how they had been at Vale, pretending to flirt with each other and dropping sexual innuendos to make the other girls nervous or to make them laugh. The only difference was that Avery just wanted to be a *provocateur.* Merritt had wanted her for real. She still did, if she were honest with herself... which Iliana said she wasn't.

"I might if I thought it would work."

"How do you know it won't?"

"So many reasons."

"You always played hard to get," Avery said, flirting casually.

Merritt pulled out of Avery's grasp. Avery looked embarrassed.

Merritt strode over to a copper drainpipe and pulled off a

piece of ivy. English ivy looked elegant, but it ate buildings like a sci-fi monster. Suddenly, she felt her throat tighten. For all the times she had driven away from Avery's house and cried because the night would never end the way she wanted, for that night at prom, for the shame of seeing Avery with Alistair and realizing how little she had meant to Avery.

"After all these years, just don't."

She didn't speak loud enough for Avery to hear her, but a second later she heard Avery's footsteps on the gravel. When Merritt turned, Avery was standing so close Merritt had to take a step back. The wall of the Elysium stopped her.

"I'm sorry," Avery said. "I'm sorry about that night."

She held Merritt's gaze, suddenly serious. Merritt had the sense that it took all Avery's effort not to look away.

"I haven't thought about it in years." She knew Avery could see the lie.

"I was an asshole."

"We were kids." Merritt forced a smile. "You were straight. Is that why you never called me? Tell me you haven't been feeling bad about that for fifteen years. I haven't."

Of course Merritt had felt bad. She had felt bad when Avery didn't return her calls and when Avery's father told her Avery had moved back to L.A. She had felt worse when Uncle Oli suffered a heart attack and the doctors said he would make it but he didn't. She had walked out of the hospital into a summer night almost like this one and realized the only person who could have comforted her was Avery, and Avery was gone.

Avery hesitated. She looked frozen with uncertainty. Merritt had seen the same expression on young carpenters cutting expensive hardwood, as though they wanted to stop time because making the wrong cut was so inevitable and so costly.

"I wasn't straight," Avery said, her voice a gasp.

Merritt must have misheard. "You were straight. That's why you chose Alistair. You can't change who you are."

"I know."

Avery was straight. That was why she had left.

Merritt tried to joke, but it just sounded bitter. "There's a signing bonus if I can get you to play for my team."

"We're on the same team."

No! Avery was straight. She'd sensed Merritt's infatuation, and it had disturbed her. If Avery was straight, she'd left because she didn't want her best friend's lust. Maybe she was even a homophobe. But if Avery was gay, she'd simply left because every single person Merritt cared about eventually realized she was unlovable.

"You're not straight?"

"No." Avery looked like she was going to run and it was taking all the fight she had in her to stand in front of Merritt.

"Since when?"

"Always."

"In high school?"

"Since I was a kid."

"And that's why you're dating Alistair King all over television."

"He's my best friend."

She and Avery had been best friends. That's what they'd called those nights by the river when Avery had stroked her hair and rubbed her shoulders—just simple, platonic affection—until Merritt thought she would die of complicated lesbian longing.

"You're not a real couple." Merritt shook her head in distaste.

"And we don't actually remodel those houses, and we certainly don't do it in one week. And there's never any dry rot. I don't even know why they put dry rot in every episode. Alistair's actually asexual, but don't tell anyone. That's not part of the brand image."

"And Alistair knows you're gay?"

"Of course."

Avery's words sank in.

"What the fuck?" Merritt's voice came out in a rough whisper.

"It's the show. Please don't tell anyone. We play straight people. It's the...thing we sell."

"Don't tell anyone? I don't care. I thought we were friends!" Anger rose up in Merritt's chest. She'd been nothing to Avery, not even a confidante. "What did you think I would say? 'I can be gay but not you'?"

"I was scared." Avery's trembling hands said she still was.

"We were in Portland. We were at *Vale*. The most liberal, hippy, kale-eating— You were gay the whole time?!" Merritt meant to say something glib, something reuniony. *Oh my gosh, what a crazy coincidence!* But it was too late. "You could have told me. You could have at least said goodbye. Did you think I'd hit on you if I knew you were gay? Was that so terrible? You couldn't say no? You had to disappear without a word?"

Avery looked stricken. "I...thought you might...I knew you wouldn't."

"What do you want with me? Did you want to clear the air? It's cleared. I don't care. Go back to Alistair. I've not been thinking about you for fifteen years. I don't want anything from you. You're on TV. I'm happy for you. Great. You did what you wanted to do. I absolve you. I—"

"I wanted to make love to you," Avery blurted.

Even in the moonlight, Merritt could see her blush.

"That's ridiculous," Merritt said bitterly. "If you wanted to, you would have. I wasn't hard to get."

She cast around for something to do or fix or touch. She should tell Avery to go so she could pull ivy. You couldn't let ivy get its fingers into lime mortar. She couldn't let Avery get her tendrils back into her heart.

"Look at me, Merritt," Avery said. "I made a mistake, and I've regretted it every day since I left Portland."

"Well, that's on you. You didn't care enough to call. You didn't care enough to text me. I'm not hard to find."

Quickly, as though she might lose her nerve, Avery clasped Merritt around the waist, awkwardly, almost like a child...but not at all like a child because it was Avery. All those times Merritt had watched her, dreamed about her, wanted her so much she had trembled with desire and the unattainability of Avery Crown.

"What the hell are you doing? You don't get to—" The air in the courtyard felt warmer, stiller, electric. Merritt thought she could hear the echo of music. "No, Avery." It came out like a question.

Did she mean yes? Her arms were encircling Avery's waist. Like on the path, she felt every cell in her body yearning for Avery.

"I'll leave if you tell me to," Avery whispered.

There was only one absolutely right answer. But she couldn't offer it. The only word on her lips was "Avery."

Avery pulled their hips together. Merritt felt the connection deep in her core.

"You're not..." Merritt said.

But Avery was. Kissing her. Every sensible thought ran through Merritt's mind. Avery was closeted. Avery was drunk and Merritt hadn't noticed. Avery had abandoned her. Avery would break her heart again. Then Avery caught Merritt's lips with a soft nip of her teeth. The move seemed unpracticed, as though Avery had seen someone kiss like this in a movie and was going to try it, quickly, before she lost her nerve. Her artlessness did not do anything to lessen the shiver of desire that seared straight to Merritt's clit. Merritt couldn't think. She could only feel. She lifted Avery onto her hips, and Avery wrapped her legs around Merritt's waist, swathing them in a cloud of tulle. Merritt spun around and pressed Avery against the wall of the Elysium, driving her tongue into Avery's mouth, pressing her hips against Avery's. She pressed her thigh between Avery's legs, straddling Avery's beautiful dress, crushing it between them. Desperately. Hungrily. For all those nights. It felt so good.

Then Merritt jolted back into the present and her good sense. She set Avery quickly down on the ground. Avery tried to pull her back into a kiss, her breath coming out in an impatient whimper that almost undid Merritt's resolve.

"No." Merritt took another step back, stumbling on the loose gravel. "It's too weird."

It's too hard. "You're practically married to Alistair King. I'm not doing this." Merritt's body said, *Please, please do this,* but she had felt something deep down inside, something raw and real. It was the heart that all those other girls said she was missing. "I'm not because..." She tried to think of a reason that wasn't the truth. *I want you. You hurt me.*

Avery grabbed Merritt's hand before Merritt could take another step back. Merritt's black belt in aikido meant she could easily have broken Avery's grasp. She could have thrown Avery over her shoulders and onto the ground without bruising the pale skin of Avery's back or disrupting a single hair on her head. Iliana would probably say that if Merritt had *really* learned the principles of peaceful resolution practiced in the dojo she would have also been able to walk away.

Avery cradled Merritt's hand in both of hers, stroking the center of her palm. The sensation made Merritt's head swim. She felt like her body was expanding and contracting at the same moment, and that feeling coalesced in the pulse between her legs. The touch was so simple, so small, and so erotic. Maybe Avery also understood the principles of peaceful resolution. You didn't have to be strong to subdue your opponent. If you believed the teachings of aikido, you didn't have to hurt them to win.

"I messed up that night," Avery whispered. "I was supposed to be with you. And I should have told you. I was so stupid. I was a kid, but that's no excuse. I wanted you, and I wanted *King and Crown*, and I didn't know how to tell you, and I was ashamed that I'd waited so long. And then...then I just blew it. I fucked up. I've regretted that for fifteen years. Is it too late?"

"Fifteen years is too late."

Avery released Merritt's hand and cupped her cheek. It was a tentative gesture, like a virgin feeling her way for the first time, but the warmth of Avery's touch reached all the way through to her heart. The right choice...the only choice was *no*. Avery held Merritt's gaze. Merritt remembered the music drifting out of the windows of the Elysium when all the lights had been lit and everyone in the Elysium had been a friend. Then they were in each other's arms again, and Merritt was filled with something that was almost anger but not quite, thinking even in that moment that she was going to push Avery away and walk out of the courtyard and never look back.

"Where do people go in Portland?" Avery gasped. "For this?"

To make love to the girl who broke your heart when you were eighteen?

"All of Portland," Merritt said. "It was made for this."

Chapter 5

Merritt rented a room at the Jupiter Hotel even though her own apartment was down the street. A motor lodge from the 1960s with retro furnishings, it was the perfect place for a one-night stand with your past.

"Do you want to get a drink at the bar first?" Merritt asked as she stepped away from the counter of the Jupiter Motel, but Avery was already outside.

Merritt followed her. Avery stood in the shadows of potted bamboo, shrinking into the darkness.

"Are you hiding?" Merritt asked.

"I have to." Avery scanned the hotel driveway and the patio with its tiki lamps and fire pits.

Merritt's heart told her to walk away. She had loved Avery too much when they were teenagers, and she sensed that those feelings could overtake her at any moment. Making love to Avery Crown (no, fucking—that was all it would be) was like walking across the top of a high roof carrying plywood in the wind. You could do it. Once. Twice. The gusts might settle down for the three minutes it took to cross the ridge. The wind might not catch the plywood like a sail, but when it did you went over.

"Come on," Merritt said because, for a second, falling off that roof would feel like flying.

When they were in their room, Merritt said, "It's not the fanciest place,"

"I'm staying in room 1313 at the Extended Stay Deluxe," Avery said. "You don't get *less* fancy than that."

"Or less lucky."

"I feel lucky."

Avery adjusted the curtains, tucking one corner between the wall and a chair.

"I'm sorry," Avery said. "There's this reporter. Dan Ponza. He's everywhere. I don't know why. Maybe he's a fan gone wrong, but he loves to hate us. Maybe he thinks there's a scandal worth waiting for."

"Is this it?" Merritt asked.

"Yeah. And, Merritt...you can't tell anyone."

"After tonight, I forget everything."

She wouldn't though.

"If anyone finds out, Alistair and I would lose everything. The show. The crew. Our producer." Avery seemed suddenly torn. "I'd get a bit part in L.A. I'd be stuck. You have my whole life in your hand. If you tell anyone—"

"You wanted this," Merritt said.

Avery drew in a sharp little breath. "You don't?" She glanced around, a look of shocked embarrassment crossing her face...as though she had not just walked a dozen blocks in nervous, erotically charged silence. "I thought...I'd understand if you changed your mind. If you didn't want to."

Merritt cocked her head. Two years in high school she'd spent pining for Avery. Fifteen years she'd spent trying not to think about her.

"Do you really think I'd be here if I didn't want to?"

"You could've changed your mind. Reunions do things to people."

They stood in the center of the small room. Merritt drew Avery to her, her hands on Avery's waist, lost in the cloud of pink frills. She couldn't believe it was happening. Of course she would remember every single detail.

"If this was what the Vale reunion did to people," Merritt said, "the alumni association would make a lot more money."

The zipper of Avery's dress was concealed beneath a plaquette of lace, but Merritt was no stranger to women's closures. She swept Avery's hair to one side and unzipped her dress with a deliberateness that said she was there for only one purpose. Beneath the pink tulle, Avery wore a pair of panties as thin and filmy as a jellyfish. She had full, round breasts and hips that swelled into a perfect hourglass. And she was short, which made her look rounder and more luscious, like the antique pin-up-girl photos Merritt collected and did not sell.

"If you don't like what you see, you don't have to look," Avery said, turning away with a little pout.

"Why wouldn't I like what I see?"

Merritt had seen Avery naked a thousand times when they

were teenagers, and every single time she had longed to touch her like this.

"You haven't changed," Merritt said.

"I'm not allowed to. That's part of my contract."

Merritt had changed. A few years of working construction followed by more years of moving woodstoves and salvaging lumber had given her once willowy body a sturdy look. She didn't mind. She was strong. The girls at the Mirage liked her hard abs. It was her heart that was too hard to love for long. But she wasn't thinking about that now. She was thinking about the film of Avery's panties, her pale skin, her sweet perfume. It smelled like cotton candy on a summer night when the carnival was still magic.

Merritt released her bra and cupped her breasts. Avery's eyes closed as Merritt brushed her fingers lightly over Avery's nipples. She felt the electricity between them, as though every inch of her skin was anticipating every inch of Avery's. Then she lowered Avery to the bed.

"I haven't..." Avery wouldn't meet her eyes, but she spoke with breathless urgency. "I have to be very careful about who I see and what I do with women, so I don't do a lot of stuff that's not okay for *King and Crown*, and I'm out of practice."

Releasing Avery for a second, Merritt turned and swept the covers off the bed, revealing taut white sheets. The air-conditioning unit in the window was silent and the room was warm. Merritt took Avery's hand and guided her to the bed, admiring how Avery's hair splayed out around her like a drift of gold-tipped autumn leaves. Merritt lay down beside her and propped herself up on her elbow, still clothed. She smoothed her hand over Avery's belly, then across the front of Avery's lace panties, then lower. The delicate fabric was damp from Avery's desire, and Merritt caressed Avery the way Avery had caressed her palm.

"Most of the time, I really don't miss sex." Avery's hips lifted to meet Merritt's touch. "I don't even think about it."

"Really?"

Merritt leaned over and took Avery's nipple in her mouth. She pushed Avery's panties aside and slid her finger inside Avery's body, savoring her warmth.

"Are you thinking about it now?"

"Merritt, of course. How could I not be...thinking...about...it...now?"

Avery clutched Merritt's shoulders. Merritt wanted to go slow, but she was alight with desire, as though all the aching of her teenage years had flooded her body.

"This is the problem with not...oh...not having sex enough." Avery gasped. "God, that feels good. Please, Merritt. Take off your clothes."

Merritt liked the frustration in Avery's voice. She rolled off just long enough to strip. Then they clung to each other, their hands and mouths racing over each other's bodies. Skin on skin. Their breath quickening, their skin flushed. Finally, Merritt couldn't stand the pressure building up between her legs. She scissored her thighs between Avery's, pressing her clitoris into the center of Avery's sex, the wet complicated folds blurring together, so that Merritt could not tell where her body ended and Avery's began, only that between the two there was such illuminating pleasure.

"Shh. Shh," Avery whispered.

Merritt was not sure if Avery was shushing her or herself.

"It's been so long." Avery grabbed Merritt's thighs. "So long. Why did I wait?"

Merritt held them tightly together, clutching Avery's hips. Then she was coming. Avery clamped a hand over Merritt's mouth and then one over her own. They were both shaking when they finally fell away from each other. And Merritt did something she had never done with any other woman: She fell instantly and blissfully asleep.

Chapter 6

Avery didn't sleep. Instead she watched Merritt lying beside her, the sheets at her feet, her arms stretched over her head. Even in her sleep, Merritt looked confident.

Avery remembered her mother explaining the magic of *King & Crown. Plain women want a fantasy. Avery Crown with Alistair King. No one gets that in real life.* Eighteen and hopeful, Avery had asked about acting in movies. *You don't always have to be beautiful in movies,* she'd said. Marlene Crown had assessed her from her too-tight curls to her soul. *But you do have to be talented. Home and garden is good for you. You're not intimidating.*

Avery wished she was intimidatingly gorgeous. Merritt was intimidatingly gorgeous. It was very clear that a woman like Merritt did not belong anywhere near a woman like Avery, especially not naked. Avery was pretty sure there'd be a split second when Merritt woke and looked like someone who'd been kidnapped. *Oh, shit. What did I do? Where's my kidney?*

Eventually, dawn light crept under the curtains. It was three a.m. and then it was four. Call was at five at the command center. Avery had two choices: sneak out like a jerk or see that look of disenchantment in Merritt's eyes. She dressed, then touched Merritt's shoulder.

"I have go to work."

Merritt woke. She looked a little blurry-eyed, not like a kidnap victim but a little sad. That was almost worse.

"Now?" Merritt glanced at the bedside clock.

"It's almost five."

Merritt smoothed her short black hair out of her eyes and it fell immediately back in place. "Take care, then," she said.

Avery's heart sank, but she mustered her courage. Her delinquent childhood friend DX (second only to Alistair in her affections) often told her to *whip life like a Peruvian cowboy lays down a jaguar, tag it with a radio transmitter, and broadcast "I was here, motherfuckers!"* Avery took it to mean *carpe diem.*

"Will I see you again after this?" she asked. "I could come by your shop."

Merritt shook her head slowly. "You know we'd only mess it up," she said, a regretful smile lifting her lips. "If we go out to Mother's for eggs Benedict, we'll kill the magic. You're leaving in six weeks. Pretend it was a dream. We don't want to be two more reunioners with nothing in common except too many mimosas."

It was a poetic way to say, *Thanks but no thanks.* Avery tried to shrug it off. "Good point. I'm going to be super busy."

She wanted to run out of the hotel room.

"I bet you are," Merritt said. "You've got a big life. You're a star."

The gentleness in her voice made it even worse. It was the same tone Avery used when she had to disengage from a fan who had convinced themselves they were best friends. Merritt rolled over and faced the wall. It was over. Avery's hand was on the door when she heard Merritt whisper, "My shop's on Burnside. We're open ten a.m. to six p.m. Don't forget."

If Avery hadn't been used to tuning her ear to Alistair's secret voice she wouldn't have heard her. "I'll stop by," she said.

Merritt said nothing else. But Avery carried her words with her as she called an Uber, waited by the window, then ducked out of the hotel, careful to scan the street for Dan Ponza. He was nowhere to be seen. She had the familiar feeling that always struck her when she first arrived in a new city, before the first person recognized her. She could be anyone, any girl going home in the morning, a girl who didn't have to watch for Dan Ponza, a girl who could cut her signature hair. *I am the girl Merritt slept with!* she thought over and over again as she rode back to the hotel seeing the city again for the first time.

* * *

Dawn was brightening when she entered her hotel room. She redid her hair. There was really too much of it, as though shampoo producers had gotten ahold of her agent and said, *It'd really cut into our profits if she didn't have so much to wash.* Then she headed back to the parking lot and caught the last van to the command center. The old diner converted into office space was already buzzing. Alistair was sitting by the window flipping through his phone. She slid in next to him.

"Whatcha got?" Avery asked, trying to act casual.

Alistair touched the screen and a video started again from the beginning. Closed captioning read, *Work is finished on the clinic in Stone, Wyoming. The America Wyoming Foundation is funding the eight-thousand-square-foot clinic, which will provide reduced-cost health care to communities in the area.*

Alistair was so good. He wasn't dreaming of his lover and the next time he'd be able to push his throbbing genitals against another person's body. He was thinking about sick children.

"They know it's you," Avery said. "Why don't you just go and cut the red ribbon?"

"They don't know it's me, and I hate all of them."

Avery snorted. "Really. One person gets out of Stone and suddenly an anonymous donor is putting up clinics and after-school programs. And you don't think they know it's you?"

"They don't watch *King and Crown*."

"You don't hate them."

"I was asexual, beautiful, and in love with the theater." Alistair fluffed his shiny blond hair. "They crucified me."

One of the production assistants came by with Avery's coffee. She didn't need it. She would never have to sleep again. *Don't forget.*

Alistair picked up the energy bar he'd been eating. The producers at TKO had struck a product placement deal with Global Body Biscuit.

"It tastes like twigs in dried marinara," he said.

"So good."

Alistair handed it to Avery, and they chewed meditatively. That was probably why Global Body Biscuits were such a good diet aid. It took hours to eat one.

"So?" he asked with a teasing lilt in his voice. "I didn't see you at the hotel."

"I didn't ruin her life," Avery whispered.

"I told you so." They were speaking in the subsonic voice only they could hear.

"But she was mad!" Avery linked her arm through Alistair's, squeezing him in her excitement.

"You're happy about that?" He scrunched his perfectly manly forehead.

Standing in the courtyard of the Elysium, she'd been so nervous she didn't think she'd be able to speak. It was Merritt's anger that had given her courage. If she was angry, it meant she cared.

"It was like we could go back in time."

"Hmm," Alistair said. "I think they're working on that at CERN, but I don't know if it's for sale at the Mac store yet. Did you go forward?"

Avery just smiled and leaned her head on his shoulder.

"You had nostalgia sex," Alistair said.

"Aw, kiddo," Greg said in his pleasantly paternal manner. "You all right?"

"I'm fine."

It felt a little sleazy lying to Greg. He knew she was gay. The crew did too. They protected her from rumors and reporters. But Greg had enough to worry about with a new house and the executive producer on set, and she wanted to keep Merritt to herself for a little longer.

*   *   *

When they neared the neighborhood, Alistair told Avery to close her eyes. He took the silk scarf from around her neck and tied it around her head.

"I know you'll peek."

"He doesn't trust me," she complained to Greg, who was riding in the front seat.

"This is pretty spectacular," Greg said. "I think this beats Austin."

Avery closed her eyes beneath the scarf. The houses were never her real passion. It was the cities. But Greg and Alistair's excitement made her smile. She loved the way they all still cared. Every episode, every city, every season, every decorative flourish, and every fixed pipe made them happy, even after fifteen years. She felt the van slow to a stop. She heard the van door open. Alistair touched her arm.

"We're going to walk up a little flagstone path," he said. He kept one arm around her waist. "I got you."

Avery remembered Merritt catching her on the stone stairs,

her body lean but strong. She had lingered in that moment longer than she should have. Alistair would have said she was playing the girl card. *Oh, my savior. Protect me.* But she couldn't lift her cheek from Merritt's breast. She couldn't pull away from the smell of Merritt's cedar cologne. Then she'd seen herself from the outside, like a full shot. She was the plain girl from a high school dramedy; Merritt was the star quarterback. Although, now that she thought about it, those movies always turned out well for the plain girl.

"All right." Alistair stopped, his arm still around her waist.

The air felt cooler. Avery smelled damp foliage and stone.

"The resale on this place is amazing," Alistair went on. "When we sell it, it'll balance the budget for the season. And you will have so much room to turn it into quintessential Portland. Right now it's Portland circa 1918, but we'll modernize it."

"Okay. Okay. Can I look?" Avery asked.

Alistair undid the knot in her scarf and swept it off her face. "Ta-da!" he said.

Avery stumbled backward. Alistair caught her against his chest.

"I know," Alistair said. "It's amazing."

The beautiful, weedy courtyard was already filled with equipment: disassembled scaffolding, C-stands, a portable generator. One of the sound guys was taking readings, walking around the space repeating, "Partridge. Dewar's. Stout. Partridge. Dewar's. Stout." Someone was setting up a table with pizza for the crew's walking lunch.

Above their heads, the sky was a lonely blue.

"We can't buy this," Avery whispered.

"We already did," Greg said. "Pam finalized the deal in the middle of the night. I don't even know how she does it."

"Happy?" Alistair asked. "It's beautiful."

Avery couldn't speak. It was horrible. It was the worst thing she had ever seen. It was Merritt's Elysium.

Chapter 7

That same morning, Merritt stood in the center of Hellenic Hardware, watching the water splashing in the Helen of Troy fountain, feeling sleepy in a way that didn't need rest. Would Avery really come by? Perhaps around closing time when Merritt was the only person in the shop? Would they go up to the retrofitted office she was using as an apartment while she finalized the purchase of the Elysium? Could she take the time to offer Avery a polite cup of coffee when her whole body ached for Avery's touch? She liked the way Avery had heard her when she'd whispered to the blank wall. *Don't forget.* Girls didn't hear her. It wasn't volume, of course. It was something else. Merritt thought she was saying, *I like you. Don't hurt me. Please stay.* Girls heard, *My heart is a glacier.*

At Merritt's side, her cochair on the Pride House board, Tate Grafton, stood with her hands in her pockets. They were organizing an end-of-summer fundraising dance, still months in the future. Hellenic Hardware would host a hipster prom for grown-ups, turning the warehouse into a wonder-land of joy and, hopefully, the inclination to give large sums of money to the youth shelter.

Tate was talking about power supplies and how they could help the Pride House kids get involved. Merritt couldn't focus on their conversation. The memory of pleasure teased her to distraction.

"I know it's way too early to think about decorating," Tate said. "We're not putting this thing on until the last day of summer, but we're trying to help the kids with preplanning, so do you mind if they come in here and scope things out?"

"Of course not."

Eventually, Tate excused herself with a friendly, "Well, I'd better be off. You have customers."

Did she? Merritt hadn't even noticed. After Tate left, Merritt took a penny out of her pocket and tossed it in the fountain. Then she sprawled across the wicker bench beneath the gazebo. She gazed up at the skylights, from where, perhaps, Uncle Oli's ghost looked down on her. A half hour later, she was still staring at the white, wrought-iron lace of the gazebo. From the front of the store she heard a cheerful voice ring out, "Meri?" Lei-Ling stretched her name out over two long syllables.

Merritt had long since given up telling her that no one had ever called her Meri and no one should. "Meri, I'm going to find you. Ready or not, here I come. Meri, your Realtor's here."

* * *

Merritt's Realtor, Trisha Hayward, met her at the front of the shop.

"I've got some bad news for you." Trisha sounded tired. "I can't sugarcoat it."

"Lay it on me," Merritt said. "The inspection get held up? Title audit?" People who treated their closing date like a wedding always got disappointed. The trick was to be patient.

"We lost the Elysium," Trisha said.

Merritt didn't hear her. She was staring out the window. On Burnside, everything looked like it was moving in peaceful slow motion. She had slept with Avery! She remembered every second, and each one filled her with a kind of excitement she had made a practice of suppressing. If she saw Avery again, she would drink in Avery's body like water. She would let Avery open her up. Merritt hadn't let a woman go down on her in years. It was too intimate when she knew, deep in her heart, this woman, like every other one, would leave. But it would be worth it with Avery, so excruciatingly good...even if Avery was leaving in six weeks. At least Merritt knew the parameters. She knew what was coming and how soon. She imagined the exact moment when Avery's tongue would first touch her. Avery might be inexperienced but she would be eager, and she would move her tongue up and down and across and in...

"Merritt?" Trisha asked.

"What?" No one was supposed to have these kinds of thoughts in front of their Realtor! "Sorry. What about the title—or was it the inspection? You were saying?"

"I found another property I thought you might like. The

neighborhood isn't as good, and it's more expensive, but I think the seller would negotiate."

Merritt came back to the conversation like a car hitting a curb.

"We're closing," she said. Suddenly Trisha's words rang in her ear. "We were done. It's all settled. They accepted my offer."

"Pending the inspection."

"I don't care if the roof fell in."

"See, the way that works..."

Merritt already knew. Either party could pull out because of a bad inspection, and it was up to the parties to define "bad." The rule was there to protect the buyer, but the seller could opt out too. Then they could list the property at a higher price. It happened all the time.

"I can up my offer," Merritt said. "How much?"

She would figure something out. She couldn't lose the Elysium and the apartment Uncle Oli had rented for almost twenty years. It was the only place Merritt had ever called home. She would buy it and live there forever. She'd run Hellenic Hardware and live in Uncle Oli's suite and wake up feeling like she belonged.

"It's not that," Trisha said. "You can't up your offer."

"Are they going over market value? Is it a company or private?"

"They didn't overbid you. I'm sorry, Merritt. We couldn't win this one." Trisha Hayward's smile was on the back of every bus in Portland, but for once she wasn't grinning. "I never saw this coming. It's a television show. They're offering

SkyBank advertising and product placement in exchange for the Elysium. It's going to be on some renovation-decorating show. I'm sure you've seen it."

"I don't have a TV."

It was like stepping on drywall and falling straight through the floor...except more painful.

"It's *King and Crown*. They're actually paying *less* than you offered." Trisha paused. "They just came out of nowhere. Literally swept in in the middle of the night. These are real pros. The Elysium had never been listed publicly. Then there they were. We couldn't have seen this coming."

Merritt looked down at her hands. They were clasped so tightly her knuckles had turned white. Avery hadn't wanted her. Avery had distracted her.

Chapter 8

Merritt headed for the staircase that led to her office apartment and slammed the door. *They swept in at night.* Avery had seduced her so her minions could steal the Elysium. That almost made her angrier than losing the Elysium itself. The thought would have startled her if she'd had an eighth of her brain to devote to reason. She had wanted the Elysium for years! Now she just wanted her sweet memories back: Avery's face surprised by pleasure, Avery's arm across her chest. But they weren't sweet memories anymore. She'd been a fool. Avery hadn't held her. Avery had held her down, lest Merritt experience a surge of psychic power telling her to run to the Realtor's office in the middle of the night.

"You didn't have to sleep with me," she said to the empty apartment. "You could have faked an emergency. You could have had some decency and just roofied me." She paced the room, her footsteps slamming into the floor. "How could you do it?!"

For one sensible moment, she considered not going. Then she marched out of her bedroom and into the stifling heat of the day.

* * *

When she arrived at the Elysium, the street was already lined with trailers. A sawhorse bore a sign reading FILM CREW BARRICADE. THRU TRAFFIC ONLY. A security guard lingered by the trailers. A dozen men in pocketed vests hurried about. One of them broke away and came over with a clipboard in hand.

"Are you with Warren Venner?" He looked like a kindly uncle who had suddenly been asked to appear in court.

"I have to talk to Avery Crown."

"Are you with the TKO contingency? I'll just need to get you a badge."

"I'm not with anyone."

"A fan? We love fans. But we've got a team of people visiting from our network. Our boss, you know." He looked apologetic. "Avery and Alistair will be visiting with fans on July nineteenth at the Bagdad Theater. They'd love to see you then."

"I'm not a fan."

Merritt caught the man glancing at security. The kindly uncle looked like a pushover, but in that glance Merritt saw all the best contractors she had worked with. He could see the whole scene with his eyes closed. Merritt pushed past him. CROWN was written on green masking tape on one of the trailers. She pounded on the door. The security guard was at her side. He grabbed for her, but her hours in Iliana's dojo were good for something and she slipped out of his grasp. A second later Avery opened the door, froze, her hand clutched to her chest.

"Merritt," she said. "I was going to come find you."

"Get away from her." The guard grabbed Merritt's shoulder.

"I know her. I know her," Avery said. "She's my friend." She pulled Merritt inside.

"I am not your friend," Merritt said. "How could you?"

Inside, the trailer contained a tiny fake fireplace, a vase of fake lilies, and fake wood veneer. But the mirror was covered in real photographs, some faded, some crisp. In each picture, Avery and Alistair stood in front of a different vista, their curved fingers held together to make two sides of a heart.

"I didn't do it." Avery's words poured out. "I was going to see you. I wanted to see you. I could have died when Alistair showed me. I would never have let them buy the Elysium if I'd known. I told them we had to give it back, but I don't have any control over anything."

Avery hurried to the window and closed the venetian blinds. Avery wore a ruffled white dress that looked like what the Kardashians thought people had worn on the Oregon Trail. Her hair was plaited in a beautiful wheat-sheaf down her back. She looked pretty and vulnerable. Merritt tried not to notice.

Merritt trailed her fingers along the wood paneling. "This place is shit," she said.

"I had no idea. You have to believe me."

"Don't even."

"I don't have anything to do with the property selection," Avery pleaded.

"I've seen your show. You pick every property by hand, and then you stick a sombrero on it and pretend you understand Texas. You're not going to make the Elysium look like Portland. You're not going to make it better. You're going to slap some paint up and then sell it to a developer who'll tear it down and put up a hundred condos. You show up somewhere for two hot seconds and pretend like that means something. You don't know anything about the places you leave. Your show is meaningless. It's a waste."

It was cruel, and Merritt wasn't a cruel person. Cold but not cruel. She'd barely even seen an episode of *King & Crown*. Somewhere deep inside she knew she couldn't bear watching Avery, even after fifteen years. But sometimes it was on at the Mirage, so she understood the setup. Buy a building. Renovate a bit. Decorate with the icons of the city. Leave.

Avery's whole face trembled. "I love those places. That's not what we do. We make people happy."

Merritt couldn't look at Avery who was trying not to cry.

"You have to believe me. Please, please believe me."

Avery touched her arm, trying to turn Merritt toward her. Merritt snatched her arm away.

"We have an acquisitions department, and we have this woman, Pam. I don't think anyone has ever seen her in real life. But if right now I said, 'I wish I had a Bluetooth speaker in the shape of a bulldog,' I would open my door and there it would be. She makes Amazon look incompetent. She buys properties and rents trailers and gets cars and vans and food and bottles of water and equipment. Sometimes she buys houses years in advance."

"You just bought the Elysium."

"There was a fire. We had to buy something on the fly."

"We." Merritt felt her face twist into a knot of anger. "The Elysium wasn't listed."

"Pam isn't a mom with 2.5 kids searching on HomeFinder. I've been doing this show for fifteen years. I never choose a building, and I don't care which one we work on. I would never mean to hurt you."

Outside, a man called out, "Where's Avery? Venner wants to talk to her."

"I can help you buy another building."

"I don't want anything you've touched."

Out of nowhere, Merritt felt a lump in her throat. She looked around the tiny room. She could smell Avery's perfume. Merritt stepped forward. Infinitesimal particles of glitter sparkled on Avery's cheeks. Merritt wiped the sheen with her thumb. Avery's skin felt feverish.

"Body glitter, really? Are we twelve? Is that the quintessential Portland?"

"I thought it was pretty," Avery said miserably.

And more than half of Merritt's soul wanted to throw her arms around Avery and hold her close. *Of course it's pretty. You're pretty. You're beautiful. You can cover me in glitter. Just don't cry.* Avery was so beautiful. Merritt's body was a traitor. She wanted to wipe away the gloss on Avery's lips. She wanted to kiss the tears that slid down her cheeks. Even now. As soon as Avery had left the Jupiter Hotel, Merritt had gone to the window and watched her Uber pulling away, consumed with tenderness and worry for every possible thing that might happen to Avery. Now *she* was the thing that was happening to Avery. Avery's face tightened, and she took a couple quick, sharp breaths. Then something in her seemed to break. She wiped her eyes with the back of her hand, but her tears flowed freely. But these tears were a ruse.

Outside a man said, "Lock it up. We're filming in two."

"What would you do if I walked out there and told all your precious producers we were fucking?" Merritt said. "What if I say, 'Avery is my lover. We just had sex. Take a DNA swab. She's all over me.'"

"You can't. The crew knows and Greg, but not the Portland hires and not the new guy from L.A."

"I'll tell them."

Even as she said it, Merritt knew she wouldn't. She was so angry. And Avery was so wrong. But she could imagine Avery crumpling to the ground outside her trailer as her life crumbled around her. She could imagine Avery sobbing into her folded knees. Despite everything that had happened, Merritt knew she couldn't do that to Avery.

"You can't do that." Avery rallied the way she had in the courtyard of the Elysium, like a shy girl mustering courage no one expected.

As quickly as they came, her tears were gone. *She's an actor,* Merritt thought.

"If you want a DNA swab..." Avery said, each word calculated.

You can't. We'll arrest you. We'll sue, Merritt filled in.

"You'd have to fuck me," Avery finished.

Merritt's surprise left her speechless.

Outside, footsteps shook the stairs and the trailer. Someone knocked the door. A man called, "Sorry, Aves, you're on."

"In a minute," Avery shot back with such ferocity even Merritt froze.

Outside, someone said, "She's got a friend in there. Give her ten."

Merritt knew it would take less than ten minutes for her to come under Avery's touch.

"I want you, Merritt."

Merritt wanted her too. Damn it, she wanted her so much. Before Merritt realized what she was doing, she had pressed Avery up against the door. Avery gripped fistfuls of Merritt's hair with a delicious force that bordered on pain and sent a current of desire down Merritt's spine. They kissed, and the kiss felt like crying and fighting and racing down an empty freeway at midnight when they were eighteen and their car was the only one on the road.

"Give me an hour." Avery clutched Merritt's back. "I'll make up an excuse. I'll come find you."

Merritt pushed up Avery's dress. The delicate fabric bunched at Avery's waist. The wall of the trailer creaked. Their legs intertwined. Merritt felt Avery's ass through lace underwear. She pressed her thigh into the apex of Avery's legs.

"Please," Avery whispered.

Iliana said make-up sex was the best. Girls never stuck around long enough for Merritt to find out. Now she understood. The urge to cry had turned into a kiss. Avery's arms comforted the same heartbreak they caused. And Merritt felt full of tenderness and rage, and touching Avery, arousing her gently and forcefully at turns, was the answer to all the feelings storming inside her.

"I'll get us a room at the Jupiter Hotel," Avery said.

She grazed her teeth along Merritt's ear. Merritt heard herself sigh in a way she never did with other women.

"Meet me there." Avery pulled away a little bit. "There's just one thing. I have to text you a contract. I don't care about it, but I owe it to Alistair and the crew. Everyone gets an NDA if they have sex. It's like using a condom for us. It's just safe. Please, it's nothing in my world. I know it sounds weird."

"An NDA?"

"A nondisclosure agreement."

Merritt untangled herself from Avery's embrace.

"It just means you won't tell anyone...officially."

Avery took her phone out of some invisible pocket in her dress and called something to the screen. She handed it to Merritt. Merritt tried to control the tremor in her hand as she scrolled to the bottom and back up. *Forfeiture of assets*, it read. *Agree to forgo legal recourse...amount of damages...* The number was more than she could conceive.

"Is this a trick?"

She had fallen for it again. She couldn't breathe. The lump in her throat was going to strangle her.

"You want my shop too? Is this how you win, Avery? This gives you everything if someone sees us."

"No! It's standard. Please, Merritt. In the industry this is nothing."

Merritt pressed her hand to Avery's chest, holding her at arm's length. She could feel Avery's heart racing.

"How are you still in the closet?"

"My fans trust me, and they feel like they know me. I can't let them down."

Avery kissed Merritt before she could protest. It was the kind of kiss that said, *This is more than sex*, soft and slow. The kind of kiss Merritt longed for and avoided because hope felt like a punch to the gut. But now she was melting into Avery's arms, letting her lead, giving in to Avery's caressing, and...

"No!"

She shook herself free. This kiss came along with a twelve-screen nondisclosure contract that, if she'd read it correctly, promised she'd relinquish her home, truck, business, and assets to *King & Crown* if she so much as called Iliana and said, *Guess what? I've got a crush on this new girl.*

"Don't touch me," Merritt said. "Don't find me. Don't come into my life again. I never wanted you to come back to Vale."

Chapter 9

Avery followed Merritt out of the trailer. The sunlight was blinding. Merritt hurried through the bustle, skipping over cables and dodging equipment dollies.

"Goddamn it. Who's that in the shot!" Venner, the executive producer from TKO, yelled.

No one in the *King & Crown* family responded.

Someone wheeled a fan past Merritt, and her white shirt blew back, outlining her body. Her black hair blew across her face.

"Security!" Venner bellowed. "Bunter, get her."

Merritt raised her voice. "I'm going."

Bunter, their security guard, had reached her. He grabbed Merritt's arm.

"Don't!" Avery called out. Her mind was racing. She had to call Merritt back. She had to explain. She would get Greg to tell her she had nothing to do with purchasing.

Bunter yanked Merritt's arm backward, twisting it behind her back. "Get off the set," he growled.

Avery saw them frozen in a single frame: Bunter scowling, Merritt's face startled by pain.

"Get off me," Merritt said.

It was her toughness that made her vulnerability so poignant.

In a flash, Avery remembered Thanksgiving at Vale. Her father had won junior-year Thanksgiving in the ever-simmering custody battle between him and Marlene. Early on Thanksgiving morning, Avery had returned to campus to pick up a book from her locker, but everything was locked. The landscaping was encased in frost. She was about to leave when she noticed the beautiful transfer student from her biology class sitting on the back of a bench, smoking a cigarette. Merritt Lessing. What luck! There were no cool girls to distract Merritt, no boy offering Merritt his pen or a soda. Avery took a deep breath and walked over.

When's your flight? Avery had asked, because Merritt was one of the residential girls who had to pack up for holidays. Not long after that, Merritt's uncle had saved her from a life of dorm food and lonely holidays, but that Thanksgiving Merritt was a woman without a home.

I got a hotel downtown, Merritt said. *And this.* She'd reached into the pocket of her leather jacket and withdrew a fake ID with the casual air of someone who floated above rules and regulations. And although Merritt was young and undeniably a girl, she reminded Avery of some of the old men Avery's mother knew. Men who had been talented, wanted, and wealthy for so long, they no longer had to flaunt the fact that the rules did not apply to them.

Merritt had always had *presence*. At Vale, the other girls had flirted with Merritt and feared her at turns. There was something dangerous about her, something rebellious, even with her A average and her lacrosse victories. She was as unmoored as her parents' yacht. No one told her what to do. No one owned her. And she played it up. So casual. So grown-up. *Christmas. Aren't we a little old for Santa Claus?*

But behind Merritt's self-assured smile, she had looked lost that Thanksgiving morning.

Avery saw that girl in Merritt now.

"Don't hurt her!" Avery yelled.

Bunter wouldn't really hurt her—you had to think about liability—but accidents happened. She couldn't bear for one more thing to come between them. How would she persuade Merritt that *King & Crown* was a lovely, harmless band of friends if Bunter dislocated Merritt's shoulder?

Bunter muscled Merritt forward, using her arm as leverage. Then somehow, unexplainably, Bunter was on his knees. He was simply upright one moment and kneeling the next. Merritt looked slightly perplexed, as though the blue sky had shed a single raindrop on her head. She held her hands up in surrender, stepping away from him.

"I don't want any trouble. I'm out of here."

"What the—"

Bunter rose and grabbed at Merritt again. She stood perfectly still. Then she wasn't in front of him anymore. Bunter was stumbling into the empty space. Avery saw Merritt's posture grow looser and more catlike. Her knees softened.

Her shoulders squared. She raised her hands before her. Then Bunter was sitting on the ground again.

Nothing Avery had ever done had that grace, and it suddenly struck her that explaining the Elysium wouldn't be enough. Merritt could have anyone. How could Avery compete? She was on television, but what did that mean to Merritt? She heard her mother's voice in the back of her mind. *I'm pulling as many strings as I can, but there's only so much we can do.* She'd thought fifteen years of *King & Crown* had proved her mother wrong. Fifteen years was exceptional. But she had never seen exceptional until she saw Merritt again.

"I'm calling the police," Greg yelled.

"Call them!" Merritt stepped away from Bunter. "And I'll call OSHA and the zoning board and the inspector." She nodded toward the film crew. "They've got their harnesses on wrong. Your painters aren't tied in. That roof isn't rated for terra-cotta shingle. I see what you have over there on that pallet."

Venner sprinted in her direction, and Avery recalled a nature show that explained how surprisingly fast the hippopotamus could run when angered...or maybe it was the crocodile. That was Venner.

"Who are you?" Venner yelled. "Who is she? Who let her on set?"

"I'm nobody," Merritt said. "I wandered in by mistake, and I'm just trying to leave."

Avery half expected Merritt to throw Venner like she had thrown Bunter...which would have been wonderful. Even through her tears, Avery was mesmerized. Every muscle in

Merritt's body broadcast glorious, brilliant, indignant rage, as though she had seen through all the world's foolishness and was ready to slam it to the ground like a football player smacking the ball down behind the end zone.

Alistair had taken his usual spot at Avery's side, a protective arm around her shoulder.

"Is Venner trying to pick her up?" Alistair whispered under his breath. "This is like the world's worst Tinder meet-up." Merritt turned toward them, and Avery felt Alistair's arm tighten around her shoulders.

Venner was trying to talk to Merritt. She stopped him with a raised hand. In L.A. Venner would have poked a finger in her chest, but here he seemed a little bit afraid of her.

"You know your show is going to ruin this place," Merritt said to Venner. "Architectural significance, antiques, beauty. You'll paste over it. Put in color-changing LED lights. You know what LED is good for? Dentistry. You don't need a Portland-glow light or blue-midnight light. Because there are actual mornings and midnights, and you don't see that. You have to stay to know it. You can't love something you have for a month. And you don't need fans to make wind, because it's not windy! It's summer in Portland..." The fire seemed to go out of her. "...and it's just beautiful."

The set had gone silent except for the buzz of the fans.

Merritt looked at Avery. "It just is," Merritt said. "And you've ruined it."

* * *

Avery felt dizzy. The dappled sunlight spun around her. Then Avery was watching the taillights of Merritt's enormous black pickup disappear down the street.

A moment later Alistair pulled Avery into his trailer. It looked exactly like hers, complete with the photos. She would've loved to show Merritt around her space, to tell her stories about the pictures. But Merritt didn't care that Avery thought that the Cariboo Mountains in British Columbia looked like a land of fairies or that the Canyonlands National Park had made her cry it was so magnificent.

"What was that?" Alistair asked. "I thought you were all happy in your nostalgia lust."

There was fear in his eyes. Avery guessed half of it was for her, but the other half was for the show. If Dan Ponza got a picture of her with a girl, the show would be over. She'd have to buy a house instead of renting villas with Alistair. They would never work together again. The crew would split up and go work on sets where producers yelled at them and people fought over the union assignments.

"It's the Elysium." Avery fell into Alistair's arms. "The building we bought. It was hers. It was supposed to be hers. She was about to close on it, and Pam just came in and took it, and now Merritt thinks it's my fault."

"How would it be your fault?"

Alistair wrapped his arms around her.

"She showed it to me," Avery said miserably. "We took a walk after the reunion, and she showed it to me. And I kissed her in the courtyard."

Avery sobbed. Alistair held her gently and stroked her hair.

Sweet, sweet Alistair, with whom she'd spent more time than most married couples spent in a lifetime. She could lie down on his bed, snuggle up to him, knowing that she could sleep in his arms and he would never try to touch her, never drink one too many and land a sloppy kiss on her neck. They would never be like those costars who secretly hated each other or dated and married and broke up all over *People* and *Star* magazine. And for the first time she thought, *What if that's not enough?*

* * *

A moment later someone pounded on the door, shaking the thin walls. The door flew open. Venner burst in. Greg followed a few paces behind him, saying, "Give her some space. You can't just walk into her trailer."

"Gold!" Venner exclaimed. He looked at Avery. "Why is she crying?"

"I'm not—"

"She's tired," Alistair said.

"Fix her." Venner looked back and forth between them.

The small space was crowded with everyone standing around like people in an elevator.

"Look at this. I mean *look at this!*" He was waving his enormous cell phone in their direction.

"Give it here," Alistair said wearily.

Venner slapped the phone down in his hand. A video froze on the screen, and Alistair restarted it.

"It's Merritt," Alistair said.

The whole scene on the set replayed in silence, but Avery knew the exact moment when Merritt had looked at her and said, *You've ruined it.*

"It's going viral," Venner said. "Look at the hits. Seriously, am I the only one who gets it? That woman who flipped Bunter is gorgeous, and she's so Portland. She's fire. She's excitement. I am the Finder. Do you know how many careers I've launched? Greg says you know her. We're putting her on *King and Crown*. She *is* the Portland edition."

Chapter 10

Two nights later, Avery lay on her bed, her face buried in the pillow. The hotel the *King & Crown* cast and crew were staying at was awful. Usually she didn't mind. She liked meeting families with kids road-tripping to Disneyland. She liked making their trip a little more special. And she liked going out early in the morning or late at night and swimming in the over-chlorinated pools and pretending she could be anyone, anywhere. But she wasn't anyone tonight. Tonight she was the woman Merritt hated. She was the woman who had had one perfect night before property-savant Pam managed to buy an apartment building in the time it took the crew to order their IPAs.

She rolled over and texted her friend DX. Texting DX was a sketchy proposition. DX was the kind of friend you were a little bit afraid of. Parties thrown by DX probably counted as terrorist acts in countries like Canada and Switzerland. But

Avery didn't want to see Alistair's poorly concealed worry. Everything she had done put *King & Crown* in jeopardy.

I messed up, she texted.

DX texted back, *Grand theft? Guns? {Tombstone emoji. Skull emoji. Dead fish emoji.} Cm on tour. China then S. Korea. Won't let them catch u.*

Avery's phone rang. The screen flashed a picture of DX's curly black hair and aviator sunglasses.

"What's up?" DX asked cheerfully. "You and Al break up?"

For a moment Avery couldn't speak. It was all too much to explain to a woman who owned a retrofitted Russian military helicopter that she might have stolen *and* was in the most remarkably healthy relationship that Avery had ever seen.

DX's voice softened. "Hey, for real? What is it?"

"I fucked up."

"Well, good. Finally, schoolgirl. Did you crash one of those comped cars you guys are always driving? Just put it in gear and pushed it over a cliff to see what would happen?"

"I'm in Portland. There aren't any cliffs," Avery said miserably. "It's a girl. She hates me."

"No one can hate you."

"It's possible." Avery picked a ball of lint off the orange-brown coverlet.

"Who was it?"

"A girl I liked"—she had to say it—"in high school."

DX hadn't even gone to high school.

"It's that reunion," DX said. "They plan them to make you feel old. Think about death. Then you'll give more to the school."

"I don't think that's true."

"Didn't they talk about *legacy giving?* Vultures."

They had talked about legacy giving.

"I've never had sex like this before," Avery blurted.

"Did you find the clitoris? I wondered whether you knew about that."

"Give me some credit!"

She told DX about her night with Merritt, the Elysium, and Merritt's arrival on set.

"Wait," DX said. "I'm googling her. Ooh, pretty. Like lesbian supermodel pretty."

"And now Warren Venner—he's a new TKO exec—he wants her on the show. But he called her, and she told him to fuck off. It blew his mind. He's kind of in love with her. *No one* tells Venner to fuck off."

"Tight!"

"But that's how much Merritt doesn't want to see me. She'd turn down a chance to be on *King and Crown.*"

"That's not absolute proof of hatred. Just ask me to hang some chintz curtains with you, and I'll show you. But this is easy. You just have to convince her to be on the show. You can go into whatever little dressing room trailers you have. Walk around in your underwear and win her back. Explain the whole thing. Be like, 'Sorry. Totes my bad. Let's get a room and make love on a waterbed full of man-of-war jellyfish.' Or go romantic. Be like, 'Marry me, you androgynous goddess.'"

Most of Avery's conversations with DX involved DX suggesting ways Avery should enrich her life and Avery saying,

No. There's actually a lot of good reasons not to do that. Except in DX's life there weren't.

"There're no jellyfish here. And it's not just about *here*." Avery sighed.

Avery remembered Merritt bursting through the doors of the Vale gymnasium like she had just run a long distance, and for a second Merritt had looked relieved and apologetic. Then Merritt had seen Alistair. Avery had read it in her eyes. First confusion, then hurt, then anger. Above Merritt, the disco ball had cast a snow flurry of white lights on the walls. Avery had wanted to throw her arms around Merritt. She had wished she had some excuse. She wished she could tell Merritt that Alistair had kidnapped her, that she had been drugged and had only now woken up, that her mother was being held for ransom and this dance was the price of her release. But, of course, she had no excuse. She only had a reason: She wanted to be on television.

"We have history."

"You never told me about her."

Of course she hadn't. When Avery had started at Vale, DX was about to go platinum. Every conversation they'd had for four years had been DX yelling over the sound of an after-party and Avery saying, *You know I can't hear you, right?*

"We were going to go to the prom together. As friends."

She was waiting for DX to mock her, but DX just said, "Classic."

"She bought me a dress. She loved antiques, and she found this old wedding dress. She said I looked like an old doll...but not the creepy kind with teeth."

"I kind of like the ones with the teeth. You're just waiting for their little eyes to blink, like, *Hello, Satan.* Did you sleep with her back in the day?"

A month before prom, Avery had spent a long, hot night in the sexuality aisle of Powell's Books, perusing advice on how to make love to women, including a book by a man named Bingo Sterling. His book *Cunnilingus! You Can!* had recommended sticking her tongue in and out of a shot glass for practice. She was pretty sure it wasn't going to be like that.

"If I'd gone with her, I think we would've. It would've been my first. Hers too."

She had written *I will!* on her hand, in her notebook, on the bottom of her pumps. It was her mantra. She would not chicken out, no matter how much she blushed and stammered. After prom they were going to rent a hotel and stay up watching television, but before they turned on the TV, Avery was going to say it: *I want to make love to you.* If Merritt said no, at least she would have tried. She wouldn't look back on her life and think *I wasn't even cool enough to ask.* Avery had felt the anticipation in every fiber of her body.

Then she'd done so much worse than not ask. She'd picked Alistair.

"I didn't even tell her what was going on," Avery said as she finished the story.

"Why'd you do it? Lesbians are sensitive about getting left for a man."

"I'd been talking to my mom about coming out. She said no one could know because it would follow me forever. Then a week or two before the prom, my mom introduced me to Alistair. I was so excited about *King and Crown*."

Avery got up and walked over to the fridge. Alistair had left her a King Cobra malt liquor. Good old Alistair. He did not understand that King Cobra was only comfort food in Stone. She cracked open the forty.

"I just kept acting like nothing had changed. I told myself Merritt should have made a move. I flirted with her all the time, and she never really went for it. I told myself my mom was right. I wasn't going to marry my high school crush. Should I ruin my career just to tell her I liked her? I thought there'd be other women."

No other woman had filled Avery with the sense of wild possibility, that feeling that she could wake up in the sunshine and grow wings.

"I felt so bad after I saw her at the prom, I just couldn't face her. I just left. I never explained anything. She was so alone."

Everyone at Vale knew rules didn't apply to Merritt. The other kids thought it was because her parents were rich. Only Avery knew it was because Merritt's parents were so definitively absent. Then one day near the end of Merritt's first year at Vale her uncle had learned of her existence and had trundled into the school office with empty suitcases. *You're coming with me.* The other girls had decried the injustice. To move into an uncle's spare room! With a curfew and dinnertime! Only Avery had heard Merritt lament, *What if he changes his mind?*

"She's not going to forgive me. If I'd only messed up once, maybe. But twice? And anyway, we're leaving. What am I going to do, leave her again? Hide her in my trailer?" Avery sipped her King Cobra. It tasted like an alcoholic tea bag. She wished she could drink straight from a bottle of vodka. "I can't come out. Yesterday a woman wrote me and said that her daughter died of cancer and the only thing that cheered them up before it happened was watching *King and Crown*. It was their last special thing. They trust me. What happens when I tell people like that that everything was a lie?"

Merritt had trusted her too.

"Damn," DX said. "You're screwed."

That was another reason why Avery hadn't gone down to Alistair's room to cry on his shoulder. She didn't want to hear that she was a good person who'd just made a mistake. She wanted DX to slap her. She deserved it.

"Don't worry," DX said. "I know what you'll do. My helicopter is getting a tune-up, but she'll be ready to fly soon. We'll kidnap your girl. Tony and I will fly you out to Taha'a. Forget Tahiti. Taha'a is so pristine, you'll want to eat the sand. And there are vanilla plantations. You can take her out into the vanilla on a full moon and ask her to marry you. Tony and I can fly over with a load of cherry blossoms and dump them on you right as you go down on one knee. You love that shit."

Avery imagined Merritt standing beneath a purple sky, the ocean lapping at a sandy beach in the distance. The petals would drift down like butterflies. But the reality was, DX would probably have to fly so low to drop the blossoms, Merritt would think they were being bombed—as though she wouldn't be terrified enough after being kidnapped.

"What do vanilla plantations even look like?" Avery asked.

"So you'll do it!"

"Of course not."

"Well, don't worry. I'm flying up to Portland. We got to wrap up this set we're recording, and then I'll be there. We'll fix this."

Coming from DX it was almost a threat, but it was a threat Avery was glad to hear.

Chapter 11

For three days Merritt told Iliana she had the flu. The old Iliana would have shoved a bottle of Sadfire Reserve at her and told Merritt to get away from her before she got Iliana sick too. Now Iliana stood at Merritt's door, a tureen of Lei-Ling's dumplings in hand. It was the third bowl of dumplings she'd brought, and each time Merritt had told herself she was too depressed to eat. Then she'd smelled fried green onion and kung pao ketchup and had eaten the whole pile in one sitting.

"Not again," Merritt said.

"You love Lei-Ling's cooking. She made the homemade ketchup you like."

"I have the flu."

It would be nice to have someone who cooked for her when she was sick or to cook with her on cold, rainy evenings in February, Merritt thought. Not someone like Lei-Ling, who loved taking care of everything (kittens, puppies, babies, sick people, dying houseplants), but someone who loved her first and most, someone who hurried home to see her, who would hold her if she cried. She hadn't cried in front of another person since she was in high school.

She remembered the exact day: her eighteenth birthday. The Vale Academy secretary had brought a package to her in homeroom. Inside was a neon pink sweatshirt and a postcard from her mother. *Wish you were here.* The banality of the sweatshirt and the obvious lie—*wish you were here*—had shocked her into tears she hadn't known she'd felt. She'd run out the room. Behind her one of the boys said, *She really hates that sweatshirt.* Avery had caught up with her just before Merritt had raced down the path. They'd sat on the steps while Merritt cried. *I wanted a family. I wanted a place. She just found a man with a yacht, and I didn't matter anymore.* A few months later Avery had moved back to California and had never spoken to Merritt again.

"You look like hell." Iliana's brow furrowed with worry. "Should I take you to the doctor?" She was wearing her white linen gi.

Merritt ran her hand through her hair. "You've got class."

"I'll cancel class if you're sick."

"I'm not sick."

"Don't be tough."

Merritt sat down on the couch. The windows of her apartment let in an unusual light. Rare summer thunderclouds had darkened half the sky, while the other half remained bright. Portland got that kind of weather only once every couple of years. You had to stay to see it.

"What is it?" Iliana asked.

"I've got to get out of this apartment," Merritt said. "Take me somewhere?"

"Of course."

* * *

But there was no *of course* about it. They were just pulling up in front of the Sadfire bar called Tiny Sorrow when the thunderclouds broke. Rain pelted the windshield, almost erasing the sound of Iliana's phone. Almost but not quite. Iliana's voice rose an octave as she answered.

"Honey Bear, what's up?" she asked. A moment later she turned to Merritt. "Lei-Ling's sister was supposed to run down to Fubonn and get a crate of clams, but she's only got her Vespa, so she asked if I could..."

The battering rain finished Iliana's sentence for her.

Half an hour later they were at the Golden Lucky Fortune, and Iliana was hurrying the clams through the back door. Next thing Merritt knew, they were seated in a booth near the window, Lei-Ling's mother fussing over them and Lei-Ling's little brother showing them a crayon drawing. Lei-Ling cuddled up to Iliana, protesting happily as Iliana shook rainwater on her.

"Are Avery and Alistair going to put me on the show?" Lei-Ling trilled.

Merritt had forgotten to tell her. "I don't think so."

Lei-Ling's face crumpled into a pout. Merritt hated Avery a little bit more for disappointing the Inner Child. There was probably a tipping point. One unhappiness after another and, eventually, Lei-Ling would become a normal human being who stayed up late worrying about global warming and whether lasting love was even a real thing.

"But you asked, right?"

"They plan these things way in advance," Merritt said. "I'm sure if they'd known about you all along, they would have loved to have your dumpling truck on the show. I tried. I really did."

Lei-Ling's face brightened. "And that's important," she said. "I have friends who'll try for me, and that's even better than being on a show. And I have my Pinyin."

That was her nickname for Iliana. Merritt thought it meant *biscuit*.

Merritt's phone rang. She rose and moved toward the door. "Hellenic Hardware."

The caller drew in a breath. "Merritt?"

It was Avery.

For a split second Merritt was a teenager again, delighted to hear Avery's voice. Then reality reasserted itself like a load of shingles sliding off a roof. There was probably a term for this in Iliana's self-help books. *Childhood happiness withdrawal.*

"I got your number from our research department," Avery said.

"You went to too much trouble. The shop number rings to my cell phone."

"I'm sorry. I know you said you didn't want to see me."

Lei-Ling looked over with bright eyes. Lei-Ling loved phones. She loved unexpected calls and dumplings and sunshine and rainbows and Hello Kitty pencils. She was so happy. It had rubbed off on Iliana. It had not rubbed off on Merritt.

Merritt moved into the glass foyer between the restaurant and the gritty sprawl of Eighty- Second Avenue.

"What part of 'I don't want you in my life' didn't you get, Avery?"

Avery's words tumbled out as though she were on a burner phone with two minutes left. "I was talking to DX, and she said I messed up big-time. And she said I should sleep with you on a bed of jellyfish, but that's just weird. I want to convince you. I want to show you I didn't do it. Even if you hate me, I just want you to know."

DX? Merritt thought everything felt surreal. Merritt had seen DX at the Moda Center, and now the singer of "Uber to Hell" was somehow listening to her personal problems. And Avery was talking so fast, Merritt could barely make out what she was saying with the rain hitting the glass foyer.

Finally, Avery took a gulping breath. "That night was special." She stopped.

"I thought you couldn't tell anyone. I thought it was so shameful you needed a twenty-page contract."

"Not shameful, Merritt. Never shameful."

Merritt wanted to believe her. Her chest tightened. Her heart raced. Maybe she would have a heart attack like Uncle Oli. She wanted Avery so much it was almost a physical pain, and it wasn't just the desire for angry, emotionally unintelligent, off-brand-hotel sex. It was the longing for Avery's words to be true. *I didn't do it. I would never hurt you.* It was that longing that made her pull the phone away from her ear and, trembling, press end.

Without looking back, she headed out into the rain.

"Come back," Iliana called out, but Merritt ignored her.

Merritt had just turned on the truck and pushed the gearshift into reverse when Iliana appeared at her window.

"Where are you going?" Iliana asked through the glass.

"Out for a drink."

"Have a drink inside."

"You have fun with Lei-Ling."

Iliana placed a palm on the window. "Stay there." She ran around to the other side of the truck and got in. "I'm sorry. You wanted to talk." Iliana glanced sheepishly back at the restaurant. "I got distracted."

Merritt leaned her arms on the steering wheel and her head on her arms. She drew in a long breath to calm herself.

"I've never seen you like this. What's going on?" Iliana said.

No one saw her like this. No one saw her true feelings. She'd held them so close even Iliana had only ever half guessed.

"I lost the Elysium."

"Shit, Meri." That ridiculous nickname! The old Iliana would never have called her anything but 'Merritt' or maybe, occasionally, 'slacker.' "Were you outbid?"

"The Historical Society is going to protect the facade. But inside who knows. Wall-to-wall carpet." The misery in her voice had nothing to do with wall-to-wall carpet.

"Who's going to put in wall-to-wall carpet?"

"It doesn't matter."

Iliana put a hand on Merritt's shoulder. "I don't want to be the asshole who says you could always buy another building, but you could always buy another building. It's kind of weird wanting to live in your dead uncle's apartment. That's the past."

"I . . ." Merritt's thoughts swirled. "It was Avery."

"What? Avery Crown bought the Elysium?"

"I took her there on the night of the reunion. Then *King and Crown* bought it." Merritt rubbed the heels of her hands across her eyes and leaned her head back against the headrest. "I slept with her."

"That's huge!" Iliana said with delight that quickly turned to anger. "She slept with you and then she bought your building for her show?"

"I think she slept with me *so* she could buy my building." It didn't seem fair that she should be embarrassed on top of everything else, but she was. She'd let her hopes grow. She'd watched Avery get in her Uber and she'd imagined a future of hot sex and homemade dinners. "It was that night. Somehow they finalized the deal in the middle of the night. She was afraid I would find out, so she slept with me to distract me."

"That's coercion," Iliana said. "That's assault." Iliana hit the dashboard with the flat of her hand. "I'll kill her. Tell me where she is. I'll kill her right now."

"That's not the *way of harmony*," Merritt said with a humorless laugh.

"No, but that's what we would have done when we were

schlepping pavers for Signa Concrete down by the port. We'll take her to Mikey's Bar, get her drunk, and bam."

Now, that was the old Iliana.

"No we won't," Merritt said.

"Okay, we won't. But I know what we'll do."

Thunderclouds still darkened the sky to the north. The halogen glow of used-car lots stood out against their darkness. Portland might be gentrifying, but Eighty-Second Avenue was still a wasteland of pawnshops and Asian funeral parlors.

"You know what I'll do?" Iliana said. "We'll go inside, and you'll tell Lei-Ling every detail. Lei-Ling will have every lesbian in America tweeting that Avery Crown betrayed her lesbian lover. Avery will go down in flames. *King and Crown* will go off the air so fast that network won't even save them a parking spot."

"I can't," Merritt said wearily.

"Of course you can."

"That show is her life."

"Merritt?" Iliana tapped her arm. "Are you crazy? She stole your dream, even though—and I did say this before—I don't think buying your dead uncle's apartment is moving you forward emotionally."

"It would destroy her to lose that show."

She imagined Avery falling to the ground in despair as Merritt exposed Avery's true sexuality. The thought that she could have done that filled her with a strange alarm.

"Are you protecting her?" Incredulity spread across Iliana's face.

"I can't use her sexual orientation against her. Isn't that against a lesbian code or something?"

The windows of the Golden Lucky Fortune glowed like a cozy snow globe. Merritt could see Lei-Ling, Lei-Ling's sister, her baby brother, her parents, and their customers. Soon Iliana would join them. Her broken attempts at Chinese would make everyone laugh. Iliana wouldn't mind because they all adored her. There had been a moment, when Merritt had woken to see Avery looking at her, that's she'd felt like Avery was family.

"Slow down. What happened?" Iliana asked. "Why don't you want to ruin this girl's life?"

Merritt told Iliana about her visit to the set and Avery's promise that she had nothing to do with the sale.

"She cried," Merritt finished. "I'm such a sucker. I still felt sorry for her."

Iliana cocked her head. "If she didn't have anything to do with the sale—"

"She had everything to do with the sale."

"You buy stuff for Hellenic Hardware and I don't have anything to do with it. Your interns don't have anything to do with it. What if someone came in and said you stole a bunch of chair rails and it was my fault?"

Merritt did not want her to be optimistic. The old Iliana would have known that people who screw you over once will do it again. As much as it hurt to be abandoned, it was the only way to guarantee a woman wouldn't eventually ruin your life.

"Did she act like she was lying?" Iliana asked.

"She's an actor."

"It's reality TV."

"It's all fake."

"But why would she bother to fake-cry? She got your building already."

"She had this nondisclosure contract. I didn't sign it, but if I had and I told anyone we'd been together, she'd take Hellenic Hardware too."

"Why would a reality television host want an antique hardware store? And Avery Crown wouldn't sleep with someone for a building. That's just messed up. She's too sweet."

Merritt was going to say, *Please don't be like Lei-Ling and believe everything you see on TV*, but she knew Iliana was right. Lei-Ling was no fool, and it was a terrible thing to accuse Avery of. Her head spun with Iliana's words and a flicker of hope, which she pushed away.

"Maybe she's telling the truth. You have to be open to possibilities," Iliana said. "I didn't think Lei-Ling and I would go anywhere. I went into her restaurant a hundred times."

It was their origin story, and Iliana loved to tell it. How many times she'd gone into the Golden Lucky Fortune. How Lei-Ling had fashioned sexually suggestive carrot flowers for her kung pao shrimp, until one day Iliana worked up the courage to bring Lei-Ling a book of Georgia O'Keeffe paintings.

"I didn't think she wanted me," Iliana went on. "But her whole family knew how she felt. They were all watching us from the kitchen. Her grandfather said, 'It is fortuitous. She has given her a book of the vagina flower.'" Iliana was about to launch into a description of their first date.

Merritt cut her off. "Please don't tell me about how happy you are."

"It could happen for you."

Rain hit the window like tears.

Even if Avery was telling the truth, she had been gone for *fifteen years*. Fifteen years and then Avery wanted to waltz back into her life like nothing had happened. She hadn't even looked for her. She had come to Portland on business, run into her by accident, and screwed her, literally and figuratively.

"I'm done with her."

"Merritt, come on," Iliana said, frustration breaking through her optimism. "You're always walking around like someone's going to hit you. Have you ever thought that maybe they won't?"

Chapter 12

A few days later Avery and Alistair were waiting in the van for the start of the Care for Kids Fun-Raiser Bike Ride. Outside the van, the grass between Naito Parkway and the river was packed with vendors. Everything was fluttering leaves and sparkling water, but nothing looked beautiful to Avery. She couldn't see the quintessential Portland she was supposed to capture in her decorating of the Elysium.

"Body Biscuit?" Alistair asked meditatively. They were both wearing spandex bicycle suits in the brand-specific green of Global Body Biscuit. Venner wanted *King & Crown* to be a *whole lifestyle brand*, which might help with their unexceptional viewership (although it might just sell biscuits).

"I haven't ridden a bike in twenty years," Avery said.

"You never forget."

Wasn't that the truth? She hadn't slept since Merritt had arrived on set, and the more tired she became, the more her memories of Merritt tormented her.

"I got you this." Alistair held out a paperback book. "It's a romance. It's got a happy ending. My mom reads them."

Alistair's mom worked in the front office of a mining company and read books about the Winchester Mystery House. Anytime Alistair had offered to take her there, she'd declined, saying, *Oh no. The good Lord gave me all I need right here,* which in Stone did not make the Lord look very good. Avery and Alistair's mom did not have much in common.

"Thanks," Avery said.

"*The Untouchable Canyon,*" Alistair said, as though the title might cheer her up. "'Lucy Sunderland was born into wealth, but she pines to run free over the moor.' You want to run free over a moor, don't you?"

Avery looked at Alistair. His blue eyes were full of sympathy, but he never got it quite right. King Cobra for grief. An enormous arrangement of plastic dahlias because he said his love for her would last forever, like plastic, which took four hundred and fifty years to biodegrade. Still, she would take his dahlias over any diamond solitaire.

"What's a moor?" Avery asked.

"It's a heath. A fen for shooting grouse."

"You miss Stone."

"Do not." He took out his phone. "Cheer you up?"

He cued up a video. The America Wyoming Foundation had put in a swimming pool for the twenty days it was warm enough to swim in Stone. The video made her feel worse. Alistair was good. The world was full of good people, and she wasn't one of them.

A loud knock on the van window startled them both. The back doors flew open.

"Hello, you beautiful Barbie dolls," DX declared.

She too was dressed in a bicycle suit, although hers was black and sleek, like the outfit of a superhero.

"I was going to come up tomorrow, but I called Greg and he said you were riding in this kids' thing, and I was like, I frickin' love kids. Here." She picked up a small cooler she had brought with her and offered it to Avery. "Hi Song sushi. Your favorite. We were in San Francisco for breakfast this morning, so I picked it up. I had to keep it on dry ice. The guy on the helicopter had some problem with that. Something about sublimated CO2. I said fuck yeah! Next time I'm filling a whole fucking bathtub with dry ice and we're flying overnight to Nepal."

"The *guy on the helicopter*," Alistair said, shaking his head with a smile. "Would that be the *pilot*?"

"No. He was just this guy we picked up in San Fran. I flew! Feminism is flying your own chopper."

Of course DX flew. DX probably prepared fugu fish for her entourage, had sex with her boyfriend in the cockpit, and recorded a new song that had gone platinum... all in the time Avery and Alistair had taken to squeeze into their Body Biscuit suits.

Alistair hopped out of the van and gave DX a full-body hug. "Cheer Avery up for me, will you? She's blue. I'll go give out our free biscuits."

DX took the seat next to Avery.

"So, you and this girl?"

"Me and this girl nothing. She doesn't want to see me."

"Did you break into her house? Tie yourself to her bed?"

"No!"

"Don't you think you should at least try?"

"To get myself arrested?"

"To get yourself arrested for *love*."

Greg appeared at the open doors.

"Sorry, Avery. You've got to get out there. Photo ops. Hi, DX." He looked wary. DX was not the person you wanted on the set of a well-organized decorating show, especially not with the TKO boss sniffing around like an auditor.

"We'll talk more," DX said. "Let's go ride the hell out of this race."

Avery made her way through the throng of vendors. One hour of hawking Global Body Biscuits and a few of hours of shooting: She could do it. Filming had always exhilarated her. A ten-hour day just made her want a twelve-hour day. But now all she wanted to do was lie in her hotel room and watch reruns of any show but *King & Crown*.

Alistair was passing out samples, his charm in overdrive. It took a lot of charm to sell energy bars that tasted like dirt and Body Biscuit's Around the World Energy Shot, which tasted like turpentine.

"You want to fly around the world?" Alistair asked a passerby. He tossed the woman a sample. "Now you can." To Avery he whispered, "Ponza is over there. I swear he doesn't have a real job. Why isn't he chasing after someone with a scandalous paternity lawsuit or a nose transplant or something? Anyway, the race starts in an hour. We'll ditch him."

Avery sat down behind Alistair and opened one of the small plastic vials of Around the World. Alistair grinned at the crowd, talking enough to make up for Avery sulking in the back of the vending tent.

Eventually, the crew arrived for a quick product-placement shot. Venner came up behind Gould, the cameraman.

"Around-the-world energy. Red Bull's a 747. This is a rocket," Venner said. "I just went to China! Bam. Japan! Bam! Paris! Bam! Let's go again."

Avery took another shot. She wasn't tired anymore, and her heart rate had sped up.

"Again," Venner said.

Gould's camera sprang at her. Alistair knocked back the same empty bottle four times. One. Two. Three. Four. DX zipped by. Venner called "action." Avery took another shot.

"Again. Action. Cut. Bam! Pow! China. Again."

Then one of the production assistants was holding the handlebars of a bike in front of her.

"It's too big," Avery said. "I don't remember how."

She felt jumpy energy sear through her body. Everything was vibrating. Maybe there really was something to the Global Body Biscuit line.

"What's in those shots?" she asked Alistair.

"You didn't actually drink all those, did you?" he asked, suddenly noticing the empty bottles. "You're supposed to pretend. Here, drink some water. Get it out of your system."

"I feel okay," Avery managed.

Someone fired a starting pistol.

"Just take it easy," Alistair said. "I think it's legal speed. It's not good for you."

He was wrong, though. The first mile was all uphill, but the shots had kicked in, and she felt light and free. Her bones vibrated. She pedaled faster. She imagined Merritt watching from the sidelines. Merritt would see her moving so fast, so gracefully, her body a flash of green. Merritt would think, *She's so strong and athletic. What a good cause. She loves children!* Merritt would be waiting for her at the finish line. *Oh, Avery. I was wrong to be so angry.* Maybe Merritt would think she looked good in green spandex. Maybe antifreeze green brought out something in her eyes.

She thought she heard Greg (or maybe it was Gould) calling, "Cut. We got it."

She pedaled harder.

"We're done," Alistair yelled.

Avery wasn't listening. She was moving fast. They had climbed a hill, and now she was on the downward slope, racing toward a conglomeration of office parks. Faster and faster she pedaled. She was at one with her bike. Forget Pilates. She needed speed.

"Woo-hoo!" someone yelled.

Avery saw a flash of superhero suit, then DX's wiry body bent over the handlebars of a BMX bike.

Avery thought she heard Alistair yelling behind her, but she couldn't stop. Stopping meant thinking. Stop and the *King & Crown* contractor was painting over vintage wallpaper in the beautiful Elysium building. Stop and the only me-

mento she had of Merritt Lessing was a memory. Stop and tomorrow would be—

"Avery, wait! No! Not that way!" Alistair's voice was far behind her. "Aves! The road!"

Alistair didn't know. Avery needed to follow DX on some wild quest. She needed to fly a helicopter full of dry ice. She needed to kiss Merritt on a busy street and not care who saw.

She saw DX flying down the road before her. They had left the other riders behind. Everything was a blur. Then, in one beautiful, sweeping movement, DX flew up the side of a concrete embankment. Avery saw her suspended against the blue sky, and then Avery was racing up the same embankment. She was soaring. She could do anything, and she would win Merritt back. She would learn to fly because she was a rocket. Avery looked down. She was airborne. Then, with a crunch of metal and gravel, she was not.

Chapter 13

It was eight o'clock that evening, and Merritt sat at the workstation in the back of Hellenic Hardware, polishing a Greenman door knocker. Soaked, polished, and oiled, the door knockers burned with the same luster they must have had when they were first forged. Ordinarily, she would have been delighted. The day before she had learned that Avery would be at the reunion, she had cleaned forty-eight ceramic fuse holders. It had taken all day. She had been perfectly happy... well, maybe not perfectly happy, but she'd enjoyed every fuse. Now everything grated on her. The heat of the day hung in the air. The Pride House interns had been dreaming of the Nostalgia-rom fundraiser they were nominally involved in planning, and they wouldn't leave. She heard something clatter.

"What are you still doing here?" Merritt called more sharply than she intended.

One of the interns bounced over to her, a mop of silky

blond hair falling in his eyes. He was nineteen. He'd been homeless for almost two years before Tate Grafton had caught him stealing scones from one of her coffee shops and had brought him to the Pride House. Merritt thought two years on the street would harden anyone, but Alex was enthusiastic, childlike, and incompetent. Usually she found the combination endearing.

"I told you to go home an hour ago."

"I love it here." Alex bounced on his toes. "Me and Cassie are working on decorations for the Nostalgia-rom, and Cassie was wondering if we could move the windows."

Merritt took off the reading glasses she wore for the detail work of restoration. She set them down with a sigh. "The Nostalgia-rom is on September twenty-second. Last day of summer. It's July. Go home."

Alex twisted his hands behind his back as he bounced. "We need room for another bar. I am going to get lit!"

"You're not," Merritt said. "You're nineteen."

"But I've got an ID."

"And I know who you are. Cut it up, or I'm telling your counselors." Merritt looked back at her work, tracing the curves of the Greenman's face with a Q-tip. "Go. It's late."

She had had a fake ID when she was a teenager. She remembered buying whiskey for Avery. They had sat beneath the Saint Johns Bridge—their bridge—drinking out of plastic cups. Merritt had felt embarrassed. All the girls at Vale nipped a little champagne, but the whiskey had suddenly seemed like a ruffian's choice. Avery looked so debonair in her pink-and-gray argyle sweater. Merritt hadn't gained any weight since she was sixteen, but she had grown taller and her jeans had exposed an inch of ankle.

Avery had sipped her whiskey. *Do your parents let you drink?*

Peach schnapps in my baby bottle. Merritt had wanted Avery to laugh, but Avery had taken her hand.

No! Really?

Merritt conceded that yes. On the yacht before her first boarding school, her mother would pour a little schnapps into a cup of juice and tell her to go play on her own. She hadn't meant to tell Avery, and she'd tried to laugh it off. Avery had put an arm around her shoulders. *That's child abuse,* she'd said very seriously. *Do you want me to tell someone?* Merritt had breathed in Avery's perfume. *What are they going to do?* she'd joked. *Take me out of the home?* Then she'd lain down on the grass and nestled her head in Avery's lap. It had felt self-indulgent, like she was taking advantage. How could kind, concerned Avery say, *I'm sorry your parents tried to liquor you up, but your head is awfully close to my crotch. Move!* But Avery hadn't seemed to mind, and she had stroked Merritt's hair and traced the contours of her face: her eyebrows, her jawline, her lips, until the pleasure of her caresses was too much and Merritt had stood up and paced down to the river.

But she was never going to see Avery again, so it didn't make sense to linger in these memories. She would never see her again, except that she kept googling images of Avery Crown. Maybe she had OCD. Compulsions: something you couldn't not do. One last time, she told herself. Then she was done. Forever.

Merritt picked up her phone. The images loaded slowly. What was she looking for? Proof that Avery hadn't stolen the Elysium? Proof that she had? Proof that Merritt herself should have been kinder?

Go back to Alistair.

I am not your friend.

I'll tell them.

I don't want you in my life.

Her own words had begun to haunt her. She accused Lei-Ling of believing everything on television. There were ten people living in a cave in Nevada who still thought reality TV was real. But maybe Iliana was right. Did reality television hosts actually do any of the things they seemed to do? She'd been mean. She never yelled at women. Iliana would say she wasn't just yelling at Avery, but she was yelling at her mother and her boarding schools and Uncle Oli for dying.

She stared at her phone. The images had loaded. She recognized most of them. A hundred glamour shots. A few outtakes. Avery and Alistair sitting on a curb looking tired but happy, Alistair passing a coffee cup to Avery and Avery looking at him as if to say, *We can do this.*

Merritt scrolled down, then stopped short. She hadn't seen the next photograph. It was Avery lying on pavement, blood on her cheek. She kept scrolling. An ambulance. A stretcher. Alistair clasping Avery's hand as EMTs carried her off. Merritt touched one of the photos and it redirected to a blog called *The Ponza Scheme.* The text read, *Singer-songwriter DX may have mastered the highest jump in the Care for Kids Fun-Raiser Bike Ride, but television hostess with the mostest Avery Crown was not so lucky. Bystanders said it was clear that the Decor Diva couldn't make the jump and she went for it anyway. Competition with her BFF, DX, or something more?*

Merritt gripped her phone. The article was dated that day. That afternoon!

Merritt raced through the possibilities. Surgery? Brain damage? She saw Avery's body in the dim light of the Jupiter Hotel. Avery had wanted her. For one delicate moment between orgasm and sleep, Merritt had been perfectly happy. Her heart seized with tenderness. She had planned on being angry at Avery for years, but not forever. Somehow she imagined they would always reconnect. At another reunion perhaps, she would see Avery at a distance, hesitate for a minute, then walk toward her, time slowing around them. *I didn't think I would see you again*, she would say. And Avery would open her arms. *Merritt, I missed you.*

Merritt's hands were trembling so much it took her several seconds to search for directions to the Extended Stay Deluxe.

"What about we paint the whole floor blue?" Alex was at her side again. "And then we get one of those projectors—"

Merritt stood up and grabbed her shop keys off a hook by the cash register. "Don't touch anything. Lock up and get out of here. You. Cassie. Now."

"You're going to let me close the shop?"

Merritt was already running for her truck.

Rush hour had slowed the city to a crawl, and Merritt beat her palm on the steering wheel. She had missed Avery so much. The realization hit her like a wrecking ball hitting a load-bearing wall: It might be too late. She thought she had time to be angry, but what if she didn't? Merritt prayed as she pulled onto I-84. *If she's okay, I'll do anything.* She would sell the hardware store. She would drive down to California, to some dusty-stucco, barred-window barrio. She would work construction like she did when Uncle Oli died. She would get a burner phone and eat from the mini-mart. She would live in a hovel. If only Avery was okay, she would give everything up. She offered a silent prayer.

* * *

She realized how foolish she was when she reached the Extended Stay Deluxe. Avery had said she was staying in room 1313. Doubly unlucky. But Avery was in the hospital. Maybe she'd been airlifted to Seattle. She wouldn't be at her motel on Airport Way.

Chapter 14

In fact, Avery was in her room at the Extended Stay Deluxe, pressing an ice pack to the side of her face. Despite Greg's protests, Venner wanted her back on set in the morning. *Thirty-five days,* he kept yelling, as if they had gotten an extension on building Rome. She limped over to the window. The hotel was only two stories high. From her vantage, she could see a row of parked cars, dying arborvitae, and beyond that the runways. She leaned her forehead against the glass.

For a moment she had lain on the pavement, staring into the blue sky and wondering if that was the end. Would her fans decorate a shrine in her honor? Would Merritt be sorry? Avery had guessed not.

Now she lay back down. The bed had been uncomfortable before. Hitting the pavement on Macadam Avenue had not improved it, but she fell asleep anyway. She wasn't sure if she woke an hour later or a day. She knew she regretted waking up. Outside her room, footsteps hurried down the hall. It was probably Venner coming to harass her. She pulled a pillow over her head. The expected pound hit the door.

"Go away. I'm dying," Avery called out.

"Do you need me to call an ambulance?"

"It's too late. You can't save me."

"It's not too late."

The voice was muffled but tense. Avery pushed the pillow off her head.

"Who is it?"

"It's Merritt."

Merritt! She was here. Avery leapt from the bed. It hurt the second she moved. The room was a mess, clothes everywhere. The bed was wrecked. Her body was still encased in irradiated-green spandex. She grabbed her robe off the floor and opened the door.

Merritt, of course, looked great. She wore black tuxedo pants and a loose white shirt unbuttoned to reveal the slight swell of her breasts.

"What are you doing *here*? I thought you were at the hospital." Merritt said. Her face read disapproval.

"How did you find me?"

"You told me your room number. Thirteen thirteen. Extended Stay Deluxe. Doubly unlucky."

Avery's voice quavered. "Come in."

"Where's Alistair? Why isn't he with you?" Anger had drained Merritt's face of color. She looked like an Armani model on a mission of retribution. Her hair and eyes so dark. Her face white and taut, shadows visible beneath her cheekbones.

"Working," Avery said.

"That's bullshit. What the hell is he doing? You're just here? In your hotel?"

Avery caught her reflection in a mirror by the door. There were women who were beautiful enough to salvage this moment, women who could play refugees and one-armed assassins and still come off looking glamorous. She wasn't one of them.

The fright of the crash hit her again. She'd gone down. Then Alistair was kneeling over her. Venner asking if she could see. Then sirens. An ambulance. Alistair was muscling Dan Ponza away, saying, *Get off her.* Then they were at the hospital. A technician took a few X-rays. A kind-faced doctor with a gray goatee shone a light in her eyes. Then Venner was saying, *I think that'll play really well on local.* Venner had dumped her off in her hotel room with a curt, *You better be ready tomorrow. Thirty-five days!* A publicity stunt! She'd thought she was dying.

Of course Alistair had tried to cheer her up. He had brought her a box of Pop Beads, which appeared to be a children's activity comprised of little plastic beads that clicked into one another so you could make necklaces. *Why?* she had asked. *To cheer you up.* It had taken an hour to convince Alistair she wanted to suffer alone.

Now Merritt glared at her in consternation.

"Look at you. You're wrecked," Merritt said. "It's exploitation. Is this all going to be on film? Is this part of the finale?"

"Merritt." Avery sat down on an ottoman, her shoulders slumped. Her whole body hurt. "I know you're mad, but

I can't do this today. I just can't." She knew she couldn't play the gorgeous assassin, but she was supposed to play the bouncy housewife. *OMG, the crash was so cringe-worthy!* But she didn't have any bounce in her. She looked up at Merritt, who still stood by the door with a look of consternation on her face. "I was in an accident. I feel like shit. I have to be back at work tomorrow. I can't—" Avery rested her head in her hands, rubbing her temples.

Merritt hated her. Venner was pissed. Greg and Alistair were working overtime to make up for the delay in filming. Her elbow was swollen. She'd accumulated scratches that would scar and her mother would insist on one of Dr. Miter's chemical peels. She knew even moving on to the next city wouldn't fix the hole in her heart.

"And I'm sorry about everything. I really am." Avery felt miserable. She'd been so excited to see Merritt at the reunion, and now everything had gone so much worse than she could have imagined. "I didn't want any of this, but I get that you don't believe me. I wish I'd given you a reason to give me the benefit of the doubt, but I know I haven't. Any other day, I'd want you to be here, even if it were just to yell at me, but you can't yell today. Please. I know you're mad, but I can't take one more thing. Today you just have to go hate me someplace else. I can't take another hit."

She closed her eyes.

She didn't hear Merritt cross the room. All she knew was that suddenly Merritt was kneeling behind her ottoman, cradling her gently against her chest.

"Baby," Merritt murmured. "I didn't mean it like that.

Sweetie, don't think I meant that. I'm not mad at *you*. I'm mad at them. Why isn't someone here with you? Why aren't you at the hospital?"

It felt like a dream. She could smell Merritt's cologne: cedar and sandalwood. Merritt lifted her effortlessly and carried her to the bed. When Merritt set her down, Avery clung to her.

"What happened?" Merritt asked.

"I didn't know about your building," Avery said. "I really didn't."

"Not the building. You. You've got blood in your hair."

Damn. It could get worse. She had so much hair, and now she was a walking biohazard, but Merritt held her, then placed the lightest kiss on her forehead.

"Sweetheart," she murmured.

"We were doing the bike ride. Me, Al, DX. I was just following DX, and she went off course and onto this ramp. She was on a BMX bike. Who does stunts in the children's hospital fun ride?"

"Did you have a BMX bike?"

"A big cruiser."

"You can't do jumps on a cruiser."

"Who knew, right? It wasn't even that big of a jump." It was all so not gloriously tragic. "When I came to, it looked like I had fallen off a curb. DX didn't even know what happened. She thought my chain broke. Alistair tried to tell me I was okay, but then Venner swooped in and started yelling about how my pupils were different. I was having a stroke. 'It's a brain bleed,' he kept yelling. I thought it was real. I was so scared." She clung to Merritt, thinking as she did that she should let go. This was too much desperation. She should have accepted a hug and pulled away, not clasped Merritt like she was drowning. But Merritt felt so good, and Avery felt so safe in her arms. "It was everything flashing before my eyes. What if I couldn't walk or I couldn't think, and I lost everything, and I...I never got to see you again? And Venner let me be scared. He loved it, and later he said he just wanted to make it look good for the camera because it gave us more drama. You're right. It's all fake. The show. The accident. God, none of it's real. I'm sorry."

I'm sorry I left.

I'm sorry I never called.

I'm sorry my company stole your building.

"Have you gotten out of this outfit? Has anyone looked you over?"

Avery had tried to squirm out of her green suit, but it hadn't been easy to get in and out of it pre-bicycle-crash. It wasn't worth the pain of extricating herself now.

"It's too tight."

"You really should." Merritt's voice was full of concern. "Do you want to wear this again?"

Avery laughed. "Do you even see where they put the logos?"

A copy of the Global Body Biscuit logo—a world with a bite taken out of it—covered each of Avery's nipples. Avery thought Merritt's eyes lingered.

"I've had those biscuits," Merritt said. "I think this is false advertising. They weren't nearly so—" Merritt stopped herself, but she smiled too.

This was who they had been at sixteen, Avery thought, teasing each other, talking dirty, letting their eyes meet over an insinuation they both understood. If only she'd had the courage to be bolder when they were kids and everything was still possible.

"I have a pocketknife. I could get you out of that thing. I'll be careful."

Avery loved the seriousness in her dark eyes. "Okay."

Very carefully, Merritt pulled the neck of Avery's suit away from her skin and sliced the tip of a tiny pocket blade through the fabric. The green spandex pulled apart faster than Avery would have liked, as though she'd been squeezed into a suit that was half a size too small. She wished she had Merritt's long bones and angular frame. Avery looked away, wincing at the thought of Merritt examining her.

"I'm a mess," Avery said. "Don't look."

"How could I not look?" Merritt said, and Avery thought she heard just a touch of awe in Merritt's voice.

Merritt offered Avery her hand and helped her out of the rest of her suit. They stood together: Avery naked, Merritt clothed. Avery remembered their night at the Jupiter Hotel, and she felt a whisper of hope. Merritt examined her carefully, first lifting her hair from her shoulders—delicately, without touching her skin—then smoothing her hand gently down Avery's arms and turning her around. Her touch was so gentle it felt like a warm breeze, but everywhere Merritt touched her and everywhere Merritt looked, Avery felt the pain of her crash fade away.

"Baby," Merritt said again. "Ah, sweetheart. You're all

bruised up and scraped. I can't believe they didn't take care of you at the hospital. I'm going to run you a bath."

Merritt disappeared into the bathroom. Avery heard the water running. A moment later Merritt returned.

In the tub, the warm water stung for a moment, and then Avery felt her muscles relax. Merritt knelt beside her and gently smoothed a washcloth along her shoulders and across her cheek. Avery longed for Merritt to release the cloth and touch her everywhere.

"I don't want to hurt you," Merritt said.

"You're not. You won't."

Finally, Merritt let the cloth swim away. She dipped her hands in the water and ran them through Avery's hair, her fingertips massaging Avery's scalp and untangling the matted curls. Avery thought it was the most delicious sensation she had ever felt. She could lay there forever. That was a feeling she couldn't remember: wanting to stay.

What she did remember were all the times she had run her hands through Merritt's silky hair. Lying by the river or in Merritt's bed. She had loved the way Merritt shifted under her caress, like a cat arching to be petted. It had sent a shiver of electricity through her. Now, as the sweet ache of arousal replaced the pain of her crash, she thought, *Did I turn her on?* Was that what Merritt's reluctant sighs had been about? Was that why it had seemed like she courted Avery's touch, laying her head on Avery's thigh or stretching her arms above her head so that Avery could not resist the urge to draw her fingernails down Merritt's lean back? Was that why sometimes she had also shaken Avery off and paced away, her face taut?

Too soon, Merritt stopped and rested her hands on the edge of the tub, gazing at her seriously.

"Let me get you out of there," Merritt said. "I should let you rest. Do you want me to call anyone for you?"

Slowly, Avery stepped out of the tub. Merritt steadied her. She held out Avery's robe and wrapped it around her. But Avery didn't want Merritt dressing her. She wanted Merritt to slide into the warm water with her. She wanted Merritt to make her forget all her bruises. She knew Merritt could, and the thought alone made her quiver.

"I should go," Merritt said.

Don't! This moment wasn't supposed end with Merritt handing her a dressing gown. They were supposed to strip the coverlet off the bed. Merritt was supposed to kiss every inch of her body. She could almost feel Merritt's fingers inside her. She had to seize the moment. She had to be like a Peruvian cowboy microchipping a jaguar . . . or something.

All Avery could manage was, "Alistair gave me a set of Pop Beads. He thought it would cheer me up."

"Pop Beads?"

Avery nodded to the kit on the table. "But you can't do them alone," she said.

"Is it like drinking?" Merritt picked up the box. "'Ages five to eight. Parental supervision suggested.' Ah, that's it. You might eat them."

"Alistair's weird. I don't think he actually knows what people give each other for gifts."

She could hear DX in the back of her mind. *I told you to tie yourself to her bed, and you came up with Pop Beads?* Merritt probably took her women to avant-garde plays. They probably crushed grapes with their feet and went to burlesque shows and walked around Merritt's apartment naked with the windows open.

Merritt wore a rueful smile. She adjusted the lapels of Avery's robe.

"I would love to make Pop Beads with you, but I should go. I just wanted to make sure you were all right."

But before Merritt stepped away, Avery mustered her courage—way more than it took to walk up a red carpet, more than it took to speak to audiences of hundreds, even a little bit more than it took to go out on the town with DX. Then she leaned up on tiptoe and planted a darting kiss on Merritt's lips.

"Avery." Merritt shook her head. "We shouldn't."

But she touched Avery's wrist, and she looked like someone wrestling with a great dilemma. With one trembling hand, Avery reached up and caressed the swirl of Merritt's ear. Merritt leaned her head into Avery's hand. Emboldened, Avery cupped Merritt's breast with her other hand, feeling the lace of Merritt's bra over her hardening nipple. Merritt sighed like someone setting down a great weight.

"It's okay," Avery whispered. She wanted to say, *I want you. Take me.* She kissed Merritt again. This was the woman she wanted to be. Bold. Free.

"I can't," Merritt murmured.

Then their tongues were moving slowly against each other, the sensation lighting a fire of desire in Avery's body. Avery stroked Merritt's back, slipping her hands under Merritt's shirt and trailing her nails down Merritt's smooth skin. Merritt could have any woman, but Avery could tell that right now Merritt wanted her. Merritt was melting in her hands. Avery might be the plain girl from the high school dramedy, but if Merritt made love to her she would be someone better. A seductress. A femme fatale. A woman with jellyfish in her waterbed.

"I think we should do what we should have done the summer after senior year," Avery said when their lips parted again. "Remember when we were kids? You could have a summer fling and you didn't break up at the end of the summer; you just...understood that summer wasn't part of your real life. You didn't expect anything to last. No one got hurt because it was magic. It wasn't real."

"I never had that summer."

Merritt leaned her forehead against the top of Avery's head.

"Neither did I. So let's have it now." Avery spoke quickly, afraid the words would freeze up in her throat and, once again, she'd fail to ask. "I'm in Portland for thirty-five more days. Be my lover. No promises. No commitments. I know you aren't going to go back into the closet."

"I never was in the closet."

"And I'm not going to quit *King and Crown*. But that night with you was..."

Merritt looked up, and her expression finished Avery's sentence for her.

"Just give me this summer," Avery said.

She ought to feel tired. She had to be on set tomorrow bruises or not. But she felt full of energy, as though she could stay awake forever. Maybe if she could coax Merritt into saying yes, this night would last forever. Maybe if Merritt said yes, the summer would never end.

"I can prove that I didn't know about the Elysium."

"I believe you."

Avery waited.

Merritt brushed a strand of wet hair off Avery's forehead. "You know, I liked you in high school," Merritt said.

Avery beamed. Merritt was going to say yes.

"A whole lot has happened since then," Merritt said. "It shouldn't matter, but it does. And, Avery Crown, you were always trouble for me."

"I want to be trouble. I haven't been trouble since we were at Vale."

"You're a sweet person."

"That's the problem."

"It's not a problem. It's lovely. I'm not sweet enough for you, Avery, even for a month. When I came to your set, I took a lot out on you. It wasn't fair. I yelled at you. I don't do that to women. I don't do that to anyone. Even people who do deserve it. And you didn't."

Now Avery wasn't sure if she was winning or crashing toward loss. Maybe if she'd dated more, she would know how much sexually charged declining was expected of old lovers getting back together for the summer. Maybe it was a thing...or maybe this was the struggle of a kind, attractive woman trying to find a better way to say *You're not exceptional.*

"You were angry," Avery said. "I don't care. What's the harm in five weeks?"

"You won't want me by the end of five weeks. Ask my exes."

"Your exes must be terrible women."

Merritt touched Avery's face, drawing her fingers along Avery's cheek, examining her the way Avery examined landmarks she left. Her last glimpse of Navy Pier. Central Park receding from view as her limo headed to the airport.

"They're not." Merritt looked sad. "Just reasonable, I guess. Come on. Let's be friends. Let's be real friends who stay in touch this time. Let's get those mimosas at Mother's and go shopping for shoes or whatever girls do."

Disappointment washed over Avery.

"Call me when you get a day off," Merritt said. "We'll go down to the river, walk around our old places."

Even though Merritt said *mimosas, shoes, and the river*, it all sounded like *goodbye*, and then Merritt was gone.

The minutes after her departure seemed to last forever. Avery heard the air conditioner clicking and whirring like a bad clock. If this were another kind of reality show, she could call DX for emergency advice. She *could* call DX for emergency advice, but it would probably involve a stolen plane. Or maybe she'd used up her SOS calls. The camera would zoom into her nostrils and the show's psychologist (whose voice would later get cut) would ask, *How does it make you feel to think you had a chance and then realize it was a no-go?* She was sick of being the bumbling, bouncy housewife-without-a-home. Maybe if she'd never gone on *King & Crown*, her face would have rearranged itself into extraordinary beauty and she'd be clever about women. She was going to read from a different script this time!

A moment later Avery burst out of the hotel, clothes hurriedly thrown on her wet body. It was a good thing the Extended Stay Deluxe parking lot went on and on, suggesting an optimism about occupancy that the hotel accommodations did not warrant. Merritt was just visible at the far end of the lot, swinging into the cab of her truck with the grace of a cowboy mounting his steed. Avery's Bellito Bellatoni flip-flops slapped across the pavement...so not awe-inspiringly gorgeous. So not gloriously tragic.

Merritt had the decency not to drive away. "What is it?" she asked, looking down on Avery from the vantage of her enormous truck.

She looked like she was talking to a crazy woman. Avery couldn't blame her. Avery clutched her side as the pain of her bike accident reasserted itself. "Wait," she gasped, trying not to double over.

Her mother always said she could never be an agent or a producer. She wasn't aggressive. She wasn't strategic. She didn't know how to read what people meant under what they said, and she didn't know how to say what she didn't mean in order to get what she wanted. But she had been on reality TV for fifteen years. As scripted as unscripted was, you still had to improvise.

"I have an idea," Avery said breathlessly.

Merritt looked guarded.

"Venner loves you."

"The guy who keeps calling me? I doubt it. I might have

told him to stick a wrench up his ass." Merritt looked embarrassed, as though this were not the kind of instructions she offered often.

"Venner wants you on the show. He thinks you're the hot new thing. You are. And he's proud of being someone who discovers new talent and fixes old shows. Negotiate. Tell him you want him to sell you the Elysium. We sell the buildings at the end of the season anyway. He'll want a bigger profit margin, but you can talk him down. Ask for the price you were going to pay. He's been bossing Greg all over the set, telling us about how sexy *Cop Brides* is and how he discovered the star of *Nail*. You're sexier than *Cop Brides*, and the girl on *Nail* looks like a gopher with breasts."

"I'm glad I beat out the gopher with breasts."

Avery thought a smile might be pulling at Merritt's lips. She took a deep breath. She could do this.

"My mother says I'm shit at business, but I've been in television for fifteen years. I know men like Venner. You can play him. I can tell you how."

* * *

It wasn't the same as winning Merritt over. It wasn't the same as Merritt's fingers in her hair (or elsewhere) or her lips on Avery's or Merritt whispering, *I can't resist you, darling.*

But Merritt did say, "Let me drive you back to your room. You shouldn't have run. Sweetie, you have to be careful."

Merritt did get out of the truck so she could help Avery up and again to help her down.

Back in her hotel room, Avery poured two plastic cups of King Cobra.

"Takes me back to someone else's misspent youth," Merritt said as she took a sip.

"Alistair's." Avery nodded. She set the Pop Beads between them on the table. "So here's what you'll have to do with Venner..."

It wasn't making love on a waterbed full of jellyfish, but she liked the admiring look on Merritt's face as she explained the pressures and personalities of television production. Merritt looked impressed. And she actually made a Pop Bead necklace, integrating all the colors in precise repetition. Avery liked that. She liked that Merritt stayed even after Avery said, "That's all I know about Venner." Merritt stayed and told her about the antique-fair zealots and a forger who had spent his career making fake faucets. And when the evening was clearly over, Merritt looped her Pop Bead necklace over Avery's head and said, "Avery Crown, you are trouble, but I always knew you'd be a star."

Chapter 15

Merritt pulled into the parking lot of the *King & Crown* headquarters. It took her a minute to confirm that her GPS was right. The "command center" looked like an abandoned 1970s diner on a stretch of McLoughlin Boulevard that was what all the rest of Portland tried not to be. Even Eighty-Second Avenue had a kind of cool, apocalyptic sleaziness about it (and you could get good dumplings at the Golden Lucky Fortune), but McLoughlin Boulevard was all off-brand tanning salons and vape parlors. Awful but not interesting.

The kind uncle who had stopped her on the *King & Crown* set poked his head out, looked both ways, and beckoned to her to enter.

"Reporters," he said apologetically as he ushered her through what had once been the restaurant's lobby. "We could use publicity, but it's just Dan Ponza looking for some scandal. I'm Greg Davis, field producer. Sorry about the other day." He pushed open the interior door. "Mr. Venner is very excited about you." He looked worried, as though Venner was excited but he wasn't. Still, he tried to hide it. "So, Avery has told you a bit about our little ship of fools?"

Inside, the place was everything Merritt hated about modern architecture. Bad linoleum. Faux-wood beams that clearly held up nothing except the vague notion that this place was supposed to look like a Swiss chalet. But the energy in the room was good. It was like the once-a-year cleaning at Hellenic Hardware. She would close the shop, and the staff and the interns would dust, polish, and rearrange, voices ringing out in collaboration, the smell of American Dream Pizza wafting around the warehouse.

"So this is show business?" Merritt asked.

"It's modest show business," Greg said. "We have to save budget for the travel. The best seasons are in the most expensive cities."

He kept talking, pointing out equipment and staff, but Merritt lost the train of conversation when she caught sight of Alistair and Avery sitting in a booth by the window. Avery wore a blue sundress. Her chestnut curls were pulled to one side in a loose ponytail. Avery caught her gaze and held it, a look of excitement in her golden-brown eyes. And Merritt wondered how she would survive five weeks of self-imposed emotional intelligence. Iliana would be proud. It had taken everything she had to walk away from Avery's hotel room, not once but twice! Avery's naked body had aroused her. Only Avery's bruises had kept her from slipping her hand into the bathwater and running her hand up Avery's inner thigh, mixing Avery's wetness with the warm water. She'd known Avery would be wet. That had turned her on too. But just as Avery awoke Merritt's desire, she stirred her loneliness. The trouble with being lonely was that it was too easy to get attached. That had been her downfall at Vale, and it would be again.

Her thoughts were interrupted by Venner bursting through the swinging doors that had once led to the kitchen.

"Merritt Lessing." He clasped a hand over his heart. "Where have you been all my life? That stunt with Bunter was priceless. When Avery told me she could get you here, I said, 'Now we're talking.'"

Avery had coached her. Venner wanted excitement. Even home shows were getting sexier. The woman on *Nail* drilled fence posts in a bikini top. *City Scions* took bombed-out warehouses and turned them into lofts. Every show ended with a guest band playing a set in the flat. In surveys, viewers liked *King & Crown*'s wholesome image. In practice, they liked to see the cohost's nipples through her wet T-shirt.

"We'll see." Merritt slid into an unoccupied booth.

Avery also said Venner liked a challenge. Everyone simpered around him. If he didn't make your career, he destroyed it. *I think he's bored with being the boss*, Avery had said. *He probably hires dominatrixes to call him a bad boy and throw grapefruits at him.* Merritt had laughed. It was so easy to laugh with Avery. That was why she had to stay away from her. After Avery left, nothing would come of that easy laughter except too much Sadfire whiskey and Decemberists songs on repeat.

Venner sat down across from her. "So, how do you know Avery?"

"We went to the same high school." *And I loved her. I pined for her. And I can't close my eyes without thinking about her.* "We took biology together."

A young woman approached their table with a pink box. "They're Voodoo Doughnuts," she said.

Venner waved the girl away, saying, "Get out of here. Can't you see we're talking business? Are you stupid?"

The girl stammered and hurried away.

"You're an asshole," Merritt said, keeping her voice mild.

Venner bristled.

"You know it," Merritt continued. "It must work for you sometimes, but it doesn't work in Portland. We're *nice* in Portland."

"We hire these locals to run errands and push doughnuts, and they don't have anything going for them. But you—" Venner folded his hands on the table and leaned in. "You have something special. I fix shows that need a little push. You know, I worked on *Cop Brides*. It was all right, but I came in and I said, if we're going to do this, we're going to *do this*. When I say—"

"I'm not here to chat. If I want to talk to assholes, I can find my own." Merritt glanced at Avery and she nodded. "You screwed me out of the Elysium, and I want it back. I had an accepted offer on it. You and your SkyBank deal killed it. I want you to sell it back to me at cost. No more than I was going to pay for it. I don't pay for whatever hideous upgrades you do. You don't mess with the exterior or any of the built-in features. And don't do anything I can't repair because it's all shit." Merritt lowered her voice. She didn't want Avery to hear. After the reunion, she'd watched a few episodes surreptitiously at the Mirage. *King & Crown* was really kind of sweet, and their decor was lovably over the top.

Venner closed his fists on the table and leaned in. Everything about him hulked. "You—" he said through gritted teeth.

Merritt saw a few members of the crew wince.

"*You* can't hurt me," she said. "I know you ruined Mabel Bartholomeus's chance at *Star Edition*." Avery had fed her the names. "You got Brian Benson thrown out of GBH. But I don't want anything you have except my building. You're the big man in a world that I don't think exists."

Venner put his elbows on the table, leaning even farther into Merritt's space. She could smell coffee on his breath. She resisted the urge to move back.

"I can't sell you the building for that price. We are going to clean house on that building. With our upgrades and it being on *King and Crown*, we'll sell for twice market value. What we're offering you is a two-hundred-dollar-a-week stipend and the best publicity your business has ever seen."

"I don't need publicity."

"Everyone needs publicity. And I'm offering you a career too. Portland is the new Hollywood. There's a production company popping up every day. You don't have to sell your hardware store; you can stay here and work in film. I'm opening a door for you."

"I run an architectural salvage business," Merritt said. "I have a lot of doors. I want my building."

"People would pay for what I'm offering." Venner pointed to the doughnut girl. "She'd do it. Don't make this harder for me than it needs to be. We've got work to do. *King and Crown*'s got thirty-four days. That's one month. They've got to roll you into the shots they've already taken. Backstory. Establishing shots. Maybe a girl fight. Nothing trashy though, more like, 'We drank too much chardonnay, and now I'm going to tell you what I really think of that engagement ring.'"

Merritt draped her arms over the back of the booth. "Are we talking business or are we just talking?"

"That's my offer," Venner said. "You. The show. Publicity. A new career."

"You know why people watch reality TV?" Merritt said. "They love story, and story is conflict."

Avery had told her Venner had been stomping around the set demanding, *Where is the conflict!* Merritt hazarded another quick glance at Avery. Damn it, she loved that feeling that they were in it together. She remembered watching Avery from across the auditorium at Vale. Avery had caught her eye and nodded and then they'd met in the hallway. *Let's go,* Avery had said. *Young ladies,* a teacher had called out to them. Avery and Merritt hadn't had to say *Run.* They'd been in Avery's Miata before they'd had a chance to look at each other, but when they had, they couldn't stop laughing. Avery'd had to pull over because tears streamed down her face. *I love you,* she'd said . . . the way straight girls said things like that, casually, without realizing what those words could mean. Except Avery hadn't been straight. Maybe if Merritt had paid more attention . . .

"You know the thing about *King and Crown?*" Merritt said. "There's no story. No drama. No passion. Yeah, Avery and Alistair are adorable. Puppy videos are adorable. Is that what you're selling? Cute?"

Avery was so much more than cute. Merritt wondered if producers saw her silver-screen beauty.

"We could increase your stipend."

Merritt shook her head.

Venner seemed to be thinking.

"We're done." He slapped the table. "Someone get her out of here."

Success had seemed inevitable as Merritt and Avery had popped beads together in Avery's room. They'd called it her *coup*. She'd stayed until late in the evening. She shouldn't have, but she did. Now it was over. She wasn't sure if she was more disappointed about the Elysium or the fact that the one good excuse she had for seeing Avery was gone. Emotional intelligence said she should be relieved. Iliana would say emotional intelligence was not her strength.

She was touched to see the disappointment on Avery's face. *It's okay*, Merritt mouthed. She started to rise, but Avery stood first.

"Sit down," Avery said.

Merritt had never heard that stern confidence in Avery's voice. It was sexy. Everything about her was sexy.

"You're just jerking her around." Avery walked over. "Our ratings aren't dropping, but they aren't going up. And you're the fixer, right? Here to fix us? And you think she's the answer, but all of a sudden you can't afford her?"

"I'm trying to put her on the show," Venner said.

"No, you are trying to screw her out of the Elysium. I'll

call Sam Grayson at TKO right now. If you don't put Merritt Lessing on the show, I'll fly down there tomorrow and tell Sam Grayson, Mark Conner, and Steven Blick that you know what to do for *King and Crown* but you won't do it."

"What the hell's gotten into you?" Venner demanded. "You don't know those guys. *I* know those guys."

After her initial charge, Avery looked scared, like someone who had wrestled a large animal to the ground and now was wondering how many seconds before it reared up. Still, Avery looked Venner straight in the eye. For an instant Merritt couldn't picture the Elysium. It was Avery's fierceness she wanted, someone to fight for her.

"You said she was the next hot thing," Avery said calmly. "You're right. She is." She squeezed Merritt's shoulder. "I thought you took risks. Alistair and I have been on set every single day your network needed us. We have filmed more seasons in a year than anyone. They're not even seasons; they're months. You paid us less. You've given Greg a budget for a local-access talk show. We've eaten a hundred Global Body Biscuits because TKO wants the product placement. And we have never complained because we love it. I love it too much to see you miss this chance."

Venner seemed to be calculating something. He picked at a hangnail on his sausage-sized thumb. The room was so quiet it absorbed sound. The road outside must have gone silent because there was so much silence in the diner.

Finally, Venner looked at Merritt like a man appraising a jewel beneath a magnifying glass . . . or pinning a butterfly to a corkboard.

"I don't know what you've done to Avery," he said.

Merritt shot Avery a startled glance. Avery snatched her hand off Merritt's shoulder. Merritt wasn't sure what she had done to Avery either, but she wanted to do it again. She remembered every luscious curve of Avery's body in the Jupiter Hotel. Had she felt Avery's clitoris touch hers? Could she tell? Could she bear the fact that Avery was probably thinking the same thing and she herself had to say no. For the sake of her heart. For the long winter that would come after Avery left, she had to say no.

"When did you grow a set of balls?" Venner demanded of Avery. He slapped the table again. "Okay. Goddamn it. Deal. She can have her goddamn building if she does everything—I mean *everything*—TKO wants out of this show. You had better be a unicorn." He stuck out his hand to shake Merritt's. "You will be. I can tell. I'm the Finder. Greg, get her a contract."

Chapter 16

Avery caught Merritt in the parking lot outside. Merritt looked as dazed as Avery had felt when she'd met Alistair at the Four Seasons and *King & Crown* was born.

"I can't believe that actually worked," Merritt said. "Why me? There are thousands of women in Portland. Like he said, they'd do it for free."

Avery admired Merritt standing in the dilapidated parking lot. She could have been a model, but it was more than that. It was that cool reserve. Had she really thought Merritt would say yes to a fling? Was it fair to be disappointed when it was so clear Merritt was out of her league? And yet there was something in the looks Merritt had given her in the command center. *We're in it together*, she'd seemed to say.

"You really don't know, do you?" Avery shook her head. "And that makes it even better."

"What's better?"

"You're A-list, Merritt. You always have been."

"There's no list in Portland."

"Ah, but there is." Avery knew. Everywhere. Every city. Every table at every restaurant. There was a hierarchy. Ask any woman in any room to list the coolest, the prettiest, the richest, and the skinniest. She could guess within the pound.

"People in Portland still wear gunnysack dresses," Merritt said. "There's no list when you're wearing a gunnysack."

Avery motioned to Merritt's perfectly creased slacks, her tank top, and her pin-striped vest, which could not have fit her more perfectly if Ralph Lauren had designed it himself. "Where's your gunny-sack?" she said flirtatiously. After all, a girl could hope.

"This?" Merritt gestured to her outfit. "This says I buy antique hinges for a living. This says I can't find the right pair of jeans."

Nothing about Merritt's slender body said *buy hinges*, and if she couldn't find the right jeans it was because she had psychologically blocked the existence of the mall...or Target...or yard sales.

"Do you have to go anywhere right now?" Avery asked.

"Back to the shop."

"Can you skip it?"

"I'm the boss."

She looked like a boss. She'd flipped Venner as surely as she'd flipped Bunter.

"Let's go." Avery said it before she could lose her nerve. She was supposed to be filming meeting-the-contractors. In two and a half minutes, Alistair would come out to see where she'd gone. But it was Merritt who made her heart race. "Hurry. My car's in the back."

Her car was a comped Mercedes Benz AMG. Bright pink.

"I am *so* not surprised," Merritt said.

"I get to drive it for free as long as I eat Body Biscuits in it."

She pushed it into second, spun out for a second, and then caught traction and turned onto the road.

"Are we escaping?" Merritt asked.

"Basically."

"Where are you taking me?"

The top was down and Merritt's short, dark hair blew around her face.

"I want you to meet my friend." Avery might not be cool herself, but she could be cool by association.

* * *

A few minutes later they were pulling up in front of the Nines Hotel. The valet opened the door to the AMG.

"Your friend is waiting for you. Here's a card to get you up to the suite. She says you're three minutes and forty seconds late."

"What's that about?" Merritt asked as they entered the retro glamour of the old department store turned luxury hotel.

"She probably put a tracking device on my car."

"Really?"

"It's DX." For Avery that explained everything.

Merritt looked curious. "DX? The singer? Is that like a Hollywood thing? You all know each other? I'd never have put you two together."

"I would never know DX except for my mom."

She wished Merritt hadn't noticed that DX and Avery were a mismatched friendship. No one thought Avery was cool enough to be friends with DX. Usually, even Avery didn't think Avery was cool enough to be friends with DX. But she wished Merritt had nodded, as if to say, *Of course. You're clearly the kind of sexy renegade who would hang out with the singer who forgot to accept her Grammy.*

"True story?" Avery said. "My mom was Jerry Xan's agent. That's DX's dad."

They waited for the bronze-plated elevator doors to open. For once, Avery was happy that no fans greeted her.

"When I was ten and she was thirteen," she said, "Jerry Xan lost DX in the Berlin Airport. He told my mom when he got back to America. Just said it, like, *We had to refuel in Puerto Rico and my daughter is somewhere in the Berlin Airport.* So my mom flew over. DX had taken a train to Amsterdam and was playing guitar outside a brothel. My mom brought her home and tried to give her a normal childhood for two hot seconds."

The elevator doors opened and then closed behind them with seductive privacy. Avery didn't look at Merritt. Her desires would be to plain to read.

"I didn't know what to think of DX," she went on. "She's crazy. Then one night I was lying in bed and I heard Marlene—my mom—and DX arguing."

She remembered the fight, her mother raising her voice to say, *Avery doesn't have your talent, DX. Let's face it. She can't throw away a brilliant career because she's not going to have one, but you can.*

"My mom was all about how talented DX was and I wasn't, and DX—she was thirteen then—just said, 'You corporate whore. You can't read the future.' I think she was the first person who ever believed in me."

"I believed in you," Merritt said quietly.

Avery wished the doors would stay closed a moment longer, so she could linger in that moment. As it was, they opened. Sunlight poured in. Before them an enormous suite spread out like Louis XIV's bedroom retrofitted for the twenty-first century.

DX greeted her with, "Avery! You lovely American Girl doll!" She turned to Merritt, lifting up the silver aviator shades she wore even at night. "And this is the girl."

Avery shot DX a look that said, *Be cool*, but DX was already so cool, scolding glances meant nothing to her.

"The *woman*," DX corrected. "Merritt Lessing." She held out her hand. "A pleasure. Avery has told me all about your prowess."

There was no doubting what DX meant. It was not Merritt's prowess at acquiring interesting lumber. Avery thought maybe she would drop dead on the yellow-and-purple-interlacing-squares carpet. She would have been mortified if Merritt *were* her woman, but Merritt wasn't. Whatever coolness Avery acquired by association with America's top-grossing female artist was lost...by association with America's top-grossing female artist.

"We'll be having dinner soon," DX said. "You two have to stay. I had a water buffalo fetus shipped over from Ban Bua Yai. The chef from Pok Pok is going to cook it up for us."

Merritt's face registered the same disbelief Avery would have felt if she hadn't known DX since childhood.

"Don't worry. It was a miscarriage," DX added. "No murder."

"I'm not sure that helps," Merritt said.

DX laughed. "We have a psilocybin etouffee. I've heard so much about you. Let's talk."

DX's band and several other people Avery did not recognize were clustered around a rat's nest of plastic tubes in the center of the elegantly over-decorated suite.

"They're making a bong," DX said. "They're trying to use a mile of tubing. It's BPA free."

DX poured Avery and Merritt a drink from a shaker on an end table and beckoned for them to join her on the porch outside. DX closed the sliding glass door behind them and leaned her elbows on the stone railing. White, canvas sun canopies shaded them. Beyond that, the blue-green high-rises of Portland reflected dazzling sunlight. They looked different in every season, Avery thought, like it was always a new city.

Merritt clinked her glass to DX's, took a sip, and said, "Water buffalo, not so sure. This drink I can do."

The drink tasted like grain alcohol and hot peppers distilled to the point of spontaneous combustion.

"Straight from Mexico," DX said. "I got it from El Chapo."

"But you didn't," Avery said. "People don't buy drinks from El Chapo."

DX's grin said, *Drink up, my little innocent.*

"So Avery says you loved her and left her at the Jupiter Hotel," DX added.

"DX! No!" Avery said. "You don't talk to people about stuff like that. In confidence, DX. *Confidence.*"

It was too late.

"You seem like the type."

Merritt looked pained. Avery's embarrassment was like the red slash across a discarded script. DX put her arm around Merritt.

"Avery's really a frickin' sweetheart. Repressed. I mean she's kind of like one of those indigenous tribes that bans homosexuality and eats twins because they think they're possessed by the devil—"

"No, DX! That isn't even a thing," Avery protested.

"But she'd knit you little things if you dated her. Little sweaters and scarves. You can't underestimate little sweaters. I mean Tony doesn't knit, but he would." DX punctuated the declaration with another swig of her atomic drink. "He *would* knit me little sweaters if I wanted because he loves me."

Avery's mortification had reached an embolism-exploding level, but Merritt was suddenly grinning. She joined DX at the stone railing and leaned her back against it, silhouetted against the high-rises. A hot breeze stirred her silky hair. They looked stylish together, like singer and drummer on the cover of *Rolling Stone.*

"I know this performance artist in Milan," DX said, "who will have sex with you in a hammock strung between two cathedral towers. And he's a hermaphrodite, so, best of both worlds. I tried to get Avery to do it, but she was always, like, 'I want a sweet woman who knows how to make miniature birdhouses for little tiny birds.'"

"There were no little tiny birds," Avery said.

Merritt laughed. DX laughed with her. And they were laughing at Avery, but somehow it didn't hurt.

"Could your hermaphrodite have sex with me *while* knitting a little sweater?" Merritt asked.

"He knit the whole hammock."

Avery had always had the inclination to correct DX, to remind her of a world that included gravity and the legal system. Merritt was just playing along. They joked back and forth a little bit more, and then Merritt held out her hand to Avery. They were almost too far away to touch, but Merritt pulled her a step closer, and for a moment all Avery could think was, *Kiss me.*

"Avery used to loan me her sweaters," Merritt said. "When we were at Vale. She said I always looked cold, and she loaned me these cute little argyle sweaters."

Avery's sweaters had always been embarrassingly loose on Merritt.

"They were so fuzzy." Merritt lifted the collar of her shirt to her nose. "And they always smelled like jasmine." She looked wistful, like someone recalling a cherished memory. "No one ever gave me a sweater besides Avery."

* * *

A few minutes later Merritt went inside to use the bathroom. It was another example of her supreme confidence. That, or the fact she didn't know there might be a python in the bathtub or the toilet or loose because DX didn't think creatures should be caged for human convenience.

When she was gone, DX said, "I like her. You like her. Good choice."

"I know," Avery said. She looked down at the shoppers and businessmen far below them. "But she's not interested."

"She's all over you."

"No she isn't."

"In her mind." DX tapped her own temple. "She's all over you in her mind."

Avery sighed and turned toward the glass door that led into the suite. The city was reflected there too. Merritt's city.

"I threw myself at her. She said we should get brunch instead."

"Ouch," DX said. "But maybe . . ."

"There's no 'but maybe.'"

"Maybe brunch is what they call it in Portland." DX stuck her tongue out between two fingers.

"She had a restaurant in mind . . . and mimosas. She's probably regretting that she slept with me at all. I mean, I think on some level she wants to, but not really. Maybe she just hasn't gotten some in a while. Maybe she's got a thing about celebrities."

"Ah, no," DX said. "Does anything about that girl say, *Star fucker?*"

"No."

"Okay then."

"I just have to not humiliate myself for five weeks. I'm not going to follow her around like some stalker fan."

DX squeezed her shoulders, much like the python might be squeezing Merritt at that very moment.

"Don't go down like that. Win her back. Send her a gift. Something big. Something she can't say no to."

"Like roses?"

"If you send her roses, you'd better send her a five-thousand-rose arrangement in the shape of your vagina." DX pulled out her phone and touched the screen. "Here it is."

"Just leave it," Avery said. "I'm not going to send her anything. She's not going to be my secret lover. I'm not going to quit the show and be a gay role model. I can't do that to Alistair. She said *no. No* doesn't mean *try harder.*"

I had fifteen years to try.

"Done!" DX said.

"What?" Avery asked.

DX held out the phone. "This thing is amazing."

The screen showed a sculpture that looked like a droplet of liquid gold, enlarged and frozen in time. It also looked phallic, as though the tip of Midas's penis was emerging from the gold. It was elegant in a way, like an art piece someone (who didn't work for *King & Crown*) might set on a coffee table. A photo illustrated the thing angled inside a woman's body.

"Get this," DX said. "It's plated in twenty-four-karat gold. It vibrates. And it has sensors so it reads your body's response. But the best part"—DX pointed to the base of the dildo—"is that this part here is weighted with Australian lead. You put it inside of you, the weight pushes it in, and it's like being fucked by a gold mine. I mean *really*! I don't want some big rubber penis when I can have the real thing, but this isn't *instead of*. This is its own thing."

Avery glanced at the image. The price was listed at $25,000. She could afford it, a fact that would probably make Merritt like her less.

"I'm not going to buy her a gold-plated dildo."

DX took a step back, texted something quickly, and drew her finger across the screen. She held the phone in Avery's direction but out of her reach. Avery squinted.

"You already did," DX said.

Chapter 17

Watching the crew take over Hellenic Hardware reminded Merritt of watching good painters prep a room. White vans lined up in the parking lot between Iliana's dojo and the loading bay at the back of Hellenic Hardware. Men in the pocketed vests that seemed to be the crew's uniform climbed out of the vans. No one moved fast, but it took only a minute until equipment filled the shop. Men tested settings and called questions and suggestions to each other with clipped efficiency. Venner was blessedly absent, and Greg took a moment out of surveying the progress to sip his coffee next to Merritt.

"It's quite a production," she said.

"Not really. We're a small operation. Unscripted makes money; it doesn't spend money. That's the motto. We fund other shows. Dramas, that kind of thing. Between comped supplies, product placement, advertising, and reselling the buildings for a huge profit"—he looked apologetic—"we make a lot of money for TKO. And Avery and Alistair have worked way under salary for such a long-running show. You know, they're such good people. It's so the crew can get more. And Alistair is *not* good with money, so it's not like he doesn't need it. It all drives Avery's agent, her mom, crazy. *She's* good with money and running people's lives. If she were my mother, I'd go into witness protection."

"I never met her." Merritt remembered Avery sitting at a coffee shop, drawing circles on the table with her finger. *My mom. It's hard.* She'd thought Avery meant getting into the industry, but maybe it was something else.

One of the pocketed men called out, "Greg, what angle do you want for the ladder?"

They'd placed a ladder up against one of the walls. A crew member—Merritt thought his name might be Setter—had climbed halfway up.

"There's nothing up there," Merritt said.

Greg laughed genially. "There doesn't have to be."

Merritt took a seat behind the counter, watching another crew member climb an A-frame ladder until his head disappeared into the forest of lamps hanging by the window. A moment later his colleague handed him a halogen lamp, and he added it to the collection.

"You know you've already got a few there," Merritt called out.

The man popped his head out. "Oh, where?"

They were fun, Merritt thought, friendly and hardworking. They had designated roles, but the hierarchy seemed flat. Greg was the boss, but he acted like a coach, tweaking settings and nodding his approval. Merritt remembered Avery strolling beside her through the tree-lined streets off Hawthorne. *We don't even own a house*, Avery had said. *The show is home.* Merritt could see it.

A soft touch on her arm brought her into the present moment. Avery stood behind her in a yellow sundress. It looked like casual cotton, but it must have been tailored for Avery. Her breasts swelled beneath the bodice. The dress accentuated her waist. Her heels were a lighter shade of creamy yellow, and even though Merritt had never been a fan of high heels, she admired the curve of Avery's leg beneath her white nylons.

"You look lovely," Merritt said.

"I'm a mess." Avery touched her cheek. "Look how much makeup Tami had to put on."

Her skin was flawless, but, on closer examination, it was heavy with foundation.

"Are you okay?" Merritt asked.

"I feel like I've been run over by a truck." She held her side. "And who wears tights in the summer? But my legs are all bruised up." She lifted one foot, but the movement unbalanced her and she stumbled against Merritt. Merritt steadied her and then let her go quickly.

Merritt remembered Avery reclining in the bathtub. She remembered the feel of Avery's hair beneath her fingers and the look of pleasure that had spread over Avery's face as she leaned her head against the rim of the tub. Merritt could have carried her to the bed and gently made love to her, at least kissed her and awoken beside her. She'd seen Avery's hurt embarrassment when Merritt had turned her down. And Merritt cared. That was the dangerous part. In thirty-three days—as Greg kept reminding everyone—Avery would sail away with Alistair, the crew that was her family, and Merritt would be left caring. Caring if Avery was hurt. Caring if Avery was happy. Caring if Avery's lovers touched her the way Merritt longed to. Would they appreciate her innocence and her fervor? Would they realize that she had not had the requisite one-night stands, bad girlfriends, and awkward firsts and lasts that left most women her age experienced in all the ways sex could go wrong (and occasionally right)? Merritt wanted to make sure all Avery knew about sex was luxuriating in pleasure. That thought solidified her resolve to say no. The more Merritt cared, the more it would hurt when Avery left. She wished her body recognized that logic, but the closer Avery stood, the more Merritt ached to touch her.

"I can't believe they made you work," Merritt said.

"The show must go on. Greg wouldn't have put me on, but Venner's stomping around talking about budget and how we're behind schedule."

"You just started filming."

"And we're already late because of Pine Street. We can pull it off. We always do."

"Have you decided what your quintessential Portland will look like?" Merritt asked.

"Maybe we'll install those carpets that look like real grass. For nature. Portland loves nature."

"Who doesn't like shag carpet that look like grass?"

"I sunbathed naked on a green roof in Berlin," Avery said a little mournfully.

It was a lovely image.

"I was fifteen. I thought I was a rebel. I think that was the last time I was."

"I don't know about that."

The thought sparked a longing that cut through Merritt's calm. Their night together. Their bodies intertwined. Oh, and that moment when she had ridden her orgasm to a gasping conclusion. Sex had never been like that before, and every fiber of her body wanted to know if it would be again.

"You know Berlin is one of the greenest cities in the world," Avery said. "You should go sometime. You should come with me." Then, as if embarrassed, she added, "Or go with a girl you like."

Someone called for Avery.

"I'm on," she said, looking relieved.

Avery headed toward Greg and the crew. Her gate was stiff, but her smile was easy. The crew greeted her with hugs and a chorus of, "There's the daredevil. Put Venner in his place, didn't you? That was epic."

* * *

Filming television was remarkably boring, Merritt discovered. After the second hour of standing in the lumber section, trying not to breathe too loudly because a man named Tom said they were getting a lot of *ambient*, Merritt was certain she would not fall in love with a life in show business. She watched Avery climb up the ladder to nowhere and exclaim, "Oh my gosh, you won't believe what I found." Then she watched her again. And again. First the crew reshot for better light, then better sound. Then Greg eyed the scene and said they needed Alistair, who was filming an exploration scene in the basement of the Elysium. Then they waited for him. When he arrived it began again.

"Oh my gosh, look what I found." Avery hung on the ladder, her pretty heels balanced on a middle rung.

"Put the picture frame in her hand," Greg said. "Where's Setter? Setter get that picture frame for Avery."

Now Avery handed an ornate gold-leaf picture frame to Alistair. He held the frame up and put his head through and beamed.

"And cut," Greg said. "Okay, go again."

By the time Avery finally climbed down from the ladder, she looked winded. She limped past Merritt and disappeared behind a tall chest of drawers, but she trailed her hand behind her as if inviting Merritt to follow. When Merritt found Avery, she was slumped in a wicker chair beneath the gazebo, one hand on her side. Merritt sat down beside her. She wanted to gather Avery up in her arms and rest Avery's head on her chest... which was exactly why she shouldn't do either of those things.

As she'd drifted off to sleep the night before, she'd fantasized about Avery kissing her ...there...where she had allowed so few women. Now she felt guilty, like she had as a teenager. Thinking, *You're so pretty*, was innocent. Imagining every twist and turn of Avery's tongue in her when Avery was a real person, sitting *right* next to her, sore from a bike crash, said, *You don't know I'm a stalker yet.* Maybe it was even worse because Avery had offered it and Merritt had turned her down. *I'll dream-stalk you, but I won't sleep with you, and I'll make you feel bad about that.*

"You sure you don't have a cracked rib?" Merritt asked.

"They checked. I'm fine," Avery said as though that were disappointing news. She looked up at the painted beams of the gazebo. "This place is beautiful. I could sit here all day."

"I do," Merritt said. "Sometimes after hours, I just come down here and listen to the fountain, think about my uncle, read a book."

"Where do you get all the merchandise?"

"People usually come to me. They can see that I love this stuff. Some salvage places treat their inventory like junk. People don't want to see their grandfather's harpsichord piled up with scrap metal in the corner...even if they don't know what to do with it themselves."

"What are your favorites?"

"The chandeliers." Merritt thought. "Or the coal stoves, the light switch covers. I once had Masonic Lodge archways. And I love the barnwood. You get twenty-by-twenty beams that were cut out of one tree. And cornices."

"That's just about everything."

"Yeah." Merritt stood up and walked to an ornate birdcage

in which she had arranged a display of old jewelry. She opened the birdcage and took out a locket. "This one's not for sale. My uncle gave it to me."

Merritt remembered her uncle standing on the balcony waving as she left for the senior prom. He had given her the locket to tuck in her pocket. *A lover's locket,* he'd said, opening the silver oval. *Friends and lovers who couldn't be together would give each other these.* Inside two women's faces were painted: one delicate, one stern. They both looked sad. Merritt had fingered the locket as she'd driven to Avery's house. She was part of that history, tied to those women, to Uncle Oli and his boyfriend, Kurt. She'd loved the whole world as she'd driven to Avery's house. Then she'd arrived. Avery's father looked surprised. *She left hours ago,* he'd said. Maybe Uncle Oli had known. Maybe that was why he had given her a gift that said, *You're not the only one who's been unhappy.*

She placed the locket in Avery's hands. Avery held it reverently.

"That's who I would have been." Merritt pointed to the stern woman.

Avery shook her head. "You're this one." She pointed to the pretty, delicate woman. "I don't know how you can't see it. You know, back at Vale I watched you for a month before I worked up the courage to talk to you."

"You were my lab partner."

"I traded with Ella Thistler. It took a while to convince her. All the girls at Vale had a crush on you."

"They did not. You're making it all up. Flatterer."

"Remember Lucy Grier?"

Merritt was surprised to realize she did.

"She had a crush on you. And Ron Craten. If guys count, there were dozens."

And you, too, but not enough.

"If you hadn't been my friend, I would have hated you," Avery said.

"I'm sure the girls lusted after you too."

"Hardly. The Hollywood Girl. That's what they called me. It wasn't a compliment in Portland."

"They were jealous. You were exotic. You had an agent." Merritt took the locket back, letting her fingertips brush Avery's palm...which she shouldn't have. The desire that warmed her body told her so. "I like the thought of these women together. Maybe they were lesbians. Maybe not. Maybe they didn't even have words for what they felt, but they had this locket. Western civilization always wants perfection. The ancient Japanese thought if something was rough or scarred, if it gave you this sense of profound, spiritual sadness, that was better than perfection. The called it *wabi-sabi*. It means 'the beauty of imperfection.' Nothing lasts forever, but nothing is finished."

"Can't something new be important?" Avery asked.

The gentle intimacy to their conversation was too alluring. Merritt changed the subject. "I said I'd let the Pride House host a fundraising dance here on the last day of summer. The Nostalgia-rom. It's like prom for grown-ups."

"With strippers?" Avery asked.

"Not that adult. It'll be very hipster. Porn-staches. Lumbersexuals."

Avery shifted a little closer to her. "I wish I had gone with you."

Above their heads the sun shone through the skylights. No matter how carefully Merritt cleaned her merchandise, Hellenic Hardware was always dusty. The dust caught in the sun's light, making shafts of gold, like the trunks of enormous, golden trees.

"If I had gone with you, it would have been special," Avery added.

If anyone had asked Merritt if she still cared about a fifteen-year-old prom, she would have scoffed. Balding football players who peaked at eighteen and had nothing else to show for themselves except a beer gut longed to go back to high school and relive the glory days. Not Merritt. Except that she did.

Someone called from the lobby.

"Avery. You're up next. You're spilling a can of ball bearings, so let's get this one right on the first take or we're stepping on balls all afternoon."

Ball bearings took another three hours. Merritt got a part in the scene. Avery reached for a can on a high shelf. Merritt said, "Don't drop—" And the ball bearings cascaded across the floor. Merritt was pretty sure she'd be picking them out of displays for years to come. Long after Avery had left, she'd walk downstairs in bare feet and step on one. That or she'd move a wardrobe, releasing a pool of ball bearings. They'd slide under her feet, and she'd go down hard.

She watched Avery reach for the can, the bruises on her arm barely covered by makeup. She wanted to draw Avery another bath. She wanted to slip her hand under the water this time. She wanted to caress Avery in places that would make her forget her everything. Who was Merritt kidding? She was already going down hard.

Chapter 18

They finished filming in record time. Merritt was amazing. Over the years, they'd invited dozens of people on the show: tour guides, contractors, home owners, crafters. They'd even had prize winners who entered competitions and then got a walk-on part in the finale. Most of those people froze up or started rambling off script, disappointed to learn that, yes, there was a script. Merritt was different. The cool that followed her like her own mountain shadow played perfectly on-screen.

Avery texted Alistair as they finished up. *Almost done.*

Alistair: *Fast. How's Nostalgia?*

They had always veiled their texts in fake names and euphemisms. There was no way to film for fifteen years and not find your phone in the crew's lost and found a dozen times.

Avery texted *Like a* ⭐.

Nostalgia give in yet? Alistair replied.

Avery: *If only I were 17*

Alistair: *Wait*

Avery: *Waited too long* 😭

Alistair: *I* 🖤 *u, she must. What next?*

She didn't have time to reply. Merritt had sidled up beside her.

"What a day," Merritt said. "I can't believe you've been doing that for fifteen years."

They watched the crew pack up.

"That was a holiday," Avery said. "We've gone until ten p.m. You were brilliant."

Merritt shrugged, as if to say, *When aren't I?*

"Your cheekbones are going to look like Cara Delevingne made love to Michelle Pfeiffer."

Artless! She was flirting with Merritt like the teenage girls who threw themselves at Alistair. Her mother was right. She was clumsy. But she couldn't help it. Merritt was gorgeous. Not mentioning it was like seeing a rainbow and not pointing it out to your friend.

"You're something else, Avery Crown," Merritt said. "Flattery . . ."

Avery hoped she would finish, *Will get you anywhere.*

But Merritt just turned away from the crew and whispered, "I bet you talk to all the girls like that."

"There is no *all.*"

It felt truer than ever. There was only Merritt, like a lone figure in a wide-angle shot.

"I'm sorry about DX the other day," Avery said. "She has no boundaries."

"I like her. She's . . ." Even cool Merritt Lessing couldn't finish the sentence. "Would you really knit me little sweaters?" She was teasing.

"If you made me a birdhouse for really tiny birds."

"First ostriches and then really tiny birds. You are a woman of contradictions. Hey," she said as though something had just occurred to her. "Do you have to go back to that miserable hotel?"

"Do you have something better?"

"I have my friends, and they are dying to meet you—and Alistair too."

Avery said she had to go back to the Extended Stay Deluxe to get Alistair, as if she had not texted him five minutes earlier. She needed to change. She needed to throw every dress out of her traveling wardrobe, try them all on, and then panic and send a production assistant to the mall to buy something that would invariably make her look like a pear.

* * *

The process took two hours. It would have taken all night if Alistair hadn't come by her room, taken a pink gingham dress out of her hands, and said, "I am fifty-fifty on whether this girl is going to break your heart and ruin your career, but if you like her, you need to know that this dress says, 'I am going to plant wheat on the prairie.' There is a line dance in Stone tonight, and I bet all the boys would like you. Some of them even have teeth."

Alistair was starting a free dental clinic in Stone. It would be up and running within the month.

"She's so—" Avery sat down on the bed. "I've got nothing to wear." She leaned her head on Alistair's shoulder. "I look like a dish detergent commercial."

"You will if you wear that one. Anyway, this morning you told me all hope was lost. If that's true, just put on that Body Biscuit suit and some Jimmy Choos. Be like, you didn't want to date me? I can still embarrass you in public."

"She cut the Body Biscuit suit off me."

"She cut it off you?" Alistair looked alarmed.

"In a sexy way."

"Okay, if you two don't wrap this up, *I* will date her. She likes you." He picked a crumpled gray tank dress off the floor. "You're beautiful. You can't get out of each other's way. Just grab her and kiss her."

"She's too wounded inside."

"Wounded!" Alistair said. "Even I have partaken of the carnal delights"—he feigned disdain—"and I know no one is too wounded for casual sex."

I don't want casual. It was what she'd asked for though. She wondered what Merritt would have said if she had thrown herself at her feet and said, *Marry me, you androgynous goddess.*

* * *

A few minutes later their driver deposited Alistair and Avery in front of King Chen's in Chinatown, Avery in her dissatisfying gray dress. Merritt greeted them at the door with a polite hug.

"You look nice," she said to Avery.

Nice! Of course she looked nice. *Nice sold wall decals. Nice did the Brattleboro Home Show.* Merritt looked like an indie director about to take the stage at Sundance, especially poised in front of the door to the dim sum restaurant. Everything in Chinatown looked like it had risen to glory, faded, and was trying to rise again. The red pagodas were faded, but the city had installed sculptures in the sidewalks.

Inside, a hostess directed them to the dining room. Servers circled the room with carts of food, and on one side of the restaurant Chinese men in business suits and young white men with long hipster beards clustered around a giant bar carved with dragons. Avery and Alistair followed Merritt, but before she got to their table, several diners leapt up.

"Are you Avery Crown?" a young woman asked.

An ancient woman, bowed over almost in half, gestured to a medallion around her neck, speaking in quick Chinese.

"Nĭ hǎo! Nĭ hǎo ma," Avery said, which was not particularly helpful since it was the only Chinese she knew, and the woman took it for confirmation that Avery understood what she was saying.

The young woman said, "My grandmother made this keepsake photo necklace from one of your kits. It's her husband in the picture. He died last year."

Avery knelt down and took the woman's hand. "Thank you," she said. "You must have loved him very much."

The young woman translated. Avery signed a dozen napkins. Only after she left the table did she catch Merritt watching her, a look of admiration on her face.

"They love you," Merritt said.

"And I love them. I love what they make. We do something when we make things like that. We put a little bit of ourselves in the world."

She thought of Merritt's locket.

"Something new that's important?" Merritt said, as if reading her mind.

"Yeah."

"That's wabi-sabi. It's new, but she's grieving. She lost something, so she made something."

"Yeah."

"You're a kind person, Avery Crown," Merritt said. "You always were."

Alistair and the hostess were waiting a few feet away, but Avery felt like the whole restaurant faded from view. Were they new or were they old? Were they anything? Was she kind enough to heal whatever hurt let Merritt sink into temptation and then pull herself back? Was it temptation, or was that Avery's wishful thinking? Maybe she was like all the housewives watching *King & Crown* and thinking, *If Avery could get a man like Alistair, anyone could.* If only they knew. No one got Alistair. Perhaps no one got Merritt either.

Avery was still thinking when they reached Merritt's friends. A woman with a long blond braid sat next to a Chinese girl with rainbow streaks dyed in her hair. The blond woman looked like she bathed in goat's milk soap and had never touched a mascara wand. Her girlfriend had glitter in her eyebrows.

"You're here! Finally!" the girlfriend exclaimed. "I thought Meri would keep you from me forever."

"Meri?" Avery asked.

Merritt closed her eyes and shook her head. "Not Meri. Never Meri. I've told them. This is Lei-Ling," she added. "And Iliana. And this is Avery and..."

Introductions were unnecessary.

"I have seen every single episode of *King and Crown*." Lei-Ling beamed at Avery and Alistair. "I keep them downloaded on my laptop. Meri said she'd ask you to put me on your show, but she said you couldn't. But now you're here...That would be my dream come true. I want to make you dumplings. I built my own food truck, and I'm so excited to meet you because I know you're leaving Portland in, like, two and a half seconds."

Avery felt Merritt glance at her. She wanted to take her hand and say, *Let's make two and a half seconds count.*

Avery said, "I'll see what I can do for your dumpling truck."

Iliana leaned back and chuckled affectionately as Lei-Ling burst into another explosion of fan-girl love. This was absolutely the best day of her life except for the day she'd met Iliana, but this was still the most exciting thing that had ever happened to anyone in the history of human joy.

"I read about the America Wyoming Foundation," she said to Alistair. "You give back so much. I want to make the world a better place too. That's why I built the dumpling cart. To help my family. I'd do anything for them."

"Alistair would do anything for his family except visit them," Avery teased.

"Oh no!" Lei-Ling cooed. "You have to visit your family."

They talked, and Avery watched Merritt out of the corner of her eye. When Merritt got up to fetch a round of drinks from the bar, Lei-Ling said, "All the girls love her, but she's such a heartbreaker."

"She's not that bad," Iliana said quickly.

"The bartender at the Mirage takes bets on who she'll go home with," Lei-Ling said. "Vita always wins. She can read people. But if the girl comes back crying, you have to give your money to a charity. Vita says it evens out karma. Meri has a heart of stone. Like glaciers. Like inside, it's February all the time, just crows sitting on power lines in the rain."

"I can hear you when my back is turned," Merritt called from the bar. "It's a superpower."

"She's so pretty, though," Lei-Ling added. "Don't you think she's pretty, Avery?"

Merritt was so much more than pretty.

Avery projected her voice. "She's the most beautiful woman in Portland."

Merritt rewarded her with a smile tossed over one shoulder. When she returned to the table with four umbrellaed daquiris and two small shots of whiskey, she said, "Flattery, Avery Crown. Flattery will get you in trouble every time."

She handed the second whiskey to Alistair. He clinked her glass. "This is the Sadfire whiskey I was telling you about," Merritt said.

Avery liked the idea of Merritt and Alistair chatting on

set, talking about whiskey or Stone or some funny thing Avery had done. She imagined them all friends—her, Alistair, Merritt, Iliana, and Lei-Ling—hanging out on Catalina Island, the two couples each sharing a chaise longue. It should have been a simple fantasy, but for her it was more or less impossible.

* * *

That night Avery flopped down on Alistair's bed.

"And now?" he asked.

She knew what he was asking.

"Now nothing. She doesn't like me."

"I'll believe that when I *don't* see it." Alistair fluffed up some pillows and lay down next to her. "I see you together. I see a lot. Be careful. I don't want to put it like this, but you"—he bugged out his eyes and lowered his voice in mock secrecy—"are really old. You're thirty-three!"

Avery gave him the same shocked look. "You are forty. For-ty."

Alistair's smile was not as lighthearted as she had hoped. "The girl on *Nail* is nineteen!" he said. "Venner's here because someone thinks we're losing our edge."

"We never had *edge*."

"We had us."

"I know. I heard about Venner coming, and, shit, I thought, 'That's no good.'"

"We're here because Greg is the best in the industry, but if someone sees you with Merritt. If they think . . . anything."

"People love *King and Crown*."

"We love this. The crew loves it. Greg loves it. Our viewers love it." Alistair's tone was paternal, and she felt the seven years between them in a way she rarely did. "But absolutely every single one of us is disposable if you and I don't play Avery and Alistair."

Avery knew what he meant. There was Al and Aves, their real selves tanning in ugly swim trunks on Catalina Island, throwing almonds to the ostriches. Then there was Alistair King and Avery Crown skipping down the streets in El Paso in matching outfits. They had *chemistry* on- and off-screen. But they had to keep their real selves behind privacy hedges. Merritt was a big secret to keep, not that Merritt would even want to travel from villa to villa with Avery and Alistair, hiding behind bougainvillea. And for the first time in her career, a tiny voice in the back of Avery's mind whispered, *I want out.*

"Don't worry. There's nothing to hide," Avery said. "She doesn't want me."

"You know why I'm worried?" Alistair asked. "Because I think she does. But, Avery, be careful. And I don't just mean the show. It's been a long time since you've really liked a girl. She's cool as hell, but she's troubled. Make sure she's not the kind of troubled who'd hurt you."

Chapter 19

A few days later Merritt walked through the peaceful neighborhoods between Hellenic Hardware and the Mirage trying to quiet her heart as well . The door to the bar was propped open, and the late-summer light showed the rips in the upholstery. Ordinarily, Merritt didn't like this kind of decor: Red vinyl masquerading as leather. Corona piñatas. Rainbow-flag Montucky Cold Snack posters. But the Mirage had that run-down imperfection that made it even lovelier than the Pearl District bars.

Iliana and Lei-Ling were already there.

"I get to bring my dumpling truck on *King and Crown.*" Lei-Ling practically bounced out of her seat. The Mirage's fraying Naugahyde had never felt such enthusiasm. "Avery called me. We're going to be on TV with Avery and Alistair."

It was an odd thought. There would be a whole season of Merritt and Avery trapesing around, pretending to stumble on interesting food carts. TKO would play rerun marathons for years after Avery left her life a second time.

Lei-Ling rested her chin on her knuckles, a perfect little angel. "They're so nice. They're just like they are on TV."

If only she knew.

"Maybe they'll come to the restaurant too. That'd be so good for Mom and Dad."

"I'm sure we can arrange it." Merritt *was* sure. As they had left the restaurant the night before, Avery had whispered, *Of course I'll get your friend on the show. Anything for you.* Then Avery talked to Greg and it was settled. If Lei-Ling wanted Avery and Alistair trying clams at the Gold Lucky Fortune, Avery would arrange that too...just because Merritt asked and because Avery was kind.

"I'll miss them when they go," Lei-Ling went on. "They're only going to be in Portland for a few days. Then they'll be gone forever."

The bartender, Vita, ambled over, bracelets jangling on her wrists, her whole body encased in leopard print.

"Hello, my beauties." Vita squatted down on her heels, resting her arms on the table, a pose that was probably meant to convey camaraderie but that looked vaguely predatory. "Merritt Lessing, you're glowing."

"She's on *King and Crown*," Lei-Ling said. "She's going to be a star."

"Hmm," Vita said. "No. It's not a job. I'd say it's a woman."

Merritt thought of the tension that hung between her and Avery. Every word they spoke seemed to be hinting at something else. It was all she could do to tear herself away at the end of each day.

"I'd say the inimitable Merritt Lessing is in love." Vita waited a beat. "That will save me a lot of time."

"I'm not," Merritt said. "How will that save you time?"

"I won't have to warn women off her," Vita said to Iliana and Lei-Ling. "I won't have to listen to them cry in their beers when she leaves."

"I don't leave," Merritt protested. "Why doesn't anyone notice that it's me who gets dumped?"

"Well," Vita said, as though this were a point she was qualified to debate. "They tell me about you. A heart of stone. Maybe this girl will get lucky. I doubt it."

"Meri's in love?!" Lei-Ling squealed.

"No," Merritt said. "Not...no. Just no."

"I'm a bartender. I know," Vita said. "I can see a bar fight start before the first punch. I can see a hookup before they even walk through the door. Don't think I don't know you, Merritt Lessing. I know *everyone*."

"Then why aren't you in love?" Merritt said.

"True enough." Vita rose and tapped the table. "Always the bridesmaid, never the bride." She strutted off.

"Can you imagine the woman who could date Vita?" Iliana asked when the bartender was back behind her bar.

"Meri, Meri, Meri, who is it?" Lei-Ling asked.

"Vita is crazy," Merritt said. "Do you see me with a girl?"

Merritt looked around. This was the Mirage. Right now there was a twenty-five-year-old gender-queer grad student with a savior complex who wanted to rescue Merritt and who would eventually dump her over Twitter. Merritt knew that story. She could play her part. It was like filming scenes from *King & Crown*, the same event looping around and around.

The conversation shifted to the end-of-summer Nostalgia-rom, which Lei-Ling thought was the *most super-fun idea ever!* and which Iliana agreed was a liability nightmare.

"And you can bring your girl," Lei-Ling exclaimed.

"There is no girl."

A few minutes later, Lei-Ling left to chat with some friends on the other side of the bar.

Iliana leaned forward. "It's Avery." It wasn't a question.

"She's a good person." Merritt sat back in the booth with a deep breath. "She didn't have anything to do with the Elysium."

"I told you that."

"I made the right choice." Merritt leaned her head against the fake leather behind her. "You'd be proud of me. I've been emotionally intelligent."

"About time," Iliana said.

Merritt had told Iliana about Avery's bike crash and her meeting with Venner. She hadn't told her about easing Avery into the bathtub and stroking her hair. She hadn't told her how her own body had cried out in protest as she'd pulled away from Avery's kiss.

"She came onto me," she said.

"That's what you wanted, right?"

"I said no. I'm not going to have a fling with her. I'm not going to sleep with her. I decided. I made one of those *life-affirming emotional choices* you're always going on about."

"No!" Iliana exclaimed, her blond braid swinging as though it, too, was appalled. "That's not the life-affirming emotional choice. The life-affirming emotional choice is to open yourself to possibilities. It's to believe in the bounty of the universe, to look around at happiness in others and know that there's enough for you. You can light a thousand candles off the flame of happiness and happiness is not diminished."

"She wants to sleep with me for five weeks. More like four now. And then she'll leave me. What part of that is emotionally intelligent?"

"You have to try. When I met Lei-Ling—"

Merritt cut her off. "Lei-Ling is out. Lei-Ling's family adores you. You both live in Portland, and her dream is to run a food truck. Avery is closeted. She works in a different city every few months. She doesn't even own a house."

Merritt glanced around the bar. It would be lovely to be there with Avery in the dark comfort of a good old-fashioned lesbian bar. Of course, it was Portland; a lesbian couple could kiss on a street corner. But there was something about the wear and tear on the Mirage. It had been here before every man in Portland had a man bun. It would be there no matter what happened in politics and in the world. And Avery couldn't come here. She had signature hair.

"I like her," Merritt said, defeated. "Do I have to spell it out? If I let her in, she's going to break my heart."

Chapter 20

It was five days before Avery got to film another scene with Merritt. She didn't know how she had stood the wait. Now Avery hoped she could get Merritt alone before they started filming, but Merritt was sitting on a retaining wall chatting with Meg, the boom mic operator and one of the few women on the crew. Avery felt a tug of jealousy. Merritt leaned in, her dark hair falling over her eyes, her posture loose and confident, as though she had spent her life on television sets. Her crisp white blouse opened to reveal a hint of her coral bra. Avery loved the contrast between Merritt's masculine style and that edge of lace. She did not like the way Merritt looked at Meg with a smile that seemed to say, *Smother me in your aftermarket boom mic windscreen.* She didn't like the fact that Meg, with her kangaroo vest and crew-cut hair, could ask Merritt out on a date, take her downtown, hold her hand without once looking over her shoulder to see if Dan Ponza was watching.

"All right," Greg called out to the assembled crew. "You've all read your call sheets."

Avery hadn't looked at her call sheet.

"We want Avery, Merritt, Mike, Tom, Setter, Chris, Tami, and Colton in van one. You're going to the Peculiarium. Don't ask. Avery, remember the line is 'keep Portland weird.' You're decorating a city that ties plastic horses to the tethering rings left in the sidewalks from 1890 and gives walking tours of the 'installation.'" He held up his fingers in double quotes. "Now, Alistair, Beth, Sean..." He continued his instructions.

Avery caught up with Merritt as Merritt hurried to the van.

"How's it going?" she asked.

"I have ball bearings in my hair."

"I liked your friends," Avery said.

One of the cameramen jostled by them. "Coming?" he asked.

Alistair called, "Be good," from the open door of his van.

Merritt climbed nimbly into her van.

Sean, the assistant photography director, had been learning to play guitar. His acoustic followed them everywhere. He plucked a few chords as they set off, and everyone groaned.

"Play 'Free Bird,'" Merritt said, leaning over the back of her seat and grinning. "I love 'Free Bird.'"

It was like she had been with the crew forever.

"No one loves 'Free Bird,'" Setter protested.

Sean struck the first chords. The crew let out a collective "nooo."

"Sean, I think your friends really support you," Merritt said. "They want to hear you practice."

Sean sang, "Biiiird," a few notes too high.

"Freeee," Merritt chimed in, actually hitting the note.

The crew laughed, and Setter and Chris joined in. Then the whole van was singing.

It was like watching Merritt at the reunion, all the linen-suited women fluttering around her. The men had crushes on her already. And so did Avery. A hopeless, teenage crush. The kind that saw no reason. The kind she should have had at eighteen when, instead, she'd sensibly agreed that no one married their high school sweetheart and it wasn't worth ruining her chances on *King & Crown* for a girl.

* * *

The Peculiarium was on the frayed end of Northwest Twenty-Third Street. A few blocks back it was designer soap shops and hand-printed stationary. But gentrification hadn't quite reached the end of the street, and the Peculiarium looked out on the industrial district and a span of highway arching over the river. A faded sandwich board outside advertised ICE CREAM. WAFFLES W/ POP ROCKS. ART. WEIRD STUFF. A rubber severed head watched them from a pedestal by the door. The entry fee was five dollars, but *King & Crown* got in for free.

"Go on. Take a look," Greg said.

Inside, the place was a tiny homemade house of horrors. The entry included a life-sized (presuming one knew what size it was in life) Krampus, various beagle-sized creatures with eyeballs protruding from stalks, and a rotary phone with the inscription THE ROTARY DIAL PHONE. THIS IS HOW PHONE CALLS USED TO BE MADE. EXCRUCIATING, ISN'T IT? GIVE IT A TRY, IF YOU CAN STAND THE PAIN.

Colton, the set manager, looked up the street.

Avery stood outside, watching the highway but glancing at Merritt.

Merritt leaned against the building beside her. Tami, in makeup and wardrobe, had done little to her. She'd traded Merritt's tuxedo pants for jeans, her white shirt for pink, but her hair was the same recalcitrant black silk, forever falling in her eyes.

"I've always liked traffic," Avery mused. "I like to think about how each one of those people could go anywhere. Seattle. Alberta."

Merritt followed her gaze. "You thinking about getting away?"

Not really, Avery realized. All those other people could go to Alberta. She wished she could take Merritt's hand and stroll up the street, maybe nip into an ice cream parlor. It was the kind of thing she would do with Alistair. She felt a twinge of guilt because she wanted to have that afternoon with Merritt instead.

"You know, we do come back to cities we like," Avery said.

"Portland will win you over today for sure," Merritt said. "I hear they have jars with organs inside and ice cream and art."

Maybe that was the little ice cream parlor they'd nip into.

"You know if they all pitched in"—Merritt nodded toward the crew—"you wouldn't be behind."

"The crew's union. We're one of the few union reality shows. They can't switch jobs."

"You mean one person's moving stuff and everyone has to stand around and watch them?"

"Pretty much. The grips move equipment. Greg is field producer. Gould is camera. Tom's sound. Meg, who you were talking to—" Avery touched her fist to Merritt's arm, a symbolic punch. Merritt pretended to look innocently confused, as though there were something between them that Meg might interrupt. Avery's heart lifted a little. Merritt was playing along. "Meg is boom mic. Solomon is assistant field producer, so if Al and I split up, he takes the easier set."

"It's all a little boring," Merritt said, not unkindly. "You spend a lot of time standing around."

Avery had never thought about it. "We're here when we're needed."

"So you travel all over the country, but when you're at work...?"

"We wait. We don't mind. It's very well organized, and the crew makes well over union wages. That's important to me and Alistair. Our contract is half the average so that Greg can pay the crew more."

"That's nice," Merritt said thoughtfully.

* * *

A few minutes later Greg called them over and identified the next shot: Avery would tiptoe into the Peculiarium. The Peculiarium really was a charming mess of campy, glue-gunned horror. Merritt would grab her by the waist and half carry, half pitch her into the dark interior. Avery would squeal, *Something's going to jump out at me.*

"You sure you don't want Alistair in this one?" Gould asked.

"I do," Greg said, "but we're behind schedule, and we have *got* to be out of here in less than a month. If we call Alistair over here, that's a day. We'll use Merritt. Make it look pally."

Avery should have told Greg about Merritt, she thought. If Merritt grabbed her and pulled her into the darkness, someone on the Peculiarium staff would see them. They'd sense Avery longing for Merritt's touch. She wanted Merritt to drag her into the dark, even if it was an exhibit that purported to be a zombie decontamination room.

"Don't you think—" She was going to say, *That would look a little gay.* But she saw Merritt examining a fake-blood-filled Magic 8-Ball in the window, the sun catching every contour of her face. Venner would make it a crass pejorative: *That's a little too gay.* She wouldn't. She would never say that because everything about Merritt was perfect.

"I'm ready when you are," she said.

"Okay. Let's get going," Greg said.

Merritt opened her arms with a cocky grin. "You ready?"

"Terrified," Avery said.

They took their places.

"Ooh, what's in here?" Avery said, a little off script. She stepped into the shadow of the Krampus. Its eyes lit up. A second later Merritt's arms closed around Avery's waist. The sensation took Avery's breath away although her grip was light. Merritt didn't seem to flex a muscle, but suddenly they were around the corner in the blackness of the zombie room. Merritt planted her neatly back on her feet.

"You forgot, 'Something's going to jump out at me,'" Greg called. "Go again."

Gould checked his light meter. Tom played back three seconds of sound. There *was* a lot of waiting, Avery thought. They ran through the scene four more times. Every time Merritt pulled her into the dark, away from the eye of the camera and the crew, Avery felt Merritt hesitate before she released her.

On the fifth take, Merritt caught her from a different angle. When they disappeared around the corner, the sweep of Merritt's movement landed Avery against Merritt's body, their lips almost kissing, Merritt's leg between Avery's thighs. It turned Avery on. Instantly. Entirely. Avery had the sense that Merritt was in complete control of every movement, just like when she'd caught Avery on the stairs of the path.

"I'm sorry," Merritt said, and pulled away.

"Are we dancing?" Avery asked, so softly the boom mic could never catch it. It was the secret voice she used only for Alistair.

"I don't know how to dance," Merritt said.

"I think you do."

"You're trouble, Avery Crown."

Then they were back outside in the clutter of equipment and the bright light of the day. Inside, Avery groaned with unrequited desire.

Chapter 21

Outside the Peculiarium, caterers were setting up long tables with white paper tablecloths. Avery's phone rang, and Merritt watched her disappear around the corner. Merritt knew she'd been wrong to tease her. Each time Greg had said, *Go Again,* she'd held Avery closer, until finally the heat of their bodies touched. She felt it. She'd heard Avery gasp. It wasn't fair. Avery didn't love her. She wouldn't stay. But Avery liked her, and Merritt didn't have a right to tease her and then say no. She'd still teased Avery though. That was the trouble with temptation. It was tempting. And her night with Avery had felt so good.

Merritt tried to muster interest in lunch. The crew was always interested. What it would be, when it would be, and would it be pasta primavera again were topics of much debate and genial complaining. The food seemed good to her. Her natural food source was popcorn shrimp from the Mirage. Sure, every few months she vowed to cook kale, but she just ended up wandering the aisles of Market of Choice, buying nothing. Sitting down to one lonely fork wasn't worth it. At least at the Mirage she could let Vita abuse her.

Instead of lunch, Merritt looked for Avery. No, she wasn't looking. She just happened to be wandering in the direction Avery had gone. She turned the corner of the Peculiarium. Half a block away, Avery was pacing back and forth, her phone to her ear. With each pass, she seemed to shrink. Even her curls seemed to sag. Finally, the call ended and she sat down on the curb. She rubbed the fading yellow paint on the concrete and ran her fingers through the gravel and dust that had collected at the edge of the road.

Merritt had only meant to catch a glimpse of Avery, but she couldn't leave her sitting on the curb picking at the gravel that had collected at the edge of the road. She hurried over. Avery didn't seem to notice her until Merritt sat down beside her.

"Not eating?" Merritt asked gently. "It might be pasta primavera. It might not. These are important issues."

"I'm not hungry." Avery picked up a pebble and placed it on the curb between them. No, I am hungry, but I'm right at my limit."

"Limit?"

"A hundred and twenty-five pounds. I told you I can't change. It's in my contract."

"That's ridiculous. You're perfect, and you would still be perfect if you gained weight."

Avery set another pebble between them. "You're sweet."

They were silent for a moment. Avery picked up a third pebble, selecting it carefully.

"Are you counting them?" Merritt touched Avery's hand.

"I don't even know how to knit," Avery said, as though this were a terrible failing that she had finally worked up the courage to share. "DX knows. I don't know why she still teases me about it. Once this woman asked me to fix this train wreck of a sweater. I had to give her this long speech about accepting yourself. *Your sweater is precious because you are. Don't compare your sweater to other sweaters.* It didn't even look like a sweater. It looked like it had crawled out of her knitting basket and died. But she said no one had ever loved her the way I did. Greg sends me a list of all the things on my blog so that I don't forget. They put a new craft up every day. How am I going to keep track if—" She sounded teary.

Merritt stopped her. "Who was it on the phone? What's wrong?"

Avery slumped even lower. "My agent...my mom."

She stared down at the gravel at her feet. She looked so sad. Merritt wanted to put her hand over Avery's, to say, *Look at me.* It was the kind of gesture she could never quite manage with the women she dated. She cared about them. She felt sorry if they were sad. But there was always this moment when there was a right thing to say or do, and she always missed it. Now everything in Avery's bowed shoulders said Merritt should put her arm around her. She wanted to. But a trio of pedestrians were walking too slowly at the end of the road.

"She says Venner's up here seeing if *King and Crown* needs a new female lead," Avery said finally.

"But it's King and *Crown*. You and Alistair are the show."

Avery looked even more despondent. "Actually, she didn't say he *was* looking for a new female lead. She said he *should be*. She said if he knew what he was doing, he'd be thinking about it, and I should be thinking about it too."

"That's crazy."

"She wants me to get a lift." Avery touched her perfectly smooth cheek, pulling it up toward her temple.

"A face-lift?"

"Yeah."

Avery was wearing the usual glitter on her cheeks. It struck Merritt as sweet and girlish. The kind of enhancement a young girl would put on and then spin around in front of the mirror, thinking she was a princess. For someone to cut into that simple happiness seemed like mowing down wildflowers.

"Don't do it!" Merritt said with passion she felt but hadn't meant to share.

"I might do it. I don't want to lose the show. I don't want to lose Alistair."

"No one in the real world notices things like that until you have a Michael Jackson nose and lumps on your forehead. Don't do it if you don't want to."

"They do notice. If it's good you just don't notice you're noticing." Avery brushed the pebbles back into the street.

"You don't need to be fixed," Merritt said. "You're not a

lumpy sweater." A thought occurred to Merritt with sudden shock. "She doesn't mean me, does she? I'm not the new lead. I'll quit if I am. I'll walk away. I won't even go back for the afternoon. I wouldn't take that away from you."

Avery looked up. "You'd lose the Elysium."

"I don't care." Merritt didn't realize how much she meant it until she spoke the words.

"I do." Avery let out a heavy sigh. "I want you to have it. Sometimes I wish I could cut my hair or just braid it. I can't take the day off. I can't go to a concert without running it by our legal department. I can only hug Alistair, even if I'm sad. And if I hug Alistair in public, it always has to be the right hug and the right sad. And it's worth it. It's just that he's not the one." She looked at Merritt. The gold flecks had faded from her eyes.

"Come with me," Merritt said.

The Peculiarium had a small storage room off the back of the store-slash-museum-slash-eatery-slash-gift-shop-of-things-you-could-only-buy-for-that-one-weird-friend. It had been offered as a dressing room, but they were dressed and Tami needed to powder them in location, to make sure the *contours accentuated the right light pattern.*

Merritt pushed open the door. The high-ceilinged room was full of Peculiarium cast-offs. She locked the door behind them. She hesitated for a moment, then put her arms around Avery. Avery sagged against her.

"Thank you," Avery whispered. "I needed this." She nestled her check against Merritt's breast.

For once Merritt knew she had done the right thing. Maybe this was what emotional intelligence felt like.

"Don't listen to them," Merritt said. "They don't have a right to tell you who to be. In the real world, you dump people like that. In the real world, if your lover acts like that, your friends hate them. They stage an intervention. You say, *No, no, I love them.* And your friends are like, *Fuck that shit.*"

"But I do love them, and they are my friends...well, not my mom." Avery sounded like she was on the verge of tears again.

Merritt wrapped her arms tighter around her, resting her cheek on Avery's head. She thought again how Avery was like the pin-up girls of the 1920s, tiny by modern standards but as luscious as that decade had ever seen. Her petite curves the perfect shape for a woman. Hollywood wanted women with the bodies of young men, but that was a waste. Young men could be young men. She wanted to say, *Get fat. Shave your head.* But she didn't think that would help. Instead she rocked Avery gently back and forth.

Then slowly Avery lifted her head from Merritt's chest, and Merritt tilted her head down. Their lips touched. Merritt's body sang with the hot desire she had stoked every time she drew Avery to her in the dark of the Peculiarium. She couldn't have stopped their kiss any more than she could have stopped the sun from rising. It was bliss, holding Avery's body close and feeling her soft lips, her tongue exploring Merritt's mouth, every sensation arousing a hungry, protective, insistent passion. She wanted Avery.

She needed her. She wouldn't care if they were making love on a pile of rubber ghoul masks. She would come with her clothes still on. But after that she'd meet Avery at the Jupiter Hotel, and she would not be able to pretend that a night at the hotel was a night out of time, that her heart wouldn't follow her into the room and it wouldn't break as Avery went out.

Her body cried out in protest, but she broke their kiss. She took Avery's shoulders and guided her away until she held her at arm's length. Avery gazed at her, her eyes wide, her lips parted in a look of nervous resolution. Then she must have seen something in Merritt's face because she covered her mouth.

"I'm sorry," she said. "Did I get it all wrong?"

"Avery, I can't."

It was the girl with the pigtails. *You'll always be alone.* It was her friends never seeing that she was the one who got hurt. It was Greg reminding them of every passing minute. It was Avery saying, *I feel free when we leave.* We: Avery and Alistair. It was the one lonely fork.

"I thought you were flirting." Avery looked despondent. "I'm hopeless. I thought...I read too much into things."

"Stop." Merritt stroked her thumb down Avery's cheek, as though tracing a tear Avery hadn't shed yet. "You can't think I don't want you. Look at me, Avery. You wreck me. I'm a mess. I can't sleep. I've never wanted anyone more than I want you. I've wanted you since we were sixteen. If I wanted you less, I'd say yes in a second. But, you see, you'll break my heart, and there's too little heart left to break."

"If there's so little...what do you lose? Wouldn't it...?" Avery didn't finish.

"Be worth it?" Between Merritt's legs, her sex throbbed. *Yes*, her body cried. "It's not that easy."

Chapter 22

It was one a.m., and the grounds of the Extended Stay Deluxe were empty. Avery sat by the pool. Occasionally, an airplane roared by overhead, but even the airport seemed to be half asleep. Soon it would be time to leave. Leaving had always made her feel better. A bad visit with her mother, a season that fell flat—the answer had been simple. Just go. But the planes looked unsteady, and the summer night would be so beautiful if Merritt were lounging in the plastic lawn chair beside her.

The water in the pool was motionless. She stood up. She was still wearing a dress, but she stepped into the shallows anyway. The dress floated around her knees. Greg would be appalled. She was wading tearfully (and fully dressed!) into a pool, right beneath a sign that said DO NOT SWIM ALONE. Dan Ponza could be in the bushes. Hotel guests could be out walking their dogs.

She took another step in, then dipped her head under the

water, holding her breath for as long as she could, listening to the water pressing against her ears. She tried to imagine herself someplace else—Atlanta, Montana—but she was right there. Her breath ran out and she popped up. Her hair hung in tangled curls. She thought about Merritt stroking it off her forehead while she lay in the bath. *I don't want to hurt you.*

"You did," she said to the empty water. Then she dipped under again, swimming the whole length underwater.

She had always been a good swimmer. She wished Merritt could see her. *You didn't give me a chance*, she thought as she surfaced, turned, and swam back. *I messed up at eighteen. You can't hold that against me forever. I won't break your heart.* She dove again, swimming down to the bottom of the pool—all eight feet of it—and sitting on the bottom. It wasn't fair to do that to a plain girl. Merritt with her slim body, her perfect face, her shop, her freedom, her friends, her effortless talent at everything. Merritt could have a career on television without Marlene Crown or plastic surgery. She forced her eyes open. The chlorinated water burned away her tears. Far away she imagined music playing, a familiar song, one of DX's softer ballads. Then it struck her: It was her phone!

She surfaced in a rush and launched out of the water. She managed to touch accept despite dripping fingers.

"Hello?"

There was a moment of silence.

"You're worth it," Merritt said.

* * *

A few minutes later Avery slid into the driver's seat of her comped pink convertible. She was a bit drier, although the dry dress she had thrown on now stuck to her legs and her hair dripped down her back. But soon she was parking behind Hellenic Hardware. She crept up to the front doors, glancing up and down Burnside. Nothing stirred inside the shop, not even the intermittent blink of a security camera, but she heard a strain of music. Avery looked up. A story above her, Merritt sat in a windowsill, outlined by the orange glow of a lamp. Her back rested against the window frame. She had tucked one leg up in front of her, her chin on her knee. The tip of a cigarette or a joint glowed at her fingertips, but she wasn't smoking. Only thinking. At least that was what it looked like from below.

Avery stood for a long minute. As a teenager, she had always felt nervous before showing up at Merritt's door. She had thought, *What if I'm not good enough? What if she's changed her mind?*

"So it's a spectator sport?" The concrete wall carried Merritt's voice like a tin-can telephone, quiet and yet right in her ear. Merritt looked down, her face in shadows. "What are you doing, Avery Crown?"

What was she doing? Dan Ponza was somewhere in the city.

"I'm coming up."

Merritt disappeared from the windowsill and returned a moment later.

"Catch." She tossed a set of keys.

For an instant Avery saw them lit by the streetlight like a

heavy snowflake. She felt more than thought that she would remember that image forever. Merritt's keys frozen in the air. The glow of Merritt's lamp. The strange sensation that she had once again become the person she was at sixteen. Then she caught the keys.

Inside, Avery made her way past the front counter. Merritt met her at the foot of the narrow staircase, fully dressed, like someone who had had no intention of going to bed. Upstairs, the apartment looked like the home of a lonely bachelor. Avery wished she could decorate the place. Even shag lawn carpet would make it look cozier.

"Why are you wet?" Merritt asked, putting her hands on Avery's waist.

"I was swimming."

"In this dress?"

"In a different dress."

"I like it."

If Dan Ponza had followed her, his camera would be glued to the window.

As if reading her mind, Merritt drew the curtains. Then she kissed her. It was wonderful. It was everything. And it was so not enough.

"I want this," Avery whispered.

She pressed herself against Merritt. She felt the same searing desire she had felt in the Peculiarium, but now it was better and more unbearable because she knew soon Merritt would touch her. Surely sensing the urgency of her need, Merritt lifted the skirt of Avery's dress over her head.

"Come to bed," Merritt said.

Avery stepped out of her heels and followed Merritt into a bedroom that was as sparse as the rest of the apartment. One pillow. One end table. One sad torchère lamp in the corner.

"Where are your antiques?" Avery asked.

"I didn't think I'd be here for so long."

"We'll be gone soon," Avery said. "It's less than a month now. God, it's only a few days really. I'm sorry you had to wait to move into the Elysium. I know how much you wanted to be there."

"Don't be sorry," Merritt said. "I'm fine here. I'm fine tonight."

The disappointment Avery had felt when Merritt strode out of the Peculiarium melted away beneath the heat of Merritt's gaze. Her dark eyes burned with desire, and the care with which she moved seemed to bely an urgency that was not careful at all. Avery was so overwhelmed with wonder—she was here! Merritt was here!—she could barely unbutton Merritt's shirt, but she did, and she cast it to the floor. They kissed for a long time while standing at the foot of Merritt's bed.

When Merritt drew away, Avery delicately nipped her bottom lip. "You're so good at everything and you're so cool and you know you're intimidating."

"Are you intimidated now?" In one graceful move that Avery didn't fully understand, Merritt fell backward on the bed, managing to carry Avery with her so gently Avery felt like she had been set down on a cloud. They lay side by side. Merritt held her, her embrace strong and light at the same time.

Merritt shed her clothes, undressing while lying down and managing to still look graceful. Then she unhooked Avery's bra and cradled one of Avery's breasts in her hand. She stayed there for a long time, massaging Avery's breasts, kissing one nipple and then the other, flicking the hardening flesh, rubbing it between her fingers. Avery felt her body grow more and more sensitive. Then very slowly Merritt kissed her way down Avery's belly and slipped off her underwear. She pressed her lips to the curls above Avery's sex and then lower. Avery thought she would faint with pleasure. Merritt was right *there* but so gentle. Merritt took her time as though there were no next step, as though this were the culmination of lesbian sex. Avery raised her hips. Merritt placed a hand on her belly and held her down.

Avery undulated between peace and frantic need until Merritt found a rhythm that spoke to both. Merritt kissed her harder. Avery felt like a wave rising and rising until it was filled with sunlight and then breaking on itself. She clasped her hand to her mouth as she came, stifling a cry that would surely have called Ponza to the window.

Avery sank into the mattress as she caught her breath. When she opened her eyes and again looked over, Merritt lay with one hand between her own legs, moving with an urgency Avery recognized.

"It's okay," Merritt whispered. "You don't have to do anything." She closed her eyes, moving faster, digging her fingers in harder. "This is enough."

The strain on her face said it wasn't.

"Slow down," Avery said. "Shh."

Avery closed her hand over Merritt's, feeling the frantic jerking of her fingers, and eased it to a stop.

"I'm fine."

"Shh," Avery said again. "I think there are other ways."

She drew Merritt's hand away, kissed her lips, her neck, her breasts, and then slid down Merritt's body until she lay between her legs. She gently parted them. "May I?"

"You don't have to. I want it. Don't think I don't want it, but it's just...I don't usually...I don't let women because...It's not you. Please know it's not you. It's just so...much more than I'm used to."

"Is that a no?" Avery leaned on one elbow.

For the first time ever, Merritt looked timid. She shook her head. "It's not a no. God, I've been thinking about it for days. I shouldn't think about you like that when we're filming, but if you go down on me...I won't know what to do."

Avery laughed deep in her throat. "You don't have to do anything. That's the point. All you have to do is trust me."

Merritt's body was swollen, beautiful, and complicated. And Avery wasn't sure she trusted herself to satisfy Merritt. Merritt made love to her like a woman who had practiced her part to perfection. Maybe *she* had read Dr. Bingo Sterling's book on cunnilingus. Avery wasn't sure she remembered the lessons she had learned at Powell's Books, and none of her other lovers had taught her much. But a career in television had taught her a few things. If the scene doesn't play well, you changed tactic. If you got it almost perfect, go again. Go again. Go again. You'd know when you got it right.

Avery dipped her tongue deeper into Merritt's body. Then kissed, sucked, and released her clit. Merritt gave a surprised "Oh!" Then Avery shifted her kiss a little bit.

"There!" Merritt said suddenly. "Harder. Slower." Then, "Oh, faster! Yes. God, yes!" Her back arched. Her hands clutched the sheets. Then she fell back. "Yes," she sighed, as though she had lost a fight she hadn't wanted to win.

But when their eyes finally met again, Merritt looked lost. "What happens now?" she asked.

"Sweetheart," Avery said. "We're women. We cuddle."

Merritt moved toward her so tentatively, it might as well have been her who nearly cracked her ribs in a bicycle accident. But when she rolled into Avery's embrace, her whole body fit perfectly, and Merritt buried her face in Avery's hair and sighed. It was only as Merritt slowly relaxed that Avery thought she might have made a terrible mistake, the one she apparently could not escape making. She had lured Merritt in, and she had touched something fragile beneath Merritt's bold swagger. And she was leaving in less than four weeks. *You'll break my heart.* Go again.

Chapter 23

Okay, we want hipster cemetery," Greg said.

Filming in a cemetery seemed a little sacrilegious Merritt thought—especially filming in Uncle Oli's cemetery—but she was too happy to care. She could still feel the exact moment when she'd given herself over to Avery completely, trusting Avery to bring her to climax and to hold her afterward. Even as she'd arched off the bed, suspended in that movement when orgasm was inevitable and so far away all at the same time, she knew Avery wouldn't say what other women had said: *Can you only come on top? It takes you so long. Are you even turned on?* It was unfair, really. Who could come with a woman holding a stopwatch over the bed? Avery made her feel like time disappeared and the only thing Avery wanted to do for eternity was to captivate her with that irresistible kiss.

Now Merritt and Avery were back at work, the *King & Crown* crew carrying equipment past them on their way to the perfectly photogenic cemetery location, but in some way everything had changed. Everything was new. The sun was brighter and softer at the same time. The air smelled sweeter. The crew's voices belonged to another world. Merritt and Avery wandered as far away as they could. Their hands were so close they were almost touching. Beside them, the headstones were set in couples. Loving husband. Loving wife.

"Uncle Oli is here," Merritt said. "On the far side with the economical plots."

"Do you hate us filming here?"

"I thought I would, but Oli would like it. He was always complaining that no one paid attention to old gay men. It was all boys, boys, boys. Dead gay men get even less attention."

Avery laughed and took off the enormous sun hat Tami had given her. They slipped behind a mausoleum.

"Was it all right last night?" Avery asked.

Merritt smiled down at her shoes, her hair falling in her eyes. She was glad she'd been too busy to cut it. *King & Crown* liked the look, and she needed someplace to hide.

"You are trouble, Avery Crown."

If Avery were a regular girl and there weren't a film crew coming up behind them, she would have leaned back against warm stone of the mausoleum, drawn Avery to her, and kissed her. Maybe there were dead lesbians hidden among the pioneer tombstones. Maybe they would cheer them on. Maybe it would be okay to bring that heat and life into the still air.

Everything else Merritt wanted to say sounded like one of Iliana's self-help books. *You make me feel safe. I live in gratitude.* In case Avery couldn't hear it in her voice, she added, "It was amazing. It's never been like that for me. I...I don't let women go down on me. Not since my ex about three years back."

"Why not?"

"It's so close, so intimate."

"Isn't sex supposed to be intimate?" Avery said, looking at Merritt with a searching smile.

"I'm not good at that part. But last night..." Merritt shook her head. She couldn't stop smiling. She wanted Avery again. She wanted her more than she had ever wanted a woman. And at the same time, she felt like a schoolgirl. "Last night I thought I would—" *Fly? Faint? Explode? Scream? Sing?* "I had a good time with you," she managed.

Avery slapped her arm lightly, the kind of flirtatious touch that turned into a caress and meant everything from a girl you had just slept with.

"I had a pleasant evening with you too, Miss Lessing," Avery said with playful formality.

They kept walking, their feet crackling in the dry grass.

"I was worried I'd get it wrong," Avery whispered a moment later. "I read a book on it when we were at Vale. It was called *Cunnilingus! You Can!* by Dr. Bingo Sterling."

Merritt was so full of giddy joy, her laughter burst out. "No? *Cunnilingus! You Can!*? Dr. Bingo?"

"Yes." Avery laughed too. "I was practicing for you." She glanced away, as though suddenly there was so much between them. "I would have loved to have been your first."

"You were amazing. Dr. Bingo did right by you," Merritt said.

"It's you who's amazing. Ever since we were in high school, you were just *better* than other people at everything. If I didn't like you so much, I'd hate you."

Merritt bumped Avery's shoulder with hers. "There are lots of things I'm not good at." *Getting women to stay*, she thought, a hint of wistfulness touching her heart like a cool breeze.

From across the cemetery, Alistair called, "Avery," with a slight hesitation in his voice. "Where are you? Remember you're working this set."

"Come on," Avery said to Merritt. "DX says I'm nine-to-fiving it. She makes it sound like I'm in prison."

Beyond the mausoleum, the crew had covered a set of gravestones in plastic marigolds and sugar skulls.

"Don't worry. We have permission from the family. Day of the Dead." Greg handed Merritt a little skeleton figurine riding a bicycle with a beer in hand. "Merritt picks this up and says, 'Classic Portland. They have IPA in the afterlife.'"

"Day of the Dead isn't until October," Merritt pointed out.

"We're running in October," Greg said.

"And the wildfire smoke from California," Gould said. "It's given this whole season an autumn feel."

That was true, Merritt thought. Time was flying by so quickly. She wondered why she had resisted Avery. She'd missed days that she could have been stretched out across her bed with Avery leaning over her, her touch firm and gentle at the same time. Days she could have caressed Avery's body, from the soles of her feet to her signature hair. Avery had been right about summer flings. Time changed. Moments lasted. But they didn't last long enough.

"Avery, you'll pick up this mask and chase Alistair to that tree there," Greg said.

The crew took their places. Merritt could imagine the shot as it would appear in the camera. They filmed the usual half dozen takes. Then the sun was in Gould's lens. Then it was right behind a cross.

"We're moving," Greg said.

Merritt knew enough not to offer to help move the equipment.

"You'd still get it done sooner if you worked together," Merritt called to the crew.

"Unions kick ass for the working class," Setter called back.

Finally, the flowers had been moved, and the mask had been worn. Alistair chased Avery across the grass, his blond hair glowing in the sunlight. Merritt picked up her skeleton hipster.

Greg said, "I don't know. Post-production might cut this. We'll have to get marketing to see if it's going to play Satanic to the Bible Belt."

The crew didn't groan. Avery and Alistair shrugged. By the time they packed up, the shadows of tombstones were stretching across the grass. Alistair gave Avery a single, almost imperceptible nod. Still Merritt could read it clearly. *Go on*, he seemed to be saying, and behind that, *Be careful*.

"Stay," Merritt whispered to Avery. "I'll drive you back in my truck."

Once the vans had pulled away, Merritt took a blanket out of her cab. "I want to show you something."

Beyond the cemetery, a huge field sloped and rolled. The grass came up to their knees. Below them, the Sunset Highway was a ribbon of gray. A distant row of trees obscured houses in the northwest hills. As they walked, the cemetery slipped from view. When they were out of sight, Merritt brushed Avery's hand. To her surprise, Avery took it.

"We have to go all the way out to the middle," Merritt said.

She knew the field well. She had paced it all summer after Uncle Oli died. Then she had slogged across it in the rain of winter. Now she only visited in the spring, when the field was covered in wildflowers.

In the center of the field, Merritt settled the blanket on the grass. She sat down and gestured for Avery to join her.

"See?" Merritt said.

Avery looked around. "What is it?"

"Nothing." Acres of wild grass surrounded them. From where they sat, the grass made a wall around them. Only their heads rose up above the sea of yellow-green.

"I used to come out here after my uncle died. I wanted to keep him in an urn at Hellenic Hardware, but Iliana said I was stuck in the past."

"What was it like after he died?"

"The shop was a mess. He'd let the books slide. I didn't know what to do. I was eighteen. Before he died I thought I'd go to community college, study business, maybe open my own shop in ten years. Then Hellenic Hardware was all mine.

But Oli had a mortgage on the shop. He had suppliers he hadn't paid. He had medical bills. And I didn't have enough money to rent an apartment. Kurt wanted to go back to his family in Florida."

"What did you do?"

"Kurt stayed long enough to make sure I was okay. He got me into construction. He knew some guys who would look after me, and then I met Iliana. Her family was shit, so she'd been on her own and working since she was sixteen. She knew how to survive, and we got along. She convinced me we should do aikido. That kind of construction is hard on you, and aikido loosens you up."

Avery touched the back of Merritt's neck, massaging her gently, and Merritt felt like her touch reached back to the stiffness of those long days.

"Kurt and I let the lease go on the Elysium. We both cried when we did the final walk-through. It had been so beautiful. We'd been happy. I slept in the shop for two years after that. I just put a mattress on one of the bedframes and slept under that gazebo."

"You were homeless."

"I had ten thousand square feet of home. I still do. Sometimes I do wonder, though," Merritt added slowly, "what my life would have been like if Oli had lived a little longer. Or if I'd stayed in one place my whole life. Maybe I'd be like you and would travel the world."

Avery took her hand and held it palm-up. "I can read your future," she said, stroking the lines that crossed Merritt's palm. "You'll be happy."

The touch shivered through Merritt's body.

"You'll make millions of dollars. You'll be loved. You'll have fifteen children."

"I don't know if they do in vitro after fourteen. Don't you think that's a little much?"

"They would in Hollywood."

Merritt closed her hand around Avery's.

"Did you know, at Vale, how much you turned me on?" Merritt asked.

She remembered Avery drawing her nails down the back of Merritt's shirt as if tracing an invisible pattern. Sometimes Avery would tickle her feet. Then the touch would become a caress. Then Avery would rub her thumb up and down the arch of Merritt's foot, activating some nerve that seared right into her core.

"I tried," Avery said coyly. "You never noticed."

"I thought it was this straight girl thing, like you were so straight it didn't even occur to you that you were driving me crazy."

"Did I really turn you on?"

"I thought about you all the time. I masturbated thinking about you."

"I was flirting," Avery said. "Why didn't you ever do anything?"

Merritt thought she should be angry. *You never told me you were gay!* But the sun and Avery's touch melted away any anger she could have felt.

"You were my best friend. I didn't want to risk anything," Merritt said. "And why didn't you? You read that book by Dr. Bingo. I didn't have that kind of insider information."

"I was working my way up to it," Avery said. "I really was. I was going to make a move, but I was afraid you'd say no."

Merritt lay down and smiled up at Avery. "*I'd* say no to *you?* What kind of lovesick teenager would I have been if I'd said no to a beautiful woman coming on to me? Come here." She touched the blanket next to her.

Avery lay down.

"Let's make up for lost time." Merritt didn't dare to hope that Avery would kiss her in the middle of a field, but her body was glowing and restless. "I want to show you what we should have done back then. Don't worry. There's no one here. I've come here for years, and I've never seen anyone."

She was certain Avery would shake her head apologetically, but Avery drew one finger down Merritt's sternum, coming to rest on the clasp of her lace bra.

"Studied more?" Avery asked.

Merritt gave Avery a close-lipped kiss. Avery didn't shrink away. "We would have done that one night in your car, and then we would have been so shy, we couldn't talk to each other for a week. Should we wait a week?"

"I think we've waited long enough."

Merritt saw her own desire reflected in Avery's eyes, and it turned her on even more.

"I'd be convinced you hated me," Merritt went on. "Then you'd invite me over. After your father went to bed, we'd do this."

She kissed Avery again slowly, her hand resting on Avery's

shoulder, not holding, just touching. She kissed her for a long time, barely slipping her tongue between Avery's lips. But each time their tongues touched, she could feel Avery stir.

"Then we wouldn't have a moment alone all week," Merritt said. "You'd read that special book of yours."

Avery leaned up on one elbow and surveyed the field. Merritt thought she might tell Merritt to stop, but she lay back down.

"Then what?" she asked.

"Then this."

Merritt rolled Avery onto her back, kissed her neck, and cupped her breast. The desire she'd felt the night before, which had subsided for only minutes after her orgasm, nearly swept her away, but she resisted. Avery wriggled beneath her touch.

"Hours," Merritt said. "Hours like this."

"I read my book. I would have made you go faster." Avery tried to press against her, but Merritt shifted so there was an inch of space between them.

"Would you really?"

"No. I'd have lost my nerve. I'd have made you make all the moves."

Merritt kissed the front of Avery's dress, then took Avery's nipple between her teeth and bit down softly through the fabric of her dress and bra. Avery moaned.

"Delinquent," Avery said.

"Undisciplined," Merritt agreed.

Merritt bit her again, palming Avery's other breast, massaging its sweet weight. Avery stretched beneath her.

"You tease," Avery said.

If only this were enough to keep her, Merritt thought. If she could tease Avery forever, maybe she'd never leave.

Avery kissed her, a hard kiss, full of affectionate irritation.

"And eventually this." Merritt put one leg over Avery and mounted her, so her legs held Avery's legs closed. Avery's hips pushed up against Merritt's in way that did not say, *Naive teenage love.* It was all Merritt could do not to pull her dress up and touch her. She kissed her lips instead. Merritt felt like her body expanded. And even though they were clothed, their bodies fit together perfectly.

"We'd have gone on and on like this, until we just wanted to pound our fists against the ground because we were so turned on and we didn't know what to do with it."

They were old enough to know now.

"Check the field," Avery said.

Merritt looked up over the tall grass that surrounded them.

"No one," Merritt said.

With that, Avery parted her legs, pulled her skirt up, and pulled Merritt to her. The seam of Merritt's pants pressed against Avery's underwear, the fabric between muffling the building pleasure.

"Oh, yes," Avery moaned. "You terrible, terrible tease. How could you?"

She shifted her hips back and forth, as if trying to find the perfect angle to relieve her longing. Then she thrust against Merritt again and again, rotating her hips.

She clutched Merritt's hips. "I'm almost there. God! I can feel you."

Merritt thought she could feel the moment Avery found exactly the right pressure, the right angle, the right pull. Avery cried out, her hands covering her mouth. Then she rolled Merritt over with the confidence of an aikido master, kissed her, and pressed into Merritt. Merritt felt the orgasm claiming her. She resisted. If she came, nothing would ever be good enough. She'd want Avery so badly she'd go crazy. And Avery would disappear in a white chem trail, just like before. *Twenty days.* If she could just stop this swell within her, hold it back the way she did with other women, refuse it and then fake it, she would—

"Yes!" Merritt cried. "Oh! Damn it, yes, yes, yes!"

She fell back on the blanket, and it felt like her pleasure filled the sky.

Avery snuggled up against her, pulling her enormous sun hat over their faces. The hat smelled of Avery's sweet perfume. Merritt could see specks of blue through the straw.

"Now we're invisible," Avery said.

If Merritt could just stay perfectly still, time would stop and they would stay there forever.

Chapter 24

Six blissfully sleepless nights later, Merritt sat on a lawn chair behind Happy Golden Fortune watching the crew set up to film Lei-Ling's food truck. The converted Slipstream RV looked like a hippie's UFO. Lei-Ling had covered it in a paisley of pink and gold. The words DUMPLING HAPPINESS IS NOW covered one side in psychedelic script. Gold wands protruded from the sides, each sporting a lumpy papier-mâché ball.

"Do they have faces?" Merritt asked Iliana, who was sitting in another lawn chair.

"They're dumplings."

That didn't answer the question.

The Slipstream was also topped with solar panels and attached to four bicycles.

"She really built that?" Merritt asked.

"Yep," Iliana said. To Lei-Ling she called out, "You need a hand, Honey Bear?"

Honey Bear. That's what love did to people. Iliana—with the tattoo of a broken heart, a sinking ship, and a skeleton in a top hat—was now one half of Pinyin and Honey Bear.

"Do we really have to bike it to the Elysium? Can't you tow it?" Merritt asked.

"It's carbon neutral. You can't tow carbon neutral. It defeats the purpose."

Alistair arrived in one of the many cars Avery and Alistair appeared to have access to. Lei-Ling knelt on top of the Slipstream.

"Yeah, Alistair!" she called out.

Alistair was so tall, his head cleared the top of the RV. Merritt had thought Iliana and Lei-Ling were an odd couple. Alistair and Lei-Ling looked like one of those photographs of the world's tallest man and smallest woman.

Lei-Ling examined her solar panels. "We need to tilt these up a little bit. We're past midsummer. The sun's shifting."

"Fourteen days left," Alistair said.

Past midsummer, Merritt thought. The sun had shifted, and soon it would be going down for the winter. She had fourteen days with Avery, and every single person on *King & Crown* seemed determined to remind her.

Lei-Ling stood up. "I'm going to jump. You have to catch me."

Lei-Ling managed to be full of fawning adoration and self-assurance at the same time, as though she and Alistair were simultaneously fan and star and brother and sister. She jumped off the top of the Slipstream. Alistair caught her effortlessly. Lei-Ling giggled.

"I love her," Iliana said dreamily. "She saw the plans for the food cart online. Then she took out the engine block, put in the solar power, built the kitchen, and hooked up the bikes."

If the whole thing didn't explode in a dumpling-shaped ball of grease fire, Merritt was going to be grudgingly impressed.

"When her folks can afford to hire another waitress, she's going to rent a spot in one of those food cart villages."

"She could park it at Hellenic Hardware," Merritt said.

Avery made Merritt feel generous. At night she gave herself to Merritt so fully and made love to her so unreservedly. Then they would lie in bed and talk, meandering through fifteen years of memories. Like a scrapbook opening between them, they talked about their classmates, old gossip, the breakups, the late-night adventures, and all the Vale Academy traditions. None of it was important, but all the memories felt magical, like Merritt had woken up next to Avery to find they had dreamed the same dream.

The other women Merritt had dated said she never talked. *You're like a stone.* She had tried, but there was just so much silence inside her, and they had never listened carefully. After every accusation—*I never know what you're thinking*—she wondered if they couldn't have made a little bit more space for her. Did they really want to know? But with Avery, every conversation flowed into the next.

Everything Avery said reminded Merritt of some small, true thing she had never told anyone. Avery seemed to hold each of Merritt's thoughts in her hands, as reverently as she had held the lovers' locket. *When did you first notice?* she might ask. *Did anyone talk to you? How did you find your way back home?* Or even, *Why don't you cook kale if you like it?*

"Really?" Iliana's face opened in an enormous smile. "You'd let Lei-Ling park in front of the shop?"

Merritt would probably regret this decision. "Absolutely."

Iliana put her hand on the arm of Merritt's lawn chair, broaching a serious subject. "Are you sure I can't tell Lei-Ling about you and Avery? She would absolutely die!"

"You haven't told her?"

"You asked me not to."

"You're a good friend, you know that?"

"The best." Iliana tipped her chair back. "I can hide a one-night stand. How can I hide you dating Avery Crown?"

"She's not my girlfriend. She's leaving."

"Come on."

"We might see each other sometime after she's gone. I don't know. Maybe she'll fly back here occasionally. You know it won't work."

"I know that love changes everything." Iliana watched Lei-Ling polish a spot on the window of the Slipstream. "You have to make it work."

"Long-distance relationships never work."

"It's not long distance if you're rich. She could buy an airplane. Get married. Go in drag so no one knows you're a girl.

With Lei-Ling—" Iliana launched into their origin story. The punch line was hope.

It wouldn't work in the real world, Merritt had said to Avery, but Avery was living in *her* real world.

Now the crew was setting up cameras in the middle of the block so they could catch the dumpling truck as it pulled out. Alistair wandered over, looking like a larger-than-life Ken doll.

"Take a walk with me, Merritt. They're having trouble with sound from the road."

Merritt patted Iliana on the shoulder. She and Alistair set off down Eighty-Second Avenue. He tucked Merritt's hand in the crook of his elbow, as though he were the lord of the manor and they were walking up the steps to the ball, not past Pussy Cats Lingerie Modeling. It felt unnatural.

"I haven't seen much of Avery," Alistair said.

Merritt said nothing. Avery had slipped out of bed around five a.m. *I have to "wake up" in the hotel.* Merritt had thought the crew knew. Avery had laughed. *Single and closeted lesbian is not the same as I-overslept-with-my-hot-lesbian-lover. I could ruin everything.* It was only after Avery left that Merritt really thought about the words.

"She's happy," Alistair said. "I haven't seen her like this. She's dated a little bit, but you're special. She's taking risks."

Happy. Special. I could ruin everything.

Alistair gazed down the road. "Eighteen to thirty-two. That's the target demographic for all shows, except for kids' shows, and the target advertising market for those are parents, and they're eighteen to thirty-two. Avery is thirty-three."

"I know," Merritt said. "We just went to our reunion."

"She's old."

"We're not old."

"*You're* not old. You sell gramophones. But TV is like mining. You wear out early."

He was older than Avery, and for the first time Merritt saw it. His makeup was heavier than hers. In the bright sun she could see where it had sunk into the lines around his eyes.

"I always knew she'd meet someone special. I knew I'd be jealous, but I wanted that for her. She's my best friend. But you...you're a kale-eating lesbian. You're a hummus and Indigo Girls lesbian. You probably went to the LP concert without a bra."

Merritt tried to remember. Maybe. She considered pointing that she never quite got to kale, but kale was not the real point of this conversation.

"She dates about once every three years," Alistair went on. "She picks girls who are as closeted as she is. She won't even do bisexuals or indie actresses. She has to know her lovers have just as much to lose. She kind of hates them because they do. And then there *you* are. You've got your shop and your friends. You walk down to the gay bar. She's a sucker for that. She thinks it's authentic. But you could ruin her career. You could ruin the only thing she's ever done. It's not even like your shop. If your shop burns down, there are more old doorknobs. There's no other *King and Crown* for her."

This is actually my life, Merritt thought incredulously. If she had only known two months ago that she'd be sleeping with Avery Crown, or that she'd be walking down Eighty-Second Avenue, getting scolded by Alistair King, she might have been ecstatic, or she might have left town. Two inflated tube men waved frantically in front of a used-car dealership. That was how she felt: bounding up and then crashing into the ground.

"Avery is standing on the edge of a cliff."

Alistair had dropped his Alistair King act. His voice lowered an octave. His posture stiffened, and he grew taller and bigger. Merritt released his arm.

"I hope that's enough to make you careful because you care about her," Alistair went on. "I see the way you look for her. I'm asexual, but I'm not blind. Other people don't see it because they're not looking, but when they start looking...You know that video with the guy in the gorilla suit? You're supposed to count the basketballs, and the first time you pay so much attention to the balls, you don't see the gorilla guy."

"I'm the guy in the gorilla suit?"

Now she was sleeping with Avery Crown and walking down Eighty-Second Avenue being compared to a man in a gorilla suit.

"Avery is a *good* person," Alistair said.

"I know."

They walked past Beyond Beauty Salon and the hundredth auto-parts shop on Eighty-Second.

"You don't lose anything," Alistair said. "You need to think about what that means and what could happen."

It was like watching a friendly dog suddenly turn fierce. Gone was Alistair's wide cartoony smile. Gone were the skip and swish in his step that said, *If I weren't with Avery, you'd think I was the gayest, gayest gay boy in the world.*

Merritt did not like thinly veiled threats. Who did? But Merritt realized she liked Alistair making them. Avery had said they were like family. Now Alistair was the older brother, taking a questionable suitor out for a long, hard talk.

"Is it that bad to be a lesbian on TV?" Merritt asked.

"It's bad to betray your viewers' trust."

They passed an empty playground. Tetherball chains clanged against their poles.

"Do you hate me?" Merritt asked.

"I should."

Alistair took up too much space on the sidewalk. Merritt kept edging onto the dried grass and cracked cement lots that lined the street.

"Whatever you do to Avery, you do to me," he said.

That was not technically true, but like the kale, Merritt did not clarify the point.

"And the crew. They don't have families most of them. We're family. They've passed that up so they could have this. And you...you get a few weeks of fun. At what expense?"

My heart. My peaceful life, Merritt thought. *The hope that someone would love me enough to stay.*

Alistair was about to start in again.

"I want you to hate me," Merritt said.

Alistair slowed his stride.

"I want Avery to have a friend who loves her most of all," Merritt said. "Back in the day, I thought it was going to be me, and it wasn't. But I want her to have a friend who hates anyone who could hurt her."

"You care about her. So leave her."

"She's leaving me," Merritt said.

"I know. Of course she is. I mean, will you leave her alone this summer? We've basically got two weeks left. If you back off now, she gets out okay."

Merritt stopped. Traffic rushed by in a spray of dust and exhaust. A bus braked loudly. Some wilted riders stepped inside. There was a right choice. There had been ever since she'd walked into the Vale reunion. *No, I won't sleep with you. No, I won't sleep with you again.* (Wasn't that how good choices went? They were hard to make the first time.) Now the good choice was, *Yes, I'll leave Avery alone.* What were a few days in a prolonged one-night stand?

They were everything.

"No," Merritt said.

Alistair glared at her. She held her ground, her eyes never wavering from his.

"I want to be with her for fourteen more days." *I want to be with her...forever.* "I'll be careful, but I won't make decisions for her. And you shouldn't have talked to me like this. You're her friend. You said she was happy. How can you go behind her back and tell me to leave?"

Alistair's eyes seemed to bore into her soul.

Finally, he nodded grudgingly. A little bit of the cute, paint-can Alistair crept back into his face. "I'm trying to hate you," he said, "but I know you're right."

With that, he turned on his heel and walked back to the set too fast for Merritt to keep up without jogging.

Chapter 25

A few days later Avery watched Greg pace around the Elysium's front unit.

"We need to tear out some dry rot! We need carpet. We need mantels," he said. "How have we spent so much time outside?"

It was a familiar grievance. Outside shots took longer. The light was tricky. The city was full of difficult sounds. Every filming season ended with Greg saying, *Inside. Inside. This is a home show*.

"We got lost in this city!" he said.

Didn't Avery know it! It was like Portland had gotten bigger and bigger the more time she spent with Merritt. She wanted to explore every dive bar, every restaurant, every park. And she wanted to lay on the grass beneath the Saint Johns Bridge forever.

"We have twelve days," Greg said. "Let's get some carpet down now."

Avery hadn't seen Merritt the night before. She and Alistair had taken a quick flight up to Seattle so they could give a two-minute speech to executives from Amazon. Now she was filming laying the carpet while Merritt was downstairs actually repairing cracks in the brick mortar.

The crew moved into the hallway. Avery and Alistair positioned themselves behind a role of green grass-like carpet. Greg had liked the idea, and it was removable. Almost everything was. Avery had made sure. The bedroom rested in the shadow of iridescent curtains. The walls were covered in velvet art depicting Portland scenes: Saint Johns Bridge, a rose for the Rose City, the Voodoo Doughnuts logo. Filament lamps danced in the corners. In the bathroom, they had replaced the clawfoot tub with a clear plexiglass wading pool, but Avery had arranged for the contractor to take the tub back to Hellenic Hardware. Sconces on the hall held curio art pieces, like friendlier versions of the exhibits in the Peculiarium, but she'd fixed the old light sockets so as not to disturb the wallpaper.

Avery and Alistair pushed the carpet roll. It was supposed to unfurl in one swoop, but it hit the wall midway down the hall. They tried again.

On the seventh try, Greg exclaimed, "Merritt could do this. Avery, look excited."

Avery grinned.

"That says serial killer. Look at Alistair. He's just unrolling the carpet with joy."

She tried again. This time the carpet rolled perfectly, but Greg protested, "Now you're making love to it."

Avery imagined Merritt's legs spread open before her, how the muscles in her thighs tightened as she reached climax. It was nothing like unrolling carpet.

"Simple. Carpet. Joy. It's not that hard," Greg said.

Everyone knew they could set a production schedule by Greg's aggravation. A little panic as they landed in each new city. Several weeks of perfect calm. A bout of frustration as the last outdoor shots wrapped up and they realized, as they always did, that they had neglected the inside of the building. Then a fatherly calm as they glided—or, more likely, ran—over their finish line. No one took his outbursts seriously, but today his words stung.

Avery's mother had called to tell her about a new renovation show that was coming out in the fall. Marlene had scheduled a consultation with Dr. Miter. *He's the very best*, she'd said in the same concerned way people talked about heart surgeons. And today on set Avery had not been able to steal a private minute with Merritt, except to get Merritt's quick invitation. *We're doing an aikido demonstration at the Alberta Arts Festival tonight. Come watch.* Besides that, Merritt had been downstairs, off set, or talking earnestly to the crew about equipment that, even after fifteen years, Avery had never once been interested in.

"This stuff is so green and so...grassy," Alistair said, smoothing his hand over the rerolled carpet. "Come on, Aves, you love lawn carpet."

* * *

When they were finally done shooting, Avery and Alistair slipped away. Alistair opened the door of his comped Lexus and closed it behind her.

"You okay?" he asked as he slid into the driver's seat.

"I guess."

"You want me to go with you?"

That was the last thing she wanted, and she felt guilty. Walking around a street festival in the twilight was just the kind of thing she and Alistair liked to do. But she didn't want Merritt to see Alistair's arm around her, and she didn't want him sitting next to them, eating up the minutes she had with Merritt. Twelve days.

"No," she said. "I'm just nervous."

"Aren't you all happy in your lesbian lust?"

Lust? Desire? Love? The word had been hovering in the back of her mind like a camera just off set.

"For twelve more days."

Avery had been excited to see Merritt off set and outside of her apartment, but now she wasn't sure.

"What if there're other women who like her?"

What if flirting with Avery on set was like flirting with a cubicle mate, just something to do to pass the time in the office? What if Avery was only good enough to be a clandestine lover? What if she wasn't exciting in a crowd full of people who probably all performed burlesque and had threesomes and hung bondage slings from trees in the forest, where they made love and plotted to get Cascadia to secede from the United States.

"What if she's happier out there? She avoided me all day

today. She's mad that we went to Seattle. What if I asked her to keep things going and she doesn't want to? I think she's pissed I went away for one day. What about months?"

"It might not be Seattle," Alistair said, watching the traffic intently.

"What else?" Avery said.

"I'm just saying it might not be Seattle."

He knew something, and he wasn't sharing. She could tell. It was a strange feeling. Avery and Alistair always knew the same things because they told each other everything. But for the first time in as long as she could remember, she didn't want to know.

"Do you think that she could fall for me?" she asked instead.

She wanted more time. That was the thing about summer: It ended so quickly. She remembered the teachers at Vale telling them how they'd never get that kind of time again. *A whole summer. You don't get that when you're working.* But kids knew as soon as you woke up that first day of vacation, you were losing the summer, breath by breath.

"Are you talking about forever?" Alistair asked.

"I don't know."

"You're very difficult," Alistair said in his British-mother voice.

"I am not." Avery feigned indignation.

"Our lives are complicated to other people," Alistair said more seriously. "You're not like dating the girl next door."

"But I look like the girl next door. It's not fair. I fail at pretending to lay carpet for a living. I'm like some bad house-wife."

Alistair was supposed to say, *Honey, don't believe the lies. You're fantastic.*

Instead he said, "We are nothing without girls next door and housewives. And your lesbian has the right to take a night off without you having an existential crisis. Do you want me to stop and get you a hidden-word puzzle book?"

Ordinarily, Alistair's puzzle book would cheer her up. Well, not the book itself. Protesting the book would cheer her up. The questions the book raised would cheer her up. Why find the hidden words? Did they have a cumulative mental health benefit, or would one do? Why had she never seen him finding the hidden word? She had asked him that once. *Men do sudoku,* he had said, as though that were an obvious fact. *I'm a feminist, but there are still rules.* But something had changed between them that a puzzle book couldn't fix.

"Just drop me off," Avery said. "Please."

* * *

The smell of patchouli and fried dough wafted down Alberta Street as Avery hurried through the crowd. Booths lined the sidewalks. A street band pounded on plastic buckets. A woman walked by with an iguana on her shoulder. Everything was coated in dust. As she strolled through the leisurely crowd, she tried to forget that it was a last-Thursday festival. She wouldn't be in Portland for the next last Thursday.

A moment later she came to an exhibition space that had

been cleared in an intersection. Iliana was speaking into a microphone, explaining the peaceful practices of aikido.

Avery's heart quavered as she watched Merritt emerge on the other side of the mats. She wore a white linen jacket and flowing black pants. She looked happy.

"Now, the thing that defines aikido," Iliana said, "is the focus on subduing your opponent without injuring him."

Two of her other students stepped forward, knelt before each other, and performed a few moves. The assembled crowd clapped politely.

A woman standing beside Avery said, "It's so elegant, isn't it?"

The woman didn't seem to notice that Avery was Avery Crown. No one did. It felt odd and liberating at the same time, as though the sky were higher, the street was longer, and the world had zoomed out in wide-angle distortion.

"We refer to the practitioners as 'uke' and 'tori.'" Iliana went on. "Tori takes the dominant role, but uke is not the victim. When they're done, they trade roles. Tori always moves to protect uke. Even as she subdues her, she carries her."

Avery knew all about that, and her heart and body thrilled at the memory of Merritt flipping her onto the bed.

"Now my friend Merritt Lessing and I will demonstrate. I am playing the role of tori and she the role of uke."

Merritt stepped forward and bowed to Iliana. Then she lunged at Iliana, and Iliana cast her to the mat. Merritt rolled and rose.

"Falling is an important part of aikido practice," Iliana said when Merritt rolled to her feet. "And no one falls as beautifully as my friend Merritt."

Merritt moved toward Iliana again, and Iliana threw her again.

The crowd cheered. Merritt and Iliana moved quickly. Merritt hit the mat every few seconds, almost on the beat. Lunge. Throw. Fall.

"How do you think they do it without hurting themselves?" the woman next to Avery asked. "I can't even do a push-up without throwing my shoulder out."

Avery drew in a breath to answer, but neither of them spoke. They were both too focused on the demonstration. Iliana whirled Merritt over her back, then pulled her forward into a somersault. Faster and faster they flew until Avery could not release her breath because it seemed impossible that Merritt would survive unscathed. Then Iliana threw Merritt one last time. Merritt rolled into a standing position and bowed to Iliana and then to the crowd.

A moment later Merritt made her way through the crowd, smiling. "It's the gorgeous Avery Crown," she said.

The woman who had been standing next to Avery looked up at Merritt like a schoolgirl. The woman was pretty, Avery suddenly noticed, with dark hair and full lips tinted with just the right amount of berry-red lipstick. Avery hoped Merritt didn't notice.

"You were so graceful," the woman said, "that blend of power and elegance. I've been thinking about starting aikido."

"You should," Merritt said. "Iliana's dojo is right behind my shop, Hellenic Hardware. Do you know it?"

"Oh, I bought tin ceiling tiles from you," the woman cooed.

"Well, we're practically friends, then." Merritt produced a business card from a hidden pocket in her gi. "I'm the top, and Iliana's number is underneath."

She was the top!

Avery guessed Merritt had not intended to smile wolfishly at the woman. It was just that her face was made for that hungry, confident smile. Avery could see the woman vibrating with delight.

"Are you a black belt? That's so amazing."

Watching Merritt was like staring into the set lights too long. In public, she was so cool, so confident. Only in private did she let her guard down. Those moments felt precious, but soon Avery would be gone, and Merritt might reveal herself to other women or not at all.

Avery was saved from these thoughts by Lei-Ling charging through the crowd.

"Oh my gosh. This is so exciting! You have to come out with us. Iliana and I have the biggest surprise."

* * *

The bar Lei-Ling chose was tucked on a side street a few blocks from Alberta. One wall was lined with pinball machines, and a blackboard advertised cocktails with names like the Troglodyte. Merritt, Iliana, and Avery piled into a booth. Lei-Ling stood up.

"Can we tell them?" Lei-Ling said to Iliana. She didn't wait for an answer but tapped a fork to her glass. "Everyone!"

The bar quieted.

"Everyone, my name is Lei-Ling Wu, and this is my girl-friend, Iliana Koslov. And we've been together for one year today, and so on August twelfth, which is twelve days from now, we are going to get married."

The bar may not have known them, but they clearly liked a love story. Cheers erupted from every table.

"We're going to get married at the Mirage because that's where we went on our first date," Lei-Ling went on. "Our friend Vita is going to marry us. She got one of those minister certificates online. And everyone should come, and you should invite all your friends, because we want to celebrate with every single person in the world!"

Merritt hugged her friends, slapping Iliana's back and ruffling Lei-Ling's rainbow-colored hair. "You two are disgustingly cute," she said. "I knew it was coming. What am I going to buy you? You've already got every Crock-Pot and Vitamix in the world."

Merritt laughed. Lei-Ling pleaded with Merritt to promise she'd be next. Merritt smiled at Avery cautiously, but as they walked back to Merritt's truck, Merritt fell silent, and Avery could not tell what was in her heart.

Chapter 26

For the next week and a bit, Avery vacillated. Sometimes her time with Merritt seemed to stretch out forever. One night was a lifetime of pleasure and laughter. Other times she felt like a giant clock counted down behind her head. A minute gone. An hour gone. A day. Avery and Merritt didn't talk about Avery's impending departure, although everything on set was *ten days left* and *nine days left* and *when we get to Cincinnati*. Then there was one week left. Pam had texted flight arrangements for Avery, Alistair, and the crew. The semitrucks that moved the equipment had arrived. They had exactly one week together.

It was too much to bear. She needed the kind of bad advice only DX could give. The morning of the seventh day before departure, Avery asked the van driver to take her to DX's studio... because, of course, in the process of visiting Avery in Portland, DX had also set up a recording studio and was at work on her next soon-to-be-platinum album. The studio was set up in a Victorian house in an old neighborhood, half houses, half old businesses. Avery pushed the door open tentatively. A young woman in a leather bra and miniscule leather shorts lounged on a sofa reading a book and smoking out of a hookah. So much for security. DX was probably too cool to need it.

"They're down there." The girl nodded toward a narrow door in the hallway.

It was clearly the stairwell to the basement. A base beat rattled the wooden steps. The stains on the walls looked like horror-movie plasma. It was just the kind of place DX loved.

And there she was. Behind a wall of recording equipment, DX belted out her latest opus while her bandmates milked every possible note of anguish and exhilaration out of their instruments. When DX saw Avery, she stopped mid-bar and stepped out of the studio.

"Avery!" She grabbed Avery around the waist. "I've been staying away so you had time to sex up that hot woman of yours."

"DX! Shh!"

The band swigged their beers and the drummer lit a joint the size of a cigar.

"They're not paying attention," DX said. "Guys, take five. I need a minute with my girl."

The band filed up the stairs.

"Isn't this place great?" DX said.

"Is it soundproofed?"

"No. That's the point. Everything is soundproofed and remastered now," DX said. "Here you're right in the middle of a love song and *bam!* Some bus rolls by overhead, and that's life. Right? You don't get ten takes. Everybody who listens to that sound is going to be, like, 'Yeah, I was there.'"

"Is that why people listen to music?"

It was DX. Of course her millions of fans would want to hear the truck go by.

"Guess what this place used to be," DX said. "Smell it."

Avery sniffed before she could stop herself. There was a faint smell of burnt metal and chemicals.

"It smells like cheap carpets."

"It was a funeral parlor, but Portlanders aren't doing funerals like they used to. They all want to get buried in burlap bags and composted. So the family rents this out as office space."

"DX, it's not an office," Avery said. "Have you ever been to an office?"

"I try not to. Those fluorescent lights suck your soul." DX grinned and perched on the back of one of the vinyl couches that lined the concrete bunker. "You look like someone stole your dog. Talk to me."

"I don't even know if I'd like a dog," Avery said.

"How about a jackal-dog? I know this guy who breeds them in Australia. A golden jackal and a dog. You can pick your dog. I'd go malamute, but you'd probably want to water it down with a pug."

Avery stretched out on the couch, staring up at the ceiling. It was like being at a really bad therapist's office.

"I don't want a jackal-dog. I'm just saying, I've never had a dog. I don't know if I'd enjoy a dog. I decorate things for a living, and I don't know how I'd decorate my own condo."

"This is about Merritt."

"She's wonderful." Avery closed her eyes. She wanted to repeat Merritt's name over and over. She wanted to have kinky sex encased in nylon bodysuits, and she wanted to watch old John Cusack movies and eat ice cream with her.

"I don't want to leave," Avery said.

DX reached over Avery's head and pulled a bottle from behind the sofa. "Real absinthe." She took a swig and held it out to Avery.

Avery shook her head. "I've only known her again her for a couple of weeks. We were just supposed to spend the summer together, but it's all gone so quickly, and I don't want it to end. When we make love...she's so tough and she's so fragile."

"Those are the best," DX said, as though she were knowledgeably picking out peaches or lobsters at the Saturday market. "Tough but vulnerable. You want to save them, but you don't have to."

"I don't know if she trusts me. Her friends are going to get married in a lesbian bar, and I can't give her that."

"What does Alistair say?"

"He says I'm complicated to someone like her. He says I have to be careful. If we stay together, I need to get her to sign a nondisclosure contract and date her like a normal person, tell people she's my trainer. But what if Dan Ponza sees us?"

DX gestured with her bottle. "Forget Dan Ponza. I know a guy who can take care of Dan Ponza."

Avery said "no" quickly and firmly. DX probably did know someone who could take care of Dan Ponza. Avery would be considered an accessory.

"I remember once when we were at Vale, Merritt and her uncle and his boyfriend went away for the weekend, and I missed her. Like everything was empty without her. So I told my dad I was going away with friends, and I drove to Astoria, where they were staying. I thought I would run into her."

She remembered standing on the boardwalk on the mouth of the Columbia, the wind whipping rain in her face, and thinking how foolish the trip had been. She wouldn't find Merritt. And then she had. At an antiques store. Merritt had been handling the receiver of an old telephone, putting it to her ear and saying, *Hello, lovely, I'll be home soon.*

I'm home now, Avery had answered, and Merritt had whirled around, delight and surprise filling her face.

"I told her I just wanted to take my new Miata out for a drive. But I thought I could die right there, I was so happy to see her. Merritt's uncle invited me to stay in their rented cottage. Merritt and I wrapped up in blankets and sat outside on the porch. The whole town is on a hill, and we could see down to the river. We could see the stars, and I almost kissed her, but I didn't. I want to do something. I want to convince her. But what if I'm not good enough? What if Merritt dumps me? What if we get caught and I wreck *King and Crown* and then she leaves me? What if she makes it and then she doesn't want me?"

"You mean on TV?"

"Yeah."

"That girl doesn't want to be a reality-TV star."

"What if she gets picked up by a real director? Venner thinks she's got what it takes."

"That's the most ridiculous thing I've ever heard. You're worried that she's going to get too famous for you? You think she cares about that stuff? You're worried that she's going to win an Emmy and dump you?"

"She could."

"That's your mom talking. All that"—DX affected a snooty accent somewhere between British aristocracy and Harvard professor—"'I know your birthweight and now I know everything.' Your mom doesn't know shit about shit."

"She knew you'd be huge."

"I was a rock star at thirteen. She doesn't get credit for discovering *me.*" DX took another sip of her absinthe. "Just quit."

"I can't do that to Alistair. He hitchhiked to L.A. from Wyoming. He slept in a sleeping bag in the snow so that he could get to Hollywood. And he made it. And he made me."

"You made yourself."

Upstairs the band had resumed their practice, and an acoustic version of DX's "Uber to Hell" filtered through the ceiling.

"What would you do if you weren't a singer?" Avery asked.

"I'd start a cult."

"No, for real?"

DX's face said, *Yes, for real.*

"What would I do?" Avery asked.

She was waiting for DX to tease her. If she had wanted grudging sympathy, she would have gone to Alistair. She hoped somewhere behind the absinthe and the bravado, DX might have an answer.

"What do you want?" DX nudged Avery's shoulder. "Sit up."

"I want to know that I'm good enough."

Avery sat. DX put the absinthe in her hand, and Avery took a small sip. It tasted like flowers and liquorish.

"Good enough is being alive," DX said.

"Says the woman who's been downloaded a million times."

"Three point two million," DX said. "But you know what? If I kicked it all and moved to some tiny island off Greece and starved to death because I couldn't fish worth shit, I'd still be a fucking rock star, even if I'd never recorded a single song."

"You ever feel old?" Avery asked. "Or like you might be getting old? One day you'll be old? Old is waiting for you?"

"Oh, don't go on about eighteen to thirty-two like Alistair. I'm going to be like my dad but without the drugs. He's sixty-seven, and when he gets onstage he rages like he's twenty-one."

"I don't even own a house."

"I have four. Do you want one?"

"Kind of. I always thought I wanted to travel with Alistair for the rest of my life. We've been together for fifteen years."

"You said she gave you a dress for prom fifteen years ago. Do you still have it?"

Eight (sometimes twelve) hard plastic wardrobes traveled by semitruck everywhere Avery went. Some were installed in her hotel, sometimes one in her trailer. There was always one she insisted on, although she never wore the clothes it held. They were hers. The camouflage sweatpants Alistair had given her. A pair of jeans with the ass ripped out that she had fantasized about wearing with a G-string. And the dress. Preserved like the wedding dress it was. She waited for it in every city.

"Yeah," she said.

"She bought it for you before you met Alistair. You've known her longer."

"That's not how you think about these things," Avery said.

"Or you fell in love with her in five weeks. You pick."

"I'm not in..."

DX's look said she wouldn't believe the lie.

Avery knocked back another swig of the absinthe. DX put her skinny hand over Avery's. She wore enough skull rings to make her own catacomb.

"This isn't hard, Aves. You tell Alistair you're sorry. You'll be careful. He'll still be your bestie. Then you tell Merritt you love her. You say, 'I'm sorry I haven't been clear. I want you to own me like the moon owns the sun. I know that I'm in the closet, but look around at these other women. I'm a frickin' star!' You don't have to go back and forth about this. Save yourself the trouble. This is just who you are."

"DX, if *good enough is being alive,* aren't all those other women moons and stars too?"

DX grabbed her by the back of the neck and gave her a shake. "Do you think I would have been friends with you for twenty-three years if you were just *as good* as everyone else?"

Chapter 27

Much to Greg's dismay, Merritt insisted on an evening off. As much as she longed to spend every remaining second with Avery, she had to breathe too, and it was getting harder and harder to breathe near Avery. She couldn't look at her without her chest tightening and her heart seizing in her chest. She was losing her. It was ending. She didn't know what she would do when Avery left.

"We have six days!" he protested, standing in the newly lawn-carpeted hallway of the apartment that would soon be hers.

In the bathroom, Alistair and Avery were submitting to Tami's expertise. The light in the Elysium was making Avery look bloated and had given Alistair dark shadows under his eyes. Gould, Tom, Setter, Colton, and Meg were standing in the bedroom waiting for their assigned tasks.

"We don't take evenings off!" Greg said. "This is television. You mortgage your life to be on television. You don't pop in at nine and leave at five."

"You work the day after you've crashed your bike," Merritt said bitterly.

Greg's face softened. "I would never have put Avery on if Venner hadn't insisted. We're not like that. We've just got work to do."

"I know," Merritt said. "But I looked at the call sheet. I'm not on after filming replacing-the-kitchen-counter."

"We might need you," Greg said.

"You're leaving in six days. There's only so much you can do in six days. By now you've done it or you haven't. If you're late now, me staring at you staring at Gould staring at Alistair isn't going to help."

Six days. Six days. Had she done what she was supposed to do? Did she know what that was? She felt like she had at boarding school. First the principal would call her into the office, sympathetic but firm. Her parents were behind in tuition. Of course it wasn't her fault, but they had found another school, with a payment plan, a better situation all around. She would count down the days until her departure, whatever little bit of comfort and security she'd developed at that school slipping away day by day.

Greg also seemed to be mulling over difficult thoughts. His dilemma, Merritt guessed, was whether to let her go despite the off chance they might need her or argue with her and lose valuable seconds.

The seconds counted more.

"Fine, fine, fine. Go. Be back here first thing tomorrow. Five a.m."

Merritt had worked construction. Five a.m. in the summer was nothing, although her nights with Avery were taking their toll. Sex could substitute for sleep but only for so long.

* * *

"What are you doing?" Iliana protested when Merritt walked through the front doors of Hellenic Hardware a little while later.

"I know you've got everything under control," Merritt said, "but I've been out of the shop for five weeks. There's billing to do. We've got shipments coming in."

Iliana grabbed her by the elbow and walked her past the interns who were sorting bolts. In the privacy of the lumber section near the loading bay, she said, "You've got a week left with your girl. Why aren't you on set?"

Avery's eyes had asked her the same question as Merritt nodded and walked out. Of course Merritt had wanted to stay. If she could stare at Avery all afternoon, she'd stay. But Alistair's words and Avery's departure hung in her heart like the last reverberations of a gong.

"I have to do something." Merritt looked around for something out of order, but Iliana kept the shop like it was her own.

"You're supposed to be making love to her every second you've got. You're supposed to be walking around the

Elysium like you're going to take her on the floor. You're supposed to tell her how you feel."

"Iliana, I need my own life back. She's leaving in less than a week, and no matter what we say, it will end." She raised her palms to the ceiling of Hellenic Hardware. "And I need this place to matter more. I have to be able to get back to the shop and love it. This is enough for me."

This all seemed a little dull. There would surely be a stack of unpaid invoices. One, maybe two, contractors who needed a little reminder from collections. A friend at the grange had texted her about an old farmhouse being deconstructed near Hillsboro. She could drive out and bid on the windows. It felt small while everything with Avery felt vast. She'd never been to Cincinnati, where *King & Crown* was going next, but she'd googled attractions. The oldest brick house in America was in Cincinnati. She'd like that...if Avery asked her to visit her in Cincinnati. And there was a museum of old signs that would be lovely...especially if Avery could forgive Merritt for taking her on the least romantic Cincinnati date ever.

"What's this about really?" Iliana said, sitting down on a neat stack of railroad ties.

Merritt sat down beside her. "Alistair talked to me."

"About what?"

"About what would happen if someone found out about us. I'd ruin everything."

Iliana grabbed her knee and squeezed a bit too hard, looking Merritt in the eye. "And Alistair is the boss of you?"

"He's her best friend."

"So he has to say shit like that. You cannot mess this up.

You've been happy for once in your life. I can tell. You look less like a bloodhound."

"I do not look like a bloodhound."

She had all of *King & Crown* to back her up. It was strange working with people forever telling her how beautiful she was in a way that made it sound like inventory on a shelf. She wondered what it was like for Avery to live in a world that told her she did not have that inventory, and she wished she could stay in Avery's life to remind her not to listen.

"Just act like a normal person and tell her how you feel," Iliana said.

"What if she says she's done with me? What if I ask her to be my girlfriend and do...girlfriend stuff? Cook. Watch reruns. What if she says she was just in it for the sex? What if she realizes that I'm okay for a few weeks, but I'm not the kind of woman you'd want to—" She shrugged.

"What?"

Merritt traced a gash in the wooden railroad ties. "Stay with."

"Why would Avery think that?"

"It's my fate."

"There is no such thing as fate."

"What's the chi, then? You say it's the energy that moves through everything. What if you get the bad energy? If you read history you'd see. One person crosses the Oregon Trail, sets up an orchard, marries the only woman in town, has ten children, and writes a blissful memoir. Another person loses everything in a fire, and then their whole family dies of the flu."

"Get a flu shot. We're not on the Oregon Trail, and you're not doomed. You're a brat." This was the old Iliana come back from the mists of pre-Lei-Ling history. "I had a shitty life," Iliana went on. "I had a dad who beat me. I had to leave my house at sixteen and buy a fake ID so I could work. You had a fake ID so you could go to Darcelle's drag club. Your parents didn't beat you. Your stepdad didn't molest you. He paid to send you to a dozen fancy boarding schools. Then your uncle willed you a business, which you happened to have a gift to turn into something really amazing."

"And every time I like a girl, she text-dumps me because she says it's the most I deserve."

"Well, you're old-fashioned."

Iliana stood up. Merritt looked up at her. "It's not old-fashioned to not want to get dumped on LinkedIn."

"Get up," Iliana said. "Everyone e-dumps. It's less embarrassing. You dump someone over dinner, and you have to figure out whether you wait until dessert to tell her. Do you tell her right away? Who pays if you've already ordered? If the girl cries, what do you do?"

"I never cry."

"So you're perfect for a repressed TV star. Come on." Iliana nodded toward the dojo. "Let's work this out. If you practiced more, you might not have to agonize over *everything*."

There was no resisting Iliana when she really wanted to practice. It was probably the strength of her chi pulling Merritt into the quiet dojo.

"If you meditated," Iliana went on. "If you practiced regularly instead of just walking in here every so often to show off."

"I don't show off."

"You show off all the time. It's a form of deflection."

Iliana took off her boots, set them by the wall, and bowed to the shrine. Merritt did the same.

"Come in from the left," Iliana instructed.

Merritt performed a rusty side approach. Iliana clasped her arm, pulled her off-balance. Merritt dropped to the ground, rolled, and regained her stance. They repeated the move a few more times. Iliana's long blond braid swung around her back, but of course no practitioner of aikido would ever yank it.

"Faster," Iliana said. She threw Merritt again.

Finally, she lunged at Merritt. It was an easy opening. Merritt was supposed to use Iliana's momentum to bring her to the floor, but she missed her chance. Iliana countered and flipped Merritt over her arm in a complete, airborne rotation. For a second Merritt saw the cloudy skylights overhead, and then she was back on her feet, her arms loosely raised because Iliana would never hurt her. She would challenge her. She would lay Merritt down on the ground with a flick of her wrist. But Iliana would always protect her as she fell.

They sparred for half an hour, and Merritt felt her muscles loosen and her body stretch. She tried to clear Avery from her mind. She tried to live in a place where there was only weight and counterweight. Fulcrum and arc. Fall and rise. The spirit of aki. Finally, they finished. Iliana bowed to Merritt.

"Now are you ready to hear reason?" Iliana sat down on the mat.

Merritt sat next to her, then flopped on her back. "What kind of reason?"

Iliana flopped down with Merritt, their heads almost touching. "I think you're hiding from her. Right now. You're telling yourself you don't need her. You want to get back to the shop. You're afraid to ask her how she feels, and you're afraid to tell her how you feel."

"I'm being realistic. I'm accepting change in the world. Isn't that what you are always telling your students to do? Let the chi move through you? Don't hold too tightly to things of this world?"

"Running away from the opponent you fear is not harnessing your chi."

"I'm not running from Avery, and I'm not afraid of her."

"I know," Iliana said again. "You're afraid of yourself."

Chapter 28

On their last night together, Avery arrived at Merritt's apartment around eight, letting herself in with the key Merritt had given her. Merritt was standing in the small, open kitchen, staring at a pile of ingredients. There was something wrapped in butcher paper, a wheel of brie, peaches, and an inordinate amount of kale, a kind of kale mountain. A few of the leaves had drifted to the floor, but that was okay because there were about two shopping bags full on the counter.

"What are you doing?" Avery asked.

"I think I'm in over my head."

Avery walked across the room and put her arms around Merritt's waist, leaning her head against her shoulder. She could feel Merritt's heart beating.

"I wanted to cook," Merritt said.

"Sure." It wasn't exactly how Avery had pictured their last night together, but it was sweet. She'd imagined tears, hers probably. Not Merritt's. But it would be nice to cook a meal first.

"I've tried to make kale before, but I never could," Merritt said.

"Cook it?"

"Buy it."

"You couldn't buy kale in Portland? Was it picking it out?" Avery teased gently. "Or carrying it to your truck? Because they'll take it out to your truck for you."

"It's stupid, and I don't actually cook. Let's just order in."

Merritt was changing the subject, but Avery wasn't sure how to coax the deep story of kale out of her.

"You bought this," Avery said. "You wanted this epic amount of kale. I don't know how to knit. But I'm not totally lost in domestic stuff. I'll show you. And you don't have to cook it, you know. You can eat it raw."

* * *

Dinner was quiet, and Merritt ate slowly. She appeared to savor each bite, although Avery doubted her brie-tilapia on a bed of peach kale was really a culinary success. And all through dinner Avery thought, *I'll ask. I'll tell her.* She wanted more. She wanted time with Merritt. The only way she might get it would be to put her desires on the table as surely as she had placed a plate in front of Merritt.

"I'm glad I got to see you doing aikido with your friends the other day," Avery said. "I like to see you in your world." There was a painful tug at her heart that said, *Maybe I'm not*. Maybe she would rather live in the privacy of Merritt's apartment where there were no other women, no friends who might warn Merritt off sleeping with a closeted television star, nothing to suggest that Merritt had a complete life before Avery arrived and would have a complete life after Avery left. Avery could still see the pretty, dark-haired woman at the last-Thursday festival leaning toward Merritt. Avery took a deep breath. She'd waited all summer, and now summer was measured in hours instead of days.

Avery leaned forward, her hands extended on the table. "What do we do now?" she asked.

Merritt took her hands. "We go to bed?"

"I mean the other now. I mean tomorrow. I want more time with you."

There. She had said it.

"I want more time with you too," Merritt said, but it sounded impossible, the way people said, *I wish I had known my father* or *I'd like to be twenty-one again.* "Alistair took me out behind the proverbial woodshed to have *a talk.* Did he tell you?"

Oh, that was it! Avery thought. Alistair had been trying to scare off her lover while offering her gender-appropriate puzzle books. For a moment she felt real anger. He should have told her!

"No. What did he say?"

"He said if I cared about you, I'd back off. You could lose your show over this."

"I told you that."

"But I didn't know how much it meant to you before. *King*

and Crown is your family. This is your life. When I'm with you—" Merritt squeezed Avery's hands. She looked pained. "All my exes say I'm cold."

"You're not cold," Avery said.

"That's why they leave. And for the first time, I think maybe I won't make the same mistakes. But, Avery, maybe I'll make worse ones. The girls I've dated say I hurt them. I never see it coming. I never think I will. What if I do it again?"

"How will you hurt me?"

"I could ruin *King and Crown*."

"I want to tell you something," Avery said, "that I never talk about, not even with Alistair. Come sit with me."

She stood up and led Merritt to the couch. It struck her again how bleak the apartment was, like every piece of furniture had been chosen because it wasn't good enough for someplace else.

"I want you to know why I never see my mother," Avery said when they were seated. "We only talk on the phone, and I don't visit. People think it's just because she's a bitch, which she is, but she's my mom, and sometimes I miss her. But there's this one moment. She and my dad," Avery went on slowly, "were about as opposite as you could get. I don't know how they had me. When I told my father I was gay, he was thrilled that I was gay. He wanted me to *subvert the cultural norm*. Although come to think of it, he probably just liked it because he knew it would piss off my mother. Then I told my mom. I remember the exact moment. I'd flown back to L.A. We were sitting outside this little restaurant with white tablecloths, white plates, and white flowers. I'd met Alistair. I wanted the show. I said, *I'm gay,* and my mom shushed me. Then she told me it was fine...morally. I asked her if I could come out and still have a career. She said they'd probably overlook the gay thing if I was really talented, but I wasn't."

"That's a terrible thing for your mother to say, and it's not true."

Avery loved the outrage in Merritt's face.

"You know I wanted to do real films when I was younger?"

"I remember," Merritt said. "You wanted to win an award at Sundance."

They sat side by side, staring at the closed curtains that hid Burnside and the city beyond. It was the perfect summer night, and they should have had the curtains open and the breeze blowing through the apartment. That would almost make up for the bad furniture.

"My mom told me I could only start my career once," Avery said, "but I could always come out. The thing is, she lied. Once I started my career, I couldn't come out. If I'd come out at eighteen, I could have been *Queer Eye for the Straight Guy* or something like that. But if I go back now, everything I've done is a fraud. My mom has closeted clients, and she should have told me what it was like for them. She never said, 'This is what you'll lose.'"

"You mean that you might lose the show?"

"That I'd lose part of myself."

Quickly, as though Avery might suddenly get up and leave, Merritt wrapped her arms around her. Merritt was so tall, it was an awkward position, like a child who was too big to be carried climbing into someone's arms. Avery never wanted to let her go.

"What is it?" Avery asked.

"Can I tell *you* something?"

"Of course."

Avery squeezed Merritt tightly.

"I'm scared." Merritt was silent for a long time. "I've been alone for so long. It feels like my fate. Iliana says that's not a thing. I'm not doomed. But every time it's harder, and when I date a girl, it's like we're replaying this story. She doesn't even know she's a part of it, but I can see the whole thing from the beginning. And I try so hard to be the kind of person who doesn't deserve that, who opens up, who has *faith in the universe*, like Iliana is always saying. But in the end, I always feel like the stuff in Hellenic Hardware, something that you can let go. So I try to let other people go first."

"Are you saying you're trying to let me go?"

Merritt pulled away. "I started trying the day you left Vale."

"Did it work?"

Merritt shook her head with a tender smile that warmed Avery's heart. "I want what Lei-Ling and Iliana have."

"To get married? Let's go. Right now. We'll get DX to fly us to Reno or Vegas. I'll wear a wig. DX is crazy-good with costumes. She'll make me look like Elvis."

As soon as the words flew out of Avery's mouth, she stopped. Had she just asked Merritt to marry her? She had wanted to make Merritt laugh. She had wanted to lift the mist of sadness from Merritt's eyes. But if Merritt had read

a different intention into Avery's words, Avery had just cata-
pulted herself into a marriage proposal. And in that second,
Avery knew that if Merritt took it as a wild declaration of
love and said yes, Avery wouldn't correct her. She would kiss
Merritt and say, *I'm sorry I don't have a ring.* After all, Avery
had never gotten a tattoo, never smoked pot, never had sex in
the woods, never bought a sports car with Bitcoin...and she
wasn't satisfied with her life. Maybe DX was right and she
needed to take a risk. She'd think about tomorrow tomorrow.
It was exhilarating.

"I want you to take me to the oldest brick house in
America," Merritt said. "It's in Cincinnati."

The oldest brick house in America was a bit of a letdown
after thinking that she would throw caution to the wind like a
virgin on prom night. Still, it was also true that Merritt asked
for the oldest brick house with the downcast gaze of someone
asking for the rings of Saturn. Maybe the oldest brick house
was a declaration of love to a hardware store owner.

"I want a life where we cook together," Merritt went on.
"I'll learn. I promise. I don't want you to dump me over
Instagram."

"Do people do that?"

"I guess Instagram is hard. It's more Twitter." Merritt
looked at Avery, her eyes dark.

Avery tucked Merritt's hair behind her ear so she could
see her face. Her hair had finally grown long enough
to stay tucked. Merritt looked pale and too thin, even
though Dr. Miter would probably use her cheekbones as
models.

"I would never dump you on Instagram."

Avery heard DX saying, *You say I'm sorry I haven't been clear. I want you to own me like the moon owns the sun.* If she didn't fight for Merritt now, she would have to answer to DX. DX who'd probably view Avery's failure as a reason to build up her confidence, like those ropes courses where corporations took their middle managers. Only DX's ropes course might be a basket hung on a vine suspended over a four-hundred-foot Amazonian chasm with snakes in it. Or maybe they'd just cross the Sahara on camel. But it wasn't really DX she was worried about. She owed it to the eighteen-year-old girl who had written *I will!* on a piece of paper she tucked into the pad of her bra and then didn't.

"DX told me to take you on vacation to Taha'a. She says they have vanilla plantations, and it's so beautiful we'd eat the sand, but if you want to go to the oldest brick house in America, that's almost as good and we could cook together and be a real couple. You and me. Everything could go wrong, but let's give it a shot. I want you to call me every night and text me pictures of your breakfast or your breasts or some crazy thing you've brought into the shop."

Merritt's smile was still tentative. There was still a shadow in her eyes, but she said, "Do you want to know what I brought into the shop? What got shipped to my shop? I'll text you a picture."

Merritt picked up her phone and disappeared into her bedroom. A moment later Avery's phone chimed. The photograph said everything about Avery's friendship with DX. Merritt returned a moment later with an ebony black box.

She opened it up and took out a red card embossed with gold ink.

"'Dear Merritt,'" Merritt read. "'Avery really is a sweet girl when she gets out of her own way. She says she knows where the clit is, but I'm saying fifty-fifty on that one.'"

Avery didn't have to ask for the name of the sender.

"'You will have a lot of work to do, but trust me. She's worth it. Here's a little something to get you two started. She's probably never used a vibrator.'"

"I have used a vibrator."

"'And by the way,'" Merritt went on. "'I don't think she can really knit, so don't hold your breath for that sweater. I'd say I'd kill you if you hurt her, but I don't think you will. XXX [skull emoji], DX.'"

"*I* will kill her," Avery said through her hands. "She has no boundaries. None."

"I've tried it," Merritt said. "It's fabulous. Come on." She pulled Avery's hands away from her face. "I saw on your blog that a girl should always spend enough time with a gift to send a sincere thank-you card."

* * *

When they were both naked and aroused, Merritt parted Avery's sex with her fingers. "Close your eyes."

Avery felt Merritt slip something inside her. A weight settled on her pubic bone and a subtle vibration caressed her inside. Merritt looked gorgeous and self-satisfied. She knelt over Avery and settled herself on top of the golden sex toy, pressing it between their bodies. In one hand, she held a pamphlet. The vibrations were delicious but faint.

Merritt read from the pamphlet. The sex toy—the Kinzan, it was called—was twenty-four-karat gold plate. Scientists had harnessed the power of ionic gold convergence.

"That's not a thing," Merritt said.

The rest of the paragraph read like an erotic novel. When seated properly, the Kinzan would place pressure on all points along the woman's labia, clitoris, and the submerged, wishbone-like extension of the clitoris that extended back on either side of her mons.

"'Woman aches for this kind of deep stimulation,'" Merritt read. "'The gold base holds Kinzan in place while she writhes with pleasure and her clitoris throbs with vibronic frequency.' That's not a thing."

But maybe it was.

"Turn it up," Avery said. "It feels good."

"You can't turn it up." Merritt's laugh was low and sultry. "That's the thing. It uses 'advanced algorithms to amplify your sexual rhythms.'"

Merritt rocked her hips gently. Her motion seemed to focus the vibrations.

The Kinzan vibrated against Avery's clit, and although the gold was heavy and hard, it seemed perfectly sculpted to contour their bodies. Merritt held up the pamphlet, still rocking back and forth as she read.

"'The ionic convergence of gold takes you to sexual enlightenment.'" Merritt gazed down at her with a droll smile, but her voice was taut. "Are you enlightened?"

Avery clasped Merritt's thighs.

"'The Kinzan...'" Merritt tried to read, but Avery reached between them and ran her fingers through Merritt's pubic hair, opening the folds of her labia so Merritt's clitoris touched the smooth gold surface.

Merritt's response was a groan.

Avery rubbed Merritt's clit, pushing it gently against the vibrating gold. Merritt closed her eyes. They hung here for a moment, each lost in their own gratification. It was the kind of moment that ought to feel lonely. There they were: getting off alone together. But Avery didn't feel lonesome. She felt like she had the few times she'd done stage theater. It had been such a joy to watch her colleagues perform well, to nail their lines. She had wanted them to succeed, just like she wanted to watch Merritt rocking herself to climax.

Then Merritt leaned back, her hands resting on the bed behind her, her hips revolving in a slow, determined circle. Avery could see the hood of Merritt's clit rubbing against the gold surface, and she loved it, and she loved the tension in Merritt's face. A moment later Merritt's body shook and she leaned over Avery, one hand braced on the bed, her arm a rope of muscle. So strong and so undone by pleasure. The sight was all Avery needed to push her over the edge.

"Tomorrow is Iliana and Lei-Ling's wedding," Merritt said when they were resting in each other's arms. "I wish you could be there. They're my life. They're my family."

"I'm sorry," Avery whispered.

"You'll be flying away."

For a second Avery feared that Merritt would take back

everything they had said. *Maybe it's not such a good idea to stay together. You know we'll only mess it up.*

But Merritt just said, "Text me a picture of the view from your airplane. Send me some clouds and say, 'Wish you were here.'"

Chapter 29

The Mirage was packed for a Sunday because Iliana and Lei-Ling were as delightful as kung pao ketchup and Pop Rocks on waffles. Tall, muscular Iliana in a white cotton dress that looked, not surprisingly, like her gi. Tiny Lei-Ling who had liked the idea of white wedding dresses but had ended up in a cornucopia of pink lace and platinum lamé. They were the best Portland had to offer: strange, charming, hardworking, in love. Everyone knew it. Well-wishers crowded around them, raising toasts.

"You give us hope," one woman said.

"To love!" someone else said.

Merritt gave a lengthier toast, describing Iliana and Lei-Ling's courtship, a story she had memorized through unsolicited repetition. Iliana hugged her.

"Avery will come back," Iliana whispered. "Believe it."

"Maybe," Merritt said. Avery hadn't texted her yet, but she

would. Merritt could feel a smile light her face, and she knew Iliana saw it too.

When the toasts were completed and the dinner of Mirage specials had been eaten, Iliana and Lei-Ling left the bar in a shower of confetti and headed to the coast for a honeymoon of clam digging and hot tubbing.

Vita brought around a tray of flaming shots. Merritt waved her away.

"You have to," Vita said. "It's the Flaming Peacock. Grape vodka and overproof rum."

"You aren't allowed to push liquor. It's against OLCC. You need to offer me a popcorn shrimp so I don't get drunk."

"Ooh," Vita said. "We'll put a shrimp in each one and then it will be a shrimp cocktail."

"No," Merritt said. "No one wants the Flaming Peacock with shrimp. I'll leave before I drink that."

"Not before we place our bets."

It was probably best she leave now, Merritt thought. If she were lucky, Vita was taking bets on the number of girls she'd caught kissing in the Mirage bathroom or the circumference of someone's cervix. Appropriate, all-ages bets that would not get them sideways with the Neighborhood Enhancement Committee...except yes, they would. But it was probably Vita's favorite theme. Merritt the bachelor. Merritt the heartbreaker. Merritt wished she could tell her the truth.

"It better not be me," Merritt said. "I'm not like that anymore, and I never was, not that you noticed."

She could hear Avery. *You're not cold.*

Vita winked at her. "We'll crowdsource that one." She

reached onto her flaming tray and pulled out the one shot that was not lit. "Your Sadfire Reserve, my dear. We are what we are."

Vita strutted away.

The crowd grew. Vita announced a DJ, and the woman took her place in the booth at the edge of the dance floor. Techno Adele filled the bar. Vita circled the bar with two coffee cans, a roll of raffle tickets, and a pen. A few minutes later the door to the bar opened, and Merritt watched a girl slip in. Eighties rocker hair covered her face, down to her lips. Jerry Xan hair. Her tights were ripped, and she seemed to be wearing three or four T-shirts, all of them shredded. Her jean vest read, ANARCHY BEGINS AT HOME. Altogether, she looked like a Halloween costume that had been put through the blender. Still, she had a body like Avery's, small and curvy in a way that made skinnier women look underfed, and Merritt longed for the feel of Avery's body on top of her.

Vita beckoned to the woman to come closer to the bar. She held out a ticket, explained something, then shook the coffee cans in front of her. Merritt thought she saw the girl say something that might have been, *That's wrong*, but it was hard to tell with her face hidden. Then the girl tossed her ticket in one of the cans.

"All right, ladies." Vita tapped a glass and gestured to the DJ to bring down the music. "I'm a bartender, so I've seen love born and love lost. Iliana and Lei-Ling are proof there is hope for all of us. How strong do you think love is?"

Women raised their glasses and whooped.

"I've put my money on love-conquers-all," Vita said. "You know our incorrigible bachelor."

"Oh, leave Merritt alone," one woman called out.

Merritt raised a middle finger in Vita's direction.

"I've got one can that says what I say," Vita went on. "Our Merritt Lessing is in love. And this can says no. You've all placed your bets. You know how this works. Winning can is a raffle. Losing can is a donation. Where's the donation going, Merritt?"

"Fuck off, Vita," Merritt called, but she couldn't muster up much indignation. This was the Mirage. These were her people. Vita had served her beers since she turned twenty-one. "The Pride House."

"The Pride House it is."

The girl with the awful eighties hair watched her from beneath lip-length bangs, or at least Merritt felt like she was watching. She could have just been lost in her hair. Maybe she was trying to find an Out in Portland coffee shop and had stumbled into the Mirage by mistake. Maybe she thought she'd woken up in a hedge.

"So, Merritt Lessing," Vita said. "I called it weeks ago. You're in love. True or false?"

There was a ripple of approval.

Someone said, "No way."

Merritt thought she heard someone else say, "You know what she did to Carlie Dewey?"

Merritt thought of Avery's plane lifting off the runway, heading for Cincinnati. She'd fly first class, direct flight. The flight attendants would ask for her autograph, and news of her presence would rustle down the aisles. Someone would bring a young girl up to her seat, and she'd shake the child's hand and ask her what kind of drawings she liked to do. So kind. So thoughtful. And she'd be thinking about Merritt.

"So," Vita prompted. "We've got sixteen fifty riding on this. This is important. What is it, Merritt?"

"Oh, well, for sixteen fifty," Merritt said.

People chuckled.

"For whatever. For a million." Merritt held up her hands in surrender. "Yeah, I am in love."

The bar cheered almost as loudly as they had for Iliana and Lei-Ling.

"There's proof, folks," Vita said. "Anything is possible."

Vita motioned to the DJ to raise the volume, and the dance floor filled. Portlanders weren't great dancers. Their parents had all been aging hippies, artists, or port workers, and they danced accordingly: heads bobbing with chicken-like exuberance, arms waving like octopuses in slow motion, or shifting their weight from foot to foot with the subtlety of hardening concrete. Merritt didn't know her mother well enough to imprint on her dancing, so she kept her seat in the corner. The girl with the eighties hair was making her way through the dancers. For the first time, Merritt knew there was no girl at the Mirage who would turn her head. Then the girl stopped in front of Merritt. And the world slowed on its axis. The dock workers' children were the only ones dancing because they danced without moving. And Merritt saw that she was wrong. There was only one woman in the Mirage. Avery tucked a hank of hideous black hair behind her ear. Merritt beamed. "You're supposed to be in Cincinnati."

"You were supposed to give me an ultimatum. Come to your friends' wedding or you'd never forgive me."

"I would never say that."

"I know. That's why I came. I pushed my flight back. I still have to go to Cincinnati tomorrow, but I wanted one more night."

Merritt felt so shy and delighted she barely knew what to say. "This is quite the outfit."

"I'm sorry I can't be me in a lesbian bar, but I wanted to be with you."

"This is so you," Merritt teased. "Where did you . . . ?" She stroked the wig. It didn't move. It was like something used to insulate houses before fiberglass.

"DX dressed me."

"In her clothes?"

"Something from her bandmates. And this"—Avery touched the wig—"is vintage Jerry Xan."

"For real? Jerry Xan doesn't have his own hair?"

"Did you think nature could do all this? Real signature hair is hard to come by." Avery tilted her chin up. The rest of her face disappeared.

Merritt drew the strands apart, found Avery's lips, and kissed her.

"Dance with me," Avery said.

Marlene Crown must have been a good dancer, even if she was a bad mother. Avery moved against her in time to the music, suggesting everything without throwing her ass around like some of the younger girls did. (Maybe their mothers had been backup dancers.)

The song slowed, and Avery put her head on Merritt's shoulder. Merritt put her arms around her. She imagined she could feel Avery's heart beating against hers. Iliana was right, Merritt thought. She'd always thought she was the only one to get hurt, to be scared. As soon as she'd seen Avery at the reunion, she'd been convinced everything had been Avery's fault. But Avery had been scared too. She'd been young. Her mother had asked her to make a decision that would change her life, and Avery had made the right decision and the wrong one. Now, tonight, in Merritt's arms, Avery had a chance to go back and take both paths at once. Maybe that was what everyone wanted, to be who they were and to go back to see who else they could have been.

Merritt closed her eyes ... and opened them only when she felt someone knock into her with the force of a bar fight. But no one fought at the Mirage.

"Hey!" Merritt said.

She didn't have time to shift into the loose opening stance of hidari hanmi or to protect Avery, who had suddenly been snatched away. By Alistair! He pushed Merritt back into the corner with one hand while he ripped Avery's wig off. Her chestnut curls cascaded down her back. He pushed her vest off too, as though he was going to take her on the floor.

"Alistair, no," Avery said.

"Ponza," he said.

"What are you doing?" Merritt cried.

Suddenly a man in a white tracksuit was pushing through

the crowd, an enormous camera raised. He pushed it in Avery and Alistair's faces, snapping pictures so fast he could have made a movie. The flash cut through the darkness.

One of the old butch dykes lunged toward Ponza.

"What are you doing?" she yelled, with a ferocity that told Merritt she remembered when a photo meant ruin. It still could. "Get out of here!"

Alistair swept Avery up in his arms. He dipped her back like a tango dancer and kissed her. Avery struggled in Alistair's arms but not enough. Above them, the disco ball whirled in a snowfall of light. Merritt felt dizzy. She tried to push Ponza aside, but her chi was gone. She wasn't a black belt anymore. She was just a tough, angry girl shuffled from school to school—fighting or flirting as best she could. Ponza held his camera in one hand, drew back his fist, and swung, landing a pathetic blow on Merritt's cheek. Being paparazzi had clearly not prepared him for street fighting. Still, the small jolt of pain knocked her back with surprise. Avery was still suspended in Alistair's grasp.

"Portland is one of the most inclusive cities in America," Alistair said to the camera Ponza had shoved back in his face. "And this is just one example, a bar where gays and straights mix. We're clubbing down the street. The Swizzle Club is next. Who's coming?"

To their credit, the women at the Mirage just frowned. No one wanted to go clubbing with Alistair King.

The Nostalgia-rom was planned for the last day of summer—September 22—but the end of summer had come early. This was it. The fall would be crisp and bright for a second. Then the sky would go gray, a spit of rain would become a sheet, and it would never stop. Merritt was back at the Vale prom, staring at Avery. She had fallen for it again. *I want someone who loves me first*, she cried inside. But Avery had her arm around Alistair's waist, and though Avery looked stricken, she was also saying, "We just love Portland. There's so much to do here."

Merritt was too proud to run. She picked up her Sadfire Reserve, looked at Avery with what she hoped read as disgust, knocked back the last of the whiskey, turned slowly, and walked out.

She was a few blocks away when she collapsed on the stone steps of an old bungalow. She didn't care if the owners saw her, if they thought she was homeless, if they called the police. She rested her head in her arms and wept.

Chapter 30

How could you?" Avery said as soon as Alistair had hustled her into the front seat of the pink convertible. The top was lowered in an accordion of pink canvas and their quick flight down the road whipped Avery's hair around her face. She had left the wig in the Mirage.

"Me?" he demanded, his tone clipped. "Avery, someone saw you there. At a lesbian bar! They tweeted. It's all over the Internet. And it looks like what it was. Thank God Greg saw it ten minutes before Ponza. This is the scandal Ponza has been waiting for. I saved your ass in there."

"But Merritt."

Avery had seen the pain on Merritt's face. Merritt had looked like she'd been stabbed. She looked like she must have the day she'd realized her mother wasn't picking her up from boarding school. It was as though the cool facade she'd always worn had been stripped away. Avery knew it wasn't Ponza's punch that had hurt Merritt.

"Fuck." Alistair sighed. "Merritt."

"Yes. Merritt! I have to find her."

"You have to come to the Swizzle Club with me and then God knows how many more clubs. We're clubbing. We were at the lesbian bar for twenty minutes. We didn't even realize what it was, but Portland's so nice. Everyone fits in."

Alistair's face was grim and his driving erratic. He swerved away from a row of orange cones in the bike lane, then drew up short behind the next car.

"No, Alistair," Avery pleaded. "We have to find her. She can't have gotten far. I love her. She can't think I didn't pick her. Don't you see? It's exactly like prom. She'll think I've done it again."

"Call her," Alistair said curtly. "Explain. She knows you and I aren't like that. You know we didn't really kiss. I've been more intimate with a bottle of 7 Up."

It was true. If Merritt had been on the inside of that kiss, she would have known how chaste it was. Alistair had held his breath. He'd tucked his tongue into the corner of his mouth.

"This isn't a government conspiracy," Alistair added. "It's pretty simple. You can't look gay right now."

Nothing felt simple. Avery felt the weight of her love, of everything that had happened at Vale, and of the fifteen years she had wasted pressing down on her. People got to make mistakes, but she'd made too many already.

"Please take me back to her place. I'll wait for her there if we can't find her."

Avery had to throw her arms around Merritt and beg for forgiveness.

"Avery," Alistair said, turning left out of the center lane and startling pedestrians in the crosswalk. "Look behind you."

Avery turned. She didn't need to pull her hair out of her eyes to see Ponza in the car behind them.

"He will follow you every single step you take in Portland," Alistair went on. "If we go find Merritt, if Ponza sees you chasing after the girl you were just dancing with, *King and Crown* is over. You can't pretend that you two are just really good friends who like each other a lot. She's your lover. It's written all over your face."

"I need to see her."

"You need to stay away from her."

All those nights she had lounged in Alistair's hotel room, reading while he tapped away at his laptop, messaging his consultants on another America Wyoming project, she'd been happy. But she wasn't happy now.

"I want to buy a house."

It occurred to Avery that she was probably the only person in the world who felt like she was betraying her best friend by buying property. Ironic, since buying property was what they had done their whole career.

"With her? Aves, you've known her for only five or six weeks. That's nothing. Do you even know what she really wants?"

"I asked her to marry me."

She wanted to rattle Alistair. This announcement would do

it. Alistair took a corner too fast and bumped into the curb. The car lurched.

"Did she say yes?"

Telling him about her not-really-a-marriage-proposal was a mistake. She realized it as soon as she'd brought it up. Merritt hadn't said yes because Avery hadn't *really* asked. Alistair didn't seem to notice the flaw in her story.

"You could have told me, Aves," he said, as though she had answered him in the affirmative.

Alistair slowed down. Ponza slowed too.

"She didn't say yes," Avery said. "Not yet. We were just talking."

"She didn't say yes? What self-respecting lesbian gets a marriage proposal from *you* and says... what? Let me check with my accountant? I've got a couple other offers on the table; I'll get back to you? She's crazy."

That was the Alistair Avery knew and loved, the Alistair who always came to her defense, the Alistair who didn't realize that Merritt could have better offers. She was still mad.

"You told her to leave me!"

She wanted to say, *You're a friend now. Why weren't you a friend then?*

"I told her to be careful because she cared about you." Whatever anger Alistair had brought to the Mirage had faded out of his brow and out of his voice. "If you go looking for Merritt right now, you will be making a decision for you, for me, and for *King and Crown*. You'll end our show." He sounded desolate. "Fifteen years, Aves. I'm not saying you can't be with her. Maybe you even want to quit. It would break my heart, but you have a right to...I think. Check your contract. But I'm just asking you not to make that big a decision right now in the Barbie-mobile, driving through God-knows-where"—he gestured toward the gray warehouses that surrounded them now that they had turned off the main road—"with Ponza tailing us like a cop. Just call her now and see her later."

"Can you lose Ponza?" Avery asked.

"Sweetie, do you see what I'm driving? The crew had every grown-up car blocked in. We need to go find some clubs and look happy. We've been *King and Crown* for fifteen years. Please give me this. Give me 'I thought about it before I called it quits.'"

Avery had seen a science fiction movie (some opening DX had dragged her to) in which a woman's blood had been replaced with a blue liquid that gave her limitless strength but eventually killed her. She felt like that now, minus the superpowers. Her body temperature had dropped. Her head swam. The street rushed by like a video game looping through the opening credits over and over again. Block after block. She couldn't say no to Alistair, who had been there for her her whole life and now just wanted her to think.

"It won't be what you want either," Alistair added. "If we go back and catch her walking home or in her apartment, Ponza's going to make it a shit show. You're not going to kiss and make up. Ponza's going to post some blurry photo of you two, and then every homophobe in America is going to trash Merritt in the comments. It'll be weeks before you get a moment alone with her. Just call her."

Avery called Merritt ten times that night and again in the morning, but the phone just rang until she reached the Hellenic Hardware voice mail.

* * *

The following day Avery stood in the master bedroom of Uncle Oli's apartment with Greg and Venner. Greg hadn't wanted to talk at the command center. They weren't leaving Portland just yet, but the way Greg had told her let her know this was not a happy development. Now Greg locked the door behind them. The decorations looked garish. The iridescent curtains lit up at night and were supposed to look like a swath of northern lights. During the day they looked like a shower curtain.

Greg sat down on one of the Swools, the bouncy stools that were supposed to enhance your abs or your posture or your moral fiber. He looked like he had no fiber left in him. Meanwhile Venner paced in front of him. In his hand he held a tablet open to the *Hollywood Insider*. The top of the screen was an innocuous story about DX's father's ex-wife, supermodel Vivan de Laris, breaking up with her boyfriend. JFK had been seen in the Heathrow Airport. Avery could lose twenty pounds of belly fat overnight by eating *This Amazing Miracle Science Food!*

"A-ver-y!" Venner said. It came out in three distinct syllables. He shoved the tablet at Avery. "What is this? What. Is. This?"

Then she saw it. An overexposed photograph of her own

terrified face looking over Merritt's shoulder, their arms still wrapped around each other. AVERY AND ALISTAIR AT THE GAY BAR! the interior headline read. AND WHO IS AVERY'S SPECIAL FRIEND?

Ponza had caught them. She should have followed Merritt home. At least then they could have spent the night together. They could have flung the windows open and made shrieking love for everyone to hear. If Avery hadn't been so distraught, the mere thought would have filled her with a hot eagerness. To release her cries of pleasure! To scream like a porn star! *Do it, baby! Right there! Don't stop!* That kind of exclamation had struck Avery as overwrought (like car salesmen on TV) until Merritt had first brought her to orgasm. Every time she came, it was harder to stifle her cries. But she wasn't thinking about that now. She was thinking about Merritt's voice mail answering again and again. No call back. No text. No knock on Avery's hotel room door.

"So?" Venner prompted.

"I don't know..." Avery looked toward the door. "I...don't..."

What could she say? *That's not me. It's not what it looks like. We were practicing...* For what?

"Avery Crown doing the nasty with some boy-band looka-like." Venner jabbed his finger at the screen.

Did he think it was a boy?

"He was...." Avery stumbled over her words. "Crew...a friend of DX's...It's nothing. I didn't...We didn't. He just attacked me, and..."

"Do you think I'm stupid!" Venner threw the tablet down

on the bed. "Do you think I accidentally produced seven of the top ten unscripted shows on TKO? Do you think they sent me up here to fix *King and Crown* because I needed to get out of the office? That's Merritt Lessing, and you have been sleeping with her since you saw her at your reunion. You stay someplace on Burnside, and I'm pretty sure she wore your Gucci rose garden print silk tank the other day."

"Are you stalking me?" Avery said.

"I know everything that goes on on my shows."

"It's not your show," Avery protested.

Greg stood up and paced across the room. "We don't live in a void, Avery." He sounded like a father whose child had been hauled into the police station.

Avery stared at the tablet glowing on the bed. It occurred to her that this was the only picture she had of her and Merritt together. The TKO transcribers had looked at hundreds of hours of the two of them on film, and this was the only picture that showed what they really were.

Greg rubbed his temples. "Why didn't you tell me you were seeing Merritt? Venner, why didn't *you* tell me she was seeing Merritt?"

Avery had the sense that Greg was in nearly as much trouble as she was.

"If you think I know about Avery and Merritt, you all get careless," Venner said. "You think I'll protect you. If you think I don't know, you're careful, but not careful enough. Clearly."

"I could have protected her!" Greg said.

"This isn't Greg's fault or Alistair's," Avery blurted.

"Alistair has the self-preservation of a teenage lemming, but it's not his fault," Venner said.

"Are you going to fire us?" Avery asked. "Or Merritt?" The thought hit her like the hardwood door slamming into its frame. Merritt had surely signed a morality contract. "You can't take the Elysium from her."

"You and Alistair are lucky," Venner said. "I don't want to fire you. We just filmed a fantastic season, and it's only going to get better." He sat down on another Swool. "America loves Avery and Alistair."

Venner wasn't talking about her. He wasn't talking about the person she'd been in the center of Merritt's field, staring up at the sky, or the person Alistair brought calm-you-down King Cobras to the way people on British dramas serve tea.

"They don't want to see you break up over some reality-TV walk-on," Venner said.

"You said Merritt was the next big thing," Avery said.

"Not if this breaks open. It's not even interesting. If you were running some sort of bondage sex club, if there was a link between you and a terrorist cell, that would be interesting. This is just..."

Venner paused, rubbing his hands together hungrily. All things considered, Avery had seen him rage more over a broken camera stand. Actually, he looked like someone who had finally hit his stride, as though all the little crises of production were beneath him. Now, finally, a hurricane had hit land. The dams had broken. The house had collapsed. And Warren Venner was in his glory.

"But married. Why haven't King and Crown tied the

knot? That's the question. The answer is your other producers were dicking around. They didn't see the possibilities. They didn't get that unscripted moves forward. It's real life, not a soap opera."

"What do you mean 'married'?"

"Married. You marry Alistair King." Venner looked happy. "It's perfect. We'll refilm the finale. Alistair will propose. You'll say yes. *Star* will leak a sneak peek. King and Crown get married. Maybe the last day of summer. That's romantic. I'll talk to TKO about a spin-off. Six episodes. Maybe on the Bride Channel. You don't want a baby, do you? That would play really well with the Midwest. After you're married, of course."

"On the show?"

"On the show. In real life. You know Dan Ponza will look up your marriage license as soon as you tweet *I do*."

"I am not marrying Alistair in real life."

"You love him," Venner said matter-of-factly.

"Like a brother. Like my best friend. I'm gay."

"It's only for two to three years. TKO won't ask for more than that. Then you can divorce. You already spend all your time together anyway. Legal will help you get an airtight prenup. The way Alistair manages his money, you'll need it."

"You can't do that," Greg said with a sigh.

"I'm not your property," Avery said. "You can't tell me who to marry in an actual legal wedding. We can do a fake wedding on TV, if you want, but I'm not... I'm just not. I have a life outside this show."

Venner looked calmer than Avery had ever seen him. He stood up and straightened the edge of his suit jacket.

"Look, Avery, you've got two options. We give the *Hollywood Insider* something that sells more copy than Avery-diddled-her-dyke-costar or you're done."

Avery opened her mouth to protest, but Venner stopped her.

"And before you get all sanctity-of-marriage on me, you need to think about Alistair. You're smart, Avery. You treat this like a job. You give twenty thousand dollars a year to breast cancer. A couple scholarships. You support the women's shelter. You wear all the stuff you get comped. Alistair has poured a million dollars into wells in Sudan. That America Wyoming Foundation will ruin him. He gets all emotional about black lung disease, and then he promises everything to everyone. The America Wyoming Foundation doesn't have enough funds to cover all the donations he's scheduled. It won't have anything if he loses this show. And no one is going to want Alistair King after he gets cuckolded. At least the gays will love you. You can do home decorating demos at Pride, and you've saved enough money. Invest smart and you can sit around eating bonbons for the rest of your life.

"But Alistair King will be forty, broke, and dumped by a B-grade TV hostess who'd rather hang out with drag queens. He's better than you, prettier, more talented. He's the heart and soul of the show, but that means he goes down hard. No one really cares about you, Avery. But they're going to hate Alistair for not being a man. And, by the way, if he goes off this show, he doesn't have enough money in savings to pay his taxes. So you might not want to marry him, but he'll be living with you, unless you send him back to Wyoming to work in the mines."

"Think about your fans too," Greg said. "They love you. There's so much wrong in the world right now. They just want a show that makes them feel safe. If they find out it's all been a sham..."

The right answer was *Of course I'll marry Alistair.* The right answer was *The Bride Channel. What fun!*

"I have to talk to Merritt," Avery said.

Greg slumped on the Swool, which was hard to do since its whole purpose was to keep you upright (and probably optimist and resilient too). She could almost see him shrink with paternal despair. It was like each of his vertebrae had collapsed into the one below, a telescope sliding in on itself.

"I'm sorry," Avery said. "I need time to think."

Chapter 31

Merritt picked up an antique door (with original hardware...an attractive add-on she would have cared about six weeks ago). She slammed it on a sawhorse she had set up at the side of the loading bay. She hoped the door would shatter into a thousand splinters. But it was hardwood, and as it hit the sawhorse, it sent a painful jolt through her shoulders. Everything was painful. She thought Avery had healed something inside her, but she'd been wrong. Merritt was like so many antiques; it was the rust and old paint that held her together. Avery had stripped those away. Now hurt and disappointment that would have stung before knocked her down. She couldn't close her eyes without reliving Avery and Alistair's kiss, and she couldn't shake the knowledge that whatever Avery said—even if Avery begged her to stay—they were over.

She hadn't even stumbled across Avery and Alistair's wedding announcement. It had jumped out at her. The day after the Mirage, she had tried to distract herself with e-mail and invoices. The interns had installed an off-brand browser on the Hellenic Hardware computer, and a banner blared news at the user. EARTHQUAKE. FIRE. THIS THING IN YOUR RE-FRIGERATOR COULD KILL YOU. AVERY CROWN AND ALISTAIR KING TO TIE THE KNOT.

It hadn't even been thirty-six hours! In one photograph, Avery held Alistair's hand as he spun her around on a parqueted dance floor. WE'VE NEVER BEEN HAPPIER, the headline read. Beneath a picture of Alistair and Avery beaming, a side box read, YOU WON'T WANT TO MISS THE NEXT KING & CROWN FINALE.

Now her phone vibrated in her back pocket. She didn't need to look at the screen to know who was calling. Twenty missed calls from Avery. It wasn't that Merritt didn't want to talk to her. She wanted to throw herself in Avery's arms and spill out all her fears and sorrows. But the only conversation they could really have now was, *Look, you know as well as I do, this won't work.* She was afraid she couldn't have that talk without yelling at Avery like she had in Avery's trailer or simply falling to the ground to cry.

Merritt picked up a planer and drew it along the surface of the door, peeling back a strip of ornate wood carvings.

"Merritt!" Alex, her intern, exclaimed from behind her.

Merritt stared down at the wood in front of her. Her planer had filed down the carved fruits and goddesses that swirled across the door's surface. She set the planer down at the very edge of the door and gauged another yard of wood.

"That's bloodwood!" Alex said. "That's high-relief nouveau-Balinese. What are you doing?"

Bloodwood. High-relief. She'd worked hard to teach him the vocabulary, to teach him that it mattered. It was hard to convince a boy who had lived behind a dumpster and now dreamed of being a YouTube makeup blogger that the Janka hardness rating meant something. She wished she cared. Instead, she handed him the planer.

"I couldn't," he whispered.

"Go ahead. Fuck it up."

Alex looked as if Merritt had held the planer to her own throat. "I'm going to get Iliana," he said.

"She's on her honeymoon. It's just a door. Finish it off. Scrape it. Paint it. You can't save it now."

"What? Why?"

"You're young and sweet. You haven't ruined anything yet. Do it now. Get your first out of the way."

Her phone rang again. It was inevitable; she would have to talk to Avery, and she'd have to be the one to say it, to break it off. Avery wouldn't have the decency to do what had to be done. Merritt pulled the phone out of her pocket and accepted the blocked number.

"I'm not ready, Avery!" she blurted.

"Avery is here!" Venner's voice boomed unexpectedly. "Avery is ready. Alistair is ready. We have a film crew costing me hundreds a minutes, and you are not here."

"We're done. The show is over. I'm out of your life and your lights and your fake world."

"You are not," Venner said. "Our people have been calling

you. We stayed in Portland for another three days. We need to film the proposal scene, and we need you there. It's in your contract, Lessing. Look it up, and get over here."

Merritt called her attorney, Kristen Brock, Portland's premiere civil rights lawyer and the wife of a customer who owed her a favor.

"You have to go," Kristen said after a brief pause. "They own you."

* * *

An hour later Merritt was once again standing at the archway that led into the Elysium courtyard. How many times had she stood there? She was days away from signing for the deed, and yet she felt like this was the end. If there had been something magic about these walls, that magic had dissipated.

Before she could enter the fray of cameras and cables, Avery rushed over, ignoring Venner's, "Get back here."

"I can explain," Avery said, clutching Merritt's hand and breaking Avery's own prohibition against touching on set.

Merritt pulled away. She could see Avery standing on Burnside looking up at Merritt's window the first night they'd made love. She saw her own keys suspended in the streetlight a second before Avery caught them. At that moment, her whole soul had cried out, *Stay.*

"You don't need to explain," Merritt said. "I know."

"I tried to tell you about the marriage, but you wouldn't answer, and now we're shooting the engagement, but it's just for show. You have to know Alistair and I aren't like that, and you're the one I want, and this isn't how it's supposed to happen, and I've messed it up again."

There were no pauses between Avery's words. Her expressive face was full of earnest concern, as though her biggest fear in the whole world was hurting Merritt. As though a really good explanation of why she had shown up at the Mirage, danced with Merritt, pushed Merritt away, kissed Alistair King, fled, and then got engaged could fix the situation.

"I need you in here," Venner called out.

She was glad for an excuse to walk away. She couldn't cry in front of Iliana; she certainly couldn't cry in front of the entire *King & Crown* crew.

As soon as they were all gathered in the courtyard, Venner launched into a lecture about his days on *Cop Brides*.

"We knew the biggest threats those officers faced wasn't on the streets of New York. It was the wedding," he said.

The *King & Crown* crew looked grim. The Portland crew had stopped whistling and hanging around the catering truck. Like guests at a stranger's funeral, they were being polite. They would move on to another Portland gig as soon as the season was over. The *King & Crown* crew—most of whom had been with the show since the beginning—were probably polishing their résumés in case a white wedding wasn't enough to save Avery's reputation. They eyed Merritt warily.

Merritt could not believe she was there. She watched Avery, her skin shimmering with pearlescent pink glitter, her hair pinned up with silk cherry blossoms, the most precious creature in the world, and Merritt felt a stab of sadness so acute she thought she would faint.

Alistair came up beside her as Venner talked. "I'm sorry," he whispered.

"You got what you wanted," she shot back, not bothering to lower her voice.

"No I didn't," he said. "She's my best friend. Look at her. You're breaking her heart. Why didn't you call her back?"

"I don't know how you guys do this for a living," Merritt said. "I can't wait to get back to the hardware store."

"Alistair, I want you over by the fountain," Venner said before Alistair could answer. "Avery, behind me. Merritt, you're helping Alistair install these flowers. You say, 'How about we just call it a day.' Then Alistair says..."

They took their places, and Merritt spoke her lines. After three more takes, Venner let the cameras turn toward Avery. She walked through the Elysium's arched entryway, carrying—for no discernible reason—a wicker basket full of glitter confetti. She tossed a handful on Alistair's head.

"Avery." Alistair knelt and reached into the pocket of his blazer. "When I'm with you, everything sparkles."

It was so corny...and it was exactly how Merritt had felt before Avery had told her she was marrying Alistair.

Venner called cut. "Goddamn it, Avery, look happier!" He clamped his hand on the back of Avery's neck. She flicked it off with speed worthy of Iliana's self-defense classes. "Alistair King just asked you to marry him! And, Merritt," Venner added, "you've got to read joy and jealousy. This is the Holy Grail of wedding proposals. You're excited but at the same time you're so jealous you could die."

That was true.

"Avery's so lucky." Venner affected a fake soprano. "And you're the one who's supposed to get the guy. How did this happen? Where did you go wrong? But the ring is so big! But you're so jealous. But the ring is so big."

He muscled Avery back toward the archway. Alistair knelt in the cascade of white flowers. Avery came in again.

"Make me the happiest man on earth." Alistair held up the ring.

Avery covered her mouth. She looked like someone witnessing a car crash. *She can't do it in front of me,* Merritt thought.

"Maybe it would work better without me," she said.

"No. You're the whole reason we're here," Venner said. "Every chubby housewife in Ohio is going to see Avery getting the guy and gorgeous Merritt Lessing out in the cold. That's a fucking portrait of hope right there."

Merritt wished she could escape. She was witnessing Avery Crown's wedding engagement over and over again like *Groundhog Day.* It was high school prom all over again, except this time she was right in the fray, squealing with glee like some coked-up housewife.

"We are not leaving here until I get ecstasy on camera," Venner said. "Go again."

Merritt couldn't watch Avery suffer anymore. She strode across the courtyard and put her arm around Avery's shoulders. Avery looked up at her with hope in her eyes.

"I wanted to go to you," Avery whispered. "But Alistair asked me to wait. He said Ponza would just follow us, and he'd harass you, and Al just wanted me to think."

"You can't talk about that here," Merritt said, her lips turned toward Avery's ear so that only Avery could hear her.

"I don't care."

She guided Avery as far away from Venner as she could, which wasn't far since they were hemmed in by crew members and hydrangeas.

"Look at me," Merritt whispered. "Let's just get this next take right so we can get out of here."

Avery looked down into her basket of glitter, her lips tightening like she was holding back tears. She hugged the basket to her chest. And Merritt felt a wave of sympathy so deep she felt her throat constrict. The old Merritt would have said something glib. The new Merritt only saw Avery's tears fall, one by one, into her basket, and she knew that nothing in the world was worse than Avery being sad. Even if Avery was leaving. Even if nothing was possible.

They shot the scene again, and Venner said it was perfect, which seemed strange since Avery's voice quavered with every word and Merritt felt her face set in a grim facade that cracked only for the ten-second bursts between "action" and "cut." But Venner said it looked like a joy-orgasm (proving once again how unreal reality television was), and the crew nodded, although whether they agreed or were simply hot and tired of packing and unpacking their equipment Merritt could not tell.

As soon as Greg said, "That's a wrap," Avery grabbed Merritt's hand.

"Please come with me."

Merritt had to go. Avery hurried them up the stairs to the

master bedroom of Uncle Oli's apartment, closed the door, and locked it. She ran to the shimmery curtains and pulled them closed. The room sank into shadows.

"I didn't kiss him." Avery was out of breath. "It wasn't a real kiss. I'll show you. I'll kiss you like Alistair kissed me, and you'll see it was like... like shaking hands or CPR. And I didn't mean to run away. It all happened so fast. Then Alistair pulled me outside, and he said if I went back to look for you, I'd ruin *King and Crown*, but I don't want to do this marriage, and I don't want you to think that there's anything between us."

"I don't think you kissed him because you're secretly sleeping together," Merritt said. "But you're getting married on September twenty-second in your house in L.A., and your colors are going to be teal and red and you can't decide whether you want a Delicata Vagrant wedding dress or a Jasmine Culture."

"Jasmine Culture. And all those dresses make you look like some kind of land-mermaid, and we don't have a house. They're renting some model home in this McMansion paradise, and it's all a publicity stunt, and I tried to call you." Avery's words tumbled out like ball bearings spilled across the floor.

Greg had told her they were staying in Portland for an extra week. Venner had cornered her in the Elysium and told her about the marriage proposal. She had to consider it; she owed it to the team. Alistair's foundation was on the verge of bankruptcy, and this would give him another season or two to get his finances in order. Her fans would love a marriage. The crew needed time to look for work if *King & Crown* was going off the air. And, yes, getting married to Alistair sounded extreme, but it was really just a simple brand-image solution.

"We'd just be putting a ring on what everyone thinks already. We're throwing a big party. We can get married, do one or two more seasons, then end it the way it should end. I wanted to wrap it up, not just have it all fall apart. I owe that to Alistair. But if you tell me not to go through with it, I won't."

"I think you already are."

"But we could..." Avery's face said she knew how hard it would be to turn back now.

"Did you plan this?"

It would be easy to fight with Avery, to make everything her fault, to pretend not to believe her. Merritt sat down with her back against the wall. In that moment she knew: If she were angrier, she could stay with Avery. If she could bring herself to yell at Avery, accuse her of cheating or being a self-involved diva, they might last. If Merritt could throw everything Avery had done back in her face—the prom, the Elysium, the show, Avery's secrecy, her nomad life—maybe they could be together. They could be one of those couples that bickered and picked on each other and stayed together because nothing better had come along or because all their fussing had worn them out and it didn't seem worth the effort to find someone new to gripe at. But she didn't want that with Avery.

"I didn't plan anything." Avery knelt before her. "I haven't planned anything in my life, but I could now. Wait for me to fix this."

Merritt stared down at her clasped hands. "Waiting? Is that what we were doing for fifteen years?"

She felt only sadness and quiet, like the empty deck of the *Astral Reveler*. Iliana thought love created more love, but love created loss. No matter what Avery tried to do, they would always end up like this, on opposite sides of their real lives. They would try, and they would apologize, and every time it would get harder until finally their affair ended, and they walked away strangers.

"We forgot this part," Merritt said. "Those teenage summer romances don't end with no one getting hurt. They end with a lot of bad poetry and listening to Death Cab for Cutie, and *then* when you're grown up you look back and think no one got hurt because you can't remember who you were before your heart broke."

Merritt heard Avery draw in a sharp breath.

"Are you breaking up with me?"

"Sweetie, were we ever going out?"

"I don't want this to end." Avery spoke quickly. "I missed you for fifteen years. I don't want to lose you again. I know that dating me wouldn't be like dating a regular girl. I know Alistair is worried about us, but he loves me. He and the crew can cover for me. I know it's going to be weird, but DX can fly you places... fly us places... that no one will find."

"That sounds like a threat," Merritt said sadly.

"I know! I don't think she even talks to the air traffic control tower or whatever, but she can do anything, and she's been my friend since we were kids. She'll help us. And I'll call my mother. I hate her, but I'll call Marlene and tell her I need to hide a gay affair. She does that. She's got gay clients. Or I can get things settled with Alistair and the show and I can come out, and we'll make it work. Please say yes."

Merritt rose and turned back to the window. "Avery," she said quietly. "I don't want to be your second choice."

"Marrying Alistair doesn't mean anything. He's not my choice. None of this is my choice."

Merritt continued as though Avery had not spoken. "You can't love the person who says, 'To have me, you can't have your own life.' I watch you every minute you're on set. You and Alistair are great together. This is your life. What kind of person would I be if I asked you to give that up? And there's no way we can be together without one of us asking for that. I don't want to pretend to be your trainer, lie to my friends, and sign nondisclosure agreements. You don't even want to buy a house. You don't want a mailing address, and I want someone who'll stay. I want someone I'm not *tying down*. I want someone whose life I haven't ruined by saying, 'Be my girlfriend.'" Tears blurred Merritt's vision, putting a filter over everything on the street below. "I can't do this."

"I wanted to take you to Taha'a," Avery said to Merritt's turned back. She sounded so sad, Merritt wanted to say, *Of course. I'll go anywhere.* But she could see beyond Taha'a.

"We would go to those exotic places and stay in a hotel room drinking margaritas with the curtains closed. And then one day we'd get caught, and it would be the end of your career. Or we wouldn't get caught, and one day I would want to go out for a coffee and a scone with you, and you wouldn't be able to. Then I'd be the woman who broke up with Avery Crown over a coffee and a scone, and you're worth so much more than that." Merritt's voice was rough. "This was the best summer of my life. Let's not drag it out until we haven't talked in nine months and we forget how good this was. Let's keep these memories perfect." She turned around and held out her hand to Avery.

"Like your locket!" Avery shot back with surprising ferocity. "You want to put us under a glass dome? In a birdcage? And say this was the past so it's better? I'm not one of your antiques. I have a future, and we could have a future. We could move forward except that you keep your heart in a box. Is it me who's not worth fighting for? If you'd found someone better, would you open your heart up? Or will no one be good enough? Is your A-list so short, you're at the top and you're the only one on it? Maybe those girls are right. You're cold. It's cold to say, 'I care about you, but you're not worth it.' It's cold to say, 'Bad things might happen, so I'm not even going to try.' If you do that, you'll always be alone."

Avery had seen the truth, as Merritt had always known she would.

"That's what you signed up for," Merritt shot back. "You knew. Of everyone in the world, you knew me best."

Merritt stepped forward. She meant to kiss Avery, to draw her into an embrace that said, *I may be cold on the inside, but I made you hot,* a kiss that would leave Avery wanting, a kiss that would make all Avery's other lovers look like sloppy middle schoolers who had learned to kiss by watching animals mating on the Discovery Channel. But she didn't manage a kiss. She just clutched Avery, holding her to her chest as though they were the last two lovers on the *Titanic*.

"I'm sorry," Merritt whispered.

Then she walked out of the room, out of the Elysium, past Venner, and all the way down to the river, where she stared at water that sparkled for everyone else except her.

Chapter 32

Winter rains came early to Portland. The city had expected another month of crisp leaves and Saturday markets full of heirloom squash. Now rain hit the windows of Hellenic Hardware, spattering the entryway as a group of bedraggled customers hurried in.

"Can I help you?" Merritt asked without looking up or listening for their answer.

Through the old glass she could see the shape of Lei-Ling's dumpling truck. It was the only spot of color on the street. Strains of Chinese pop music tinkled from a speaker. Nothing about Super Junior-M and Jay Chou said *buy more vintage hardware*, but she didn't care. Lei-Ling had even shown her a video by Acrush, a Chinese boy band comprised of cross-dressing girls. They were cute, but they were in China, and Avery was in Los Angeles, getting married to Alistair King in a few weeks. And Merritt was here, in her uncle's shop, hawking fixtures. She took another brass light switch cover from the pile at her elbow and dipped it in mineral oil.

The door flew open, and Iliana and Lei-Ling rushed in, bringing a wave of rain with them.

"The wind!" Iliana held her coat over Lei-Ling's head.

"The rain!" Lei-Ling exclaimed.

They looked flushed and happy. The rain was an excuse for hot chocolate and impromptu fires in the barrel behind Happy Golden Fortune.

Lei-Ling looked at Merritt. "Oh, you're so sad!" She raced to Merritt and folded her arms on the counter, resting her head on her arms and looking up at Merritt. "I want you to be happy. Can I make you a dumpling? I'll put anything in it you want. Name your five favorite foods. It can be anything."

"I'm not sad," Merritt said.

"Starburst?" Lei-Ling suggested helpfully. "Bacon!"

"I'm fine."

"But you aren't," Lei-Ling said.

Of course Lei-Ling was right. Merritt had said goodbye to Avery and walked all the way down to the river. She had stared at the water. It had sparkled in the late-summer sunlight, but it wasn't sparkling anymore. If you were not in love, winter in Portland was a long, dismal slog. And Merritt wasn't in love, she told herself. She didn't even miss Avery.

"Happy? Happy? Happy?" Lei-Ling said, as though Merritt had just forgotten the word.

"Merritt is depressed," Iliana said, "because she's made bad life choices."

"I have not made bad life choices."

"Why haven't you moved into the Elysium?" Iliana asked.

"You said living in my uncle's old apartment was morbid."

"You're living in your uncle's retrofitted office," Iliana said. "You have a beautiful, three-bedroom apartment."

"I'm working on the..." She could not think what she was working on. The apartment was special. Avery had made sure of that.

Merritt was saved by a group of customers. Another group rang the bell outside Lei-Ling's dumpling truck. Lei-Ling hurried outside to provide dumpling happiness for those still able to find cheer in carbohydrates. Once the customers had spread throughout the shop and Lei-Ling was busy at her steamers, Iliana pulled up a stool next to Merritt.

"You want to go over to the dojo? Practice a little?"

"No," Merritt said. "Thanks."

"Discipline is good for you. It's good for everyone."

"I am disciplined."

"Would you please just call her and get it over with?" Iliana said. "Nobody can stand you."

"Who has to stand me? Go hang some chandeliers if you can't stand me."

"I'm serious. You've been moping around since you told her to get out of your life."

"I didn't tell her to get out of my life. You make it sound so bad."

"I don't *make* it sound anything. I can't even take you to the Mirage. You're miserable. I'm sure she's miserable. Just suck it up. You're not going to be any less happy if you call her."

Merritt knew from experience that that was not true. Being alone was like the brisk, cold days of autumn. Button up your coat and hold your head up, and it was not that bad. Nothing was worse than the empty ring of an unanswered call or the awkward question on the other end. She remembered her mother picking up. *Why are you calling, Merritt?*

Because it's my birthday.

Because it's Christmas.

Because I'm ten and I'm lonely.

"You know, you think your problems are so bad," Iliana went on. "I get that. They feel bad. But look at me and Lei-Ling. It's not always easy. We're not happy every single minute of the day. When we first met she—"

"I called her!" Merritt shot back. "Okay? I called her."

"You called her?" Iliana looked surprised.

"Of course I called her." Merritt slumped over the counter, her chin in her hands. "I'm not a total idiot."

She had been disciplined for a week. For a week, she had considered deleting Avery's phone number. But a week after Avery left, Merritt had taken out her phone. If a dour, almost-forty-year-old Russian-American aikido sensei could find love with the world's most optimistic dumpling waitress, Merritt thought, why couldn't she hope that there was someone in the world who wouldn't leave her? *Why not me?* After all, it was she who had sent Avery away, she who had said never, she who had somehow let her mother and the *Astral Reveler* and all the girls who had dumped her stand in the way of the woman she loved.

Merritt had called, giddy with the prospect of telling Avery she would make the sacrifice. She would be in the closet. She would pretend to be Avery's trainer. She would go to Taha'a with Avery (and Alistair as cover for their affair). It would be seductively clandestine. She had thrilled with the thought. Avery's kisses would replace the dull ache in her body. Avery's tenderness would make up for everything. Merritt would devour her and worship her and, at some point, they would tumble into laughter and Merritt would feel like she was sixteen again.

Avery's voice mail had answered, *You guys are too much! I've been getting so many congratulations about the engagement, I've routed my calls to my agent for now, but don't worry. You're still my BFFFFFF. Leave a message.* It didn't even sound like Avery. Merritt had left a coy message and then another. Then a week had gone by and then a month.

"When did you call her?"

"After she left."

"That was weeks ago." Iliana looked confused. The new Iliana believed in love conquering all, and this wasn't part of the script.

"She never called back."

"What? She's crazy. She loves you."

"Yeah, and my mom loved me until I was five. Then she met someone better."

"Your parents were yacht rats who sent you off to boarding school because they didn't have souls. Avery's not like that. Call her again. I know this is all going to work out. You're a pessimist. You always expect the worst. Lei-Ling is right. You've got crows on power lines sitting in your heart, but"—

Iliana put a hand on Merritt's shoulder—"one day those crows are going to open their wings and fly."

"Oh, good Lord!" Merritt said. "*I'm* going to go hang chandeliers. You can't stand *me*? They're going to fly away," she muttered as she stomped off. "Wind beneath my fucking wings."

That was the new Iliana, and her old friend showed no signs of coming back. Merritt hurried to the top of one of the ladders in the Land of Lamps and hid her face in the vintage crystal so Iliana would not see her fighting back tears.

* * *

That evening after Iliana and Lei-Ling had left, Merritt wandered the aisles of Hellenic Hardware until she came to the antique birdcage that contained the lover's locket. NOT FOR SALE, the card read. She opened the door in the wire-framed dome and took out the locket. She smoothed her thumb over the surface, then tucked it in her pocket, rubbing it like a worry stone. She resumed her pacing. Finally, she stopped by the fountain. The water splashed, and Helen of Troy's vacant eyes stared at her.

"Uncle Oli?" she said to the sound of the fountain and the HVAC. "Uncle Oli, are you there? What do I do?"

Above Merritt's head and on every window frame, trellis, and chandelier, the little cardboard price tags fluttered in a faint breeze. That was all it was. Not spirits. Not the past.

"Uncle Oli, I'm so sad." She opened the locket and stared

at the women's faces. They gazed at each other in profile, one innocent, one stern. "She'll always choose Alistair."

She could just imagine how she looked. Staring at someone else's locket. Talking to her dead uncle, who surely had better things to do in heaven. She would have been pitiable at eighteen. It was downright pathetic at thirty-three. She might as well have put on the Amazon music playlist Top 50 Most Miserable Songs Ever.

It couldn't get worse.

She pulled her phone out of her pocket and touched Avery's name. The call went straight to voice mail.

"You're still my BFFFFF. Leave a message."

What the hell are the extra Fs for?

She stood up. That was it. She was sick of sleeping in the office apartment. She was sick of feeling sad. She was sick of Iliana telling her to call Avery like it was that simple. Most of all she was sick of the sinking feeling that it was all her fault. Avery had begged for her love, and she had turned her away. She had kissed Avery for the last time without even realizing it was the last. Merritt had been so wrapped up in her own hurt she had done to Avery what every single person in her life had done to her.

"She would never have stayed with me," she said out loud.

The price tags fluttered.

She raised her voice. "She would have strung me along, and then she would have left. Damn you, Avery," she said to the dark skylights. She pulled the locket out of her pocket. "We're not like this. We were never going to be forever."

Had it been true? Merritt had made it true.

* * *

She didn't remember the drive to the Elysium. When she got out of her truck, it was raining. Her tenants were already tucked into their apartments, their windows glowing like Christmas cards. The single mom with her quiet daughter. The old professor. The drag queen with her windows festooned with feather boas. Slowly, Merritt mounted the stone stairs to the third floor. Uncle Oli's apartment was at the front of the building. She unlocked the door. The grass carpet absorbed her footsteps. The little curio sculptures in the sconces goggled at her. In the bedroom, she touched the light switch. Everything came on at once. The filament lamp. The weirdly iridescent, glowing plastic curtains that looked remarkably like the northern lights. Even the bed seemed to glow as the sparkly comforter caught the light. Come to think of it, the bed must have been supplied by the show. She had never slept in it. She lay down, took out the locket, and stared at the picture of the two women. Then she tried Avery's number one more time.

"You're still my BFFFFFF. Leave a message."

But she didn't, because there wasn't anything to say. She deleted the contact and pressed her face into the decorative throw pillows, each one embroidered with a thousand heart-shaped sequins.

Chapter 33

Avery sat on an enormous white velvet divan in a Canyon Creek mansion TKO purported to be Alistair's. The train of her Delicata Vagrant wedding dress trailed over the divan, showcasing forty-two meters of lace and fifteen pounds of sustainably harvested pearls. Outside in the garden, an intimate gathering of friends and family (that was how the announcement on the *King & Crown* website described the hundred and fifty TKO executives, Hollywood reporters, and film crew members) were enjoying Veuve Clicquot and Royal Ossetra caviar. It was the end of summer, but the sky was blue and the palm trees were absolutely motionless.

The uninvited DX was probably offering to fill Marlene Crown's vagina with blocks of cocaine just for the pleasure of watching Marlene's Botoxed face attempt to register shock. A few months ago the thought would have made Avery laugh, but she'd been fighting back tears since she'd left Portland.

She was homesick, but there was no home waiting for her in the Rose City.

She picked up a layer of lace and let it fall back on her lap.

"If this house catches fire, I will die," she said to Alistair, who was seated next to her on the divan. "I can't move."

"If this house catches fire, you can smother it with that thing," Alistair said amiably.

Avery had signed a comp agreement saying she would not eat, drink, fornicate, or engage in strenuous physical activity while wearing the gown. It was hard to imagine. If the wedding party deserted her, she would die trying to crawl to water. Alistair got a spot on the divan as well, but his outfit did not double as a tent, and at the end of the night he got to keep his cream-colored suit.

"Need a drink?" Alistair asked.

"Body Biscuit shots?"

Alistair pulled a flask out of his breast pocket. "It's that killer whiskey your girl likes."

Avery took the flask. At least the Delicata Vagrant dress was sleeveless. She could still move her arms. She took a sip of whiskey. It tasted like smoke and regret. "She's not my girl."

"I'm sorry," Alistair said. "But maybe someday. You never know. There'll be another reunion." He leaned over to hug her, but several tons of lace blocked his way. "This is like a chastity dress. What do people do if they actually want to have sex?"

Another reunion. Alistair had been saying that since they left Portland, as though Merritt were a tourist attraction Avery could catch on her next trip. *Next time you're in Paris, you've got to see the Musée d'Orsay.* But Merritt wasn't a transaction or a fling, and Avery had had her second chance with Merritt and she had blown it, just like she had at Vale.

A knock on the door signaled another round of photographers. Alistair tucked the flask back in his jacket. Avery blinked quickly.

"This should be *Vanity Fair,*" Alistair said.

They ran through their poses for the photographer.

"Nice. Good. Very nice," he kept saying.

Avery and Alistair moved into their final pose. Avery stood. Alistair put his arms around her.

"Can you kiss?" the photographer asked.

Avery puckered her lips a millimeter from Alistair's.

"Warren Venner said we could get tongue."

"I think we're done here," Alistair said. "Avery and I don't kiss on camera. Some things are private."

The photographer left. A muffled clapping from the window behind them startled Avery. She turned. DX had climbed onto the windowsill and now sat on the other side of the glass like a sprite from an urban fairy tale.

Alistair yanked open the window. "Well, just come in, Peeping Tom," he said.

DX jumped in. She was dressed in leather (probably vegan) chaps and vest and studded belt that wrapped around her breasts and crotch.

"You look like a gladiator," Alistair said.

DX carried a wooden jewelry box. "It's almost like prostitution, but I'm glad you've got some kissing principles," she said cheerfully. "All that white. It's like you're a child bride and your family sold you into an arranged marriage, and now your new family is going to melt that dress down and sell it for money to put your brothers through school."

"DX, stop," Alistair said.

"Do you think they'll actually make you sleep together?" DX asked.

"Of course they won't," Alistair said.

DX stalked around the room, the jewelry box balanced on her upturned hand.

"What are you wearing?" Avery asked. "They're going to kick you out. There's a dress code."

"For your fake wedding? Tragic," DX said. "Don't worry. I'm not sticking around to watch you throw away your chance at love. There's a guy down in Monterey who will hook a fishing line through your tongue and drag you around behind his trawler, and I think I'm going to do that this afternoon instead. More fun." She clicked her tongue.

"Avery's going through a hard time," Alistair said. "Either step up and be a friend or get out of here. Merritt left her. Remember? Don't make her feel worse."

"She wouldn't fight for us," Avery said quietly. "I wasn't worth it to her."

"She's a lesbian," DX said. "It's like a monastic order. The whole marriage thing threw her off. It's called epigenetic memory. She's probably never been dumped for a man, but think about all the lesbians who have. She's inherited their trauma."

It was usually Avery who corrected DX, but she was too sad, so Alistair performed that futile task.

"That implies Avery comes from a long line of lesbians, like they all share the same DNA. You know that's not how it works, right?"

"And here Avery is"—DX waved her hand dismissively—"picking Alistair King again."

"Avery told her she'd quit the show," Alistair said with exasperation in his voice. "And I tried to tell Merritt too, but she wouldn't take my calls. I wasn't going to let Avery throw away the love of her life. This is Merritt's fault."

"It's not her," Avery said. "She's just been hurt so many times."

Alistair and DX weren't listening.

"But it's so much bigger than that," DX said. "You don't get symbolism. Yeah, you guys are adorable, but what does it all mean? I'm an artist. I get it. This wedding symbolizes everything Merritt's lost."

"I know symbolism," Alistair said. "I worked in the mines. You get one tattoo for your girl, one for each baby, one for your dad when he dies and another for your mom, and then one day the pick throws a spark and someone gets a tattoo for you."

"Merritt is not asking Avery to work in the mines in Wyoming," DX said.

"She's asking Avery to do the impossible," Alistair said. "She's asking Avery to promise nothing bad is ever going to happen."

"She's not asking me anything," Avery said. "It's just over."

"She's asking her to do indie films or local theater," Alistair said as though the Wyoming mines were preferable.

Avery had a sudden image of a simple soundstage and a bunch of hipsters drinking coffee and laughing. Merritt would be there. Maybe she would help build a set or run lights. After filming they'd all go out, and Avery would curl up in a booth at the Doug Fir Lounge with Merritt by her side. Everyone would know they were lovers. No one would mind.

"Merritt wants her to live an authentic life," DX went on. "Avery could do anything. She could open a line of legal weed shops or breed designer piranha. You can genetically modify them so they glow in the dark. Avery is a talented woman. She could do a lot of things."

Alistair's personal assistant appeared at the door. "We've got thirty minutes till go," she said.

"We're almost ready," Alistair said, and his assistant disappeared again.

DX held up the box she had been carrying.

"Guess what you get to do after this is all over. They have a room with all the presents fans sent you, and you have to pose for a picture with each one. I bet they made you stuff with macramé."

"They're nice," Avery said.

She wasn't looking forward to sitting in her wedding dress for hours while someone snapped photos of her with the presents. But her fans were sweet. She could guess the contents: knitted potholders and kids' drawings. Little bits of normal people's lives. Maybe her wedding made them happy. Maybe they were a little kinder to their spouses because they believed in King and Crown's love story.

"I dug around to see if there was anything I wanted," DX said. "I found this."

The box was inlaid with gold filigree but scuffed and dented like it had traveled the seas. DX set it in Avery's lap.

"I don't think that thing should touch your dress," Alistair said, but he was leaning over to examine the box.

It was old and battered and more beautiful because of the walnut-colored stains in the grain of the wood. Hope expanded in Avery's chest like a balloon. She ran her hand over the top.

"Did you buy this?" she asked DX.

"I told you. I stole it from your gift table."

Avery stared at DX, trying to read her eyes, which, of course, she couldn't because they were hidden behind mirrored sunglasses and an explosion of dark curls.

"You have to tell me." Avery's voice trembled. "You have to tell me if you bought this."

If it was another one of DX's stunts—if she opened the box and it contained tickets to Antarctica or a tiny replica of DX's kidney—the disappointment would kill her. She would slide down into her gown and suffocate. That must have happened at least once in the history of Delicata Vagrant wedding dresses.

DX lifted the lid.

It wasn't from DX. It was the one present even DX couldn't procure.

Inside lay Merritt's locket, open to the two photographs: the stern woman with a jaw like George Washington and the delicate girl with the high lace collar. She thought she smelled a hint of cedar. She turned the locket over. On the back, engraved in fine cursive script, were the words *I'd rather have the future.*

"These presents have been coming in for weeks," Avery said. "This could have been at Marlene's office for months. Was there a postmark?" She had missed Merritt's gift! "If she thinks..."

Calls, e-mails, and presents had been coming in at such a spectacular rate, Marlene had stepped in to manage the deluge, but that meant she had had access to Avery's phone. She had read her mail, organized her wedding presents. Had she deleted Avery's messages? Merritt had sent the locket. She had sent this token, this offer, this invitation to love and had heard nothing back. Avery could see Merritt sitting at the counter of Hellenic Hardware, scanning the mail, fiddling with her cell phone, waiting. And nothing. Which is what Merritt always expected.

She thought DX and Alistair might be talking. Maybe they had asked her if she was all right. She couldn't hear them. Avery closed the locket and squeezed it in her hand.

"I don't want to do this," she whispered.

She remembered taking Merritt back to her father's house shortly after they met. They were sixteen. Merritt had seemed so debonair, so grown-up, Avery had hesitated to invite her for a sleepover. She'd felt like a kid compared to Merritt, but Merritt had accepted quickly. After Avery's father had gone to bed, they had stood out on the deck drinking coffee, watching the city below, and talking. *You're so pretty. Why aren't you dating?* Avery had asked. Merritt had tossed her scarf over her shoulder and looked up at the cold October sky. *There's only one person you can count on.* Avery had thought, *I'm going to change your mind.*

She had failed again.

"I don't want to get married." Had she said it out loud, or was she dreaming?

DX and Alistair were still arguing like siblings at a holiday dinner.

"I just see more possibilities than you do," DX said.

"DX, you shred everything you touch," Alistair said.

"I break things that need to be broken."

I don't want to do the show, Avery thought. With or without Merritt, she was done.

"I don't want to do the show." She heard bagpipes start up in the garden. "I'm sorry, Alistair. I love you. I love what we do, but I've loved her since I was sixteen." The Delicata Vagrant wedding dress squeezed her like a giant white anaconda. "I want my own life." She could not imagine how the strapless gown stayed up except that it was taped to her with industrial-strength adhesive. "I need to go outside," Avery gasped. "I want to be out. I want her to be proud of me. I want *this* wedding with her." She clutched the antique locket to her chest. "I can't breathe without her."

"Avery?" Alistair turned toward her in slow motion.

She drew in a breath. The dress just tightened around her. She could exhale, but she could not take in more air. Outside, the bagpipes were playing "Here Comes the Bride," but it was too early because there was no one to carry her dress, and she could not walk without help.

DX cocked her head. Alistair stood frozen.

"I can't breathe," Avery gasped.

"You wanted this," DX said. "Nobody forced you into that monstrosity."

"I really can't breathe! Alistair, help me." The edges of her vision were going dark. "DX...DX, it's my fault." Avery swayed on the divan. "She sent this to me."

The locket slipped from her hand. Her field of vision shrank down to a single point of light, like looking into the front of a camera lens.

"Alistair, I'm sorry. I can't..."

Suddenly, Alistair was spinning her around, pulling at the pearl buttons on her dress. They were buried in lace.

"You're okay," he said. "You're okay. DX, call someone!"

Alistair wrestled with the closure.

Avery heard her own voice as if from outside her body. "There are three hundred and sixty-five buttons. It's symbolic."

"DX, get me a knife. I'm going to cut this dress," Alistair yelled.

"Why would I have a knife?"

"You have a military helicopter. You have drug lords' phone numbers! Why don't you have a knife?"

DX's answer was lost in the sound of ripping seams, as Alistair sent three hundred and sixty-five pearl buttons spraying across the room.

"Oh my God. That's a Delicata Vagrant wedding dress," DX said.

Avery caught her breath. The room came slowly back into focus.

"Can you forgive me?" Avery asked Alistair.

He sat beside her, his massive arm wrapped around her bare shoulders. The silence stretched between them as long and wide as the Pacific Ocean.

"Aves, I know you. I see you. Your heart broke when we left Portland. You're great on camera, and your fans love you, and Venner thinks we're better than ever. But it's no good if you're not happy. If you're not happy, it's not *King and Crown*. And I know you were protecting me. I know I haven't been good with money and you think you owe me something because I worked hard to get here. But I'm from Stone. I grew up in the mines. They took us down there when we were kids so we could see where our dads worked. There's nothing in this world"—he gestured to the divan and the large room that was supposed to be theirs even though they had never seen it before that day—"like being ten when they shut off the lights in the mines to show you your future. After Stone, everything is easy. I'll be fine."

"But what will you do?"

"I always wanted to do a food show."

"Can you forgive me for picking her?"

Alistair put his other arm around her and pulled her close. His body was as familiar as the Hollywood hills, but she knew this would be the last time he held her like this. They'd be friends. They would hug. But not like this.

"You're my best friend," Alistair said. "I want you to be happy."

A knock on the door signaled the arrival of the six teenage models who would carry Avery's dress.

"Can we tell them I got sick?" Avery asked.

"I think we have to tell them it's off," Alistair said.

"But what about our contracts? What about Merritt's contract? What if they go after her or after you?"

Alistair smiled sadly and put his hands over hers. "They last until the end of the show, and the show ends when you quit. E-mail Venner, Greg, your mom, the casting producer, legal, the other executive producers."

"You can do it from the helicopter," DX said. "It's the last day of summer. There's that dance at Merritt's shop." She pulled out her cell phone and checked the time. "It's five o'clock. I can get you there by midnight. I'll get the band to cause a distraction. We run."

"You flew a Russian military helicopter to my wedding?" Avery asked.

"I landed a fifty-two-foot helicopter on a sixty-square-foot lawn. I am a goddess of war."

"What about you?" Avery asked Alistair.

Alistair rose. He looked impossibly elegant in his suit. "I think I might rent an old Ford and take a trip up north."

"Wyoming," Avery said.

"Yeah."

"You want to go back to Wyoming?" DX asked. "I'll take you. We'll drop Avery off and then we'll go land in some massive snowstorm with the lights on, and everyone in—where do you live? Pit? Stick?—will think it's UFOs, and then *BAM*, it's you."

"I am not going to be the asshole who shows up in Stone in a helicopter."

"But you *are* the asshole whose friend flies the most epic retrofitted military helicopter in American airspace," DX said without a hint of criticism in her voice. "We're all that asshole. Whatever. I don't want to be like one of those douchebag Quotable Cushions you two are always hawking on my Twitter feed, but I'm going to say it. *Forgiveness is the sunshine that dries the rain.* You just have to be who you are and hope everyone forgives you for it. You're not going to get a better offer. That's life."

Avery looked down at the remains of her dress. "Will she forgive me?"

"I don't know," DX said. "But you have to try."

"I have to go home and change."

"Forget that." DX was already heading for the door. "I have some latex body paint in the helicopter. You'll be fine."

"I have to wear the dress she gave me."

DX paused midstride. Her face lit with something Avery had not seen for a long time: approval.

Chapter 34

O h my gosh, it's like everything you learned you learned from Avery Crown!" Lei-Ling exclaimed.

Iliana put a hand on Merritt's shoulder.

It was the last day of summer, and they were standing on the newly cleared dance floor that surrounded the Helen of Troy fountain. Tate Grafton, from the Pride House board, had joined them. Some interns had too.

"Wow," Tate said as she surveyed the interior of Hellenic Hardware with a look of apprehension.

"Don't worry. It's all properly wired," Merritt said. "I've shut off the power to the back of the shop so we don't blow a fuse."

"It's not that. Everyone will love it." Tate eyed the artificial cherry trees Merritt had fashioned out of scrap metal and pink Christmas lights. "It looks great. It's just not what I expected from you."

"I know."

Merritt hadn't meant to buy a small welding station and weld together twelve cherry-tree frames in honor of Portland springtime. She hadn't meant to circle the fountain with fake grass. Or powder coat the concrete sculpture of Helen of Troy in opalescent silver. Or replicate the Portland White Stag sign in neon tubing. She should probably have canceled the Nostalgia-rom and just donated the decorating budget to the Pride House. It looked like hipsters had made love in her fountain. It looked like...*King & Crown* had been there.

"It's a feminine aesthetic," Lei-Ling told Tate knowledgeably. "Merritt just did a whole season with *King and Crown*, and she and Avery totally hit it off...again, because they were friends before. And this is totally Avery Crown."

Merritt had even used a can of *King & Crown* paint. She hadn't meant to. She had sent one of the interns to the store for paint, and when she pulled it out of the paper bag, Avery and Alistair's cartoon faces had grinned out at her, their eyes sparkling with drawn-on stars. She had almost dropped it on her foot.

"You okay?" Tate asked, half joking, half serious.

"No. Yeah. Of course. Decorating is great stress relief," Merritt said.

Stress relief. Stress was finding out the interns had been polishing bronze pieces with vinegar instead of mineral oil. Stress was arguing with contractors over the tile work in the entryway of the Elysium. She could handle stress without cracking a beer. This was like waiting for spring and then realizing it was going to rain forever. The only spring she was going to get were the scrap-metal trees.

"Well, it looks great," Tate said. "We've got the bartender setting up at six. Catering at seven. Doors open at eight." She ran through logistics.

When Tate left, Iliana said, "Now you can relax, right?"

Lei-Ling stepped onto the dance floor and spun around, arms flying. Above her, nets of white lights covered the dark skylights.

"I think you guys should totally be friends again," Lei-Ling said. "I think Avery has a girl crush on you. She was like, 'Where's Merritt? What does Merritt think? Doesn't Merritt look amazing?'"

Merritt glanced at Iliana. She had not told Lei-Ling. Lei-Ling had loved *King & Crown* since she was in elementary school. And Merritt had seduced Avery, slept with her, almost dated her, and lost her through her own stupidity, and faithful Iliana had never said a word.

"They're getting married today. Avery and Alistair." Lei-Ling stopped twirling suddenly. "Oh! I bet it's on Twitter." She pulled out her phone in its pink Hello Kitty case. "Oh, she looks so beautiful!"

The picture showed Avery in a wedding gown the size of an iceberg. Merritt felt like she had been hit by an iceberg.

"Gaudy," she said, and passed the phone back to Lei-Ling.

"She looks sad," Iliana said.

"Why would she be sad?" Lei-Ling cooed. "She's marrying Alistair King."

Merritt glanced at Iliana, who looked pained. It wasn't fair. Iliana told Lei-Ling everything.

"Lei-Ling," Merritt said. "Can I talk to you about something?"

Lei-Ling was flicking through pictures. "Look at these presents. They say Avery and Alistair have been getting presents every day since they announced their engagement, and they're all here. That's, like, a thousand presents!"

"Lei-Ling." Merritt put her hand over Lei-Ling's phone.

Lei-Ling's expression changed suddenly. Her mouth formed a perfect, adorable O of surprise.

"You mean really talk? Of course we can really talk, Merritt. I always want to really talk to you. What is it?"

Merritt sat down on the bench beneath the gazebo. "Can I tell you something and you'll promise not to tell anyone?"

"Of course."

"It's important. If you did tell someone, anyone who might spread it around, someone I...care about could get really hurt."

Merritt wondered if getting outed would hurt Avery as much as she had hurt her. She thought of Avery's clumsy, spontaneous kisses. How many times had Merritt turned her down while Avery was in Portland? And yet Avery had launched herself at Merritt again and again, at the possibility of happiness. No wonder Lei-Ling liked her. They had a lot in common.

"I'll never say anything to anyone," Lei-Ling said earnestly. "Iliana can tell you. I keep secrets."

"Avery and Alistair aren't really a couple," Merritt said

slowly. "I mean, they are getting married, but it's just for the show."

Lei-Ling's eyes shone with the delight of newly acquired celebrity gossip, and Merritt almost stopped. But Lei-Ling scooted in beside her and set her phone down.

"What is it?" Lei-Ling asked.

"You know how Vita was convinced I had a crush?"

"Yeah."

"It was Avery." There. That wasn't so hard. It was just a passing crush. "I asked Iliana not to tell you because if people find out about Avery, her career is over. But you and Iliana are beautiful together, and I'm happy for you, and I don't want her to keep secrets from you."

Lei-Ling cocked her head to one side, her eyes surprisingly discerning behind fronds of pink mascara. "You didn't just have a crush on her."

"I didn't just have a crush on her," Merritt said.

"And that's why you're so sad."

"It's over," Merritt said. "It was just a summer thing."

Merritt wanted Iliana and Lei-Ling to stop looking at her. She had done her part. She had told Lei-Ling. Now Lei-Ling and Iliana could go forward into a happy, secret-free marriage. If they would stop looking at her.

"Really, I'm back in the game," Merritt said. If the game was waiting for her heart to wither like the last leaves on the winter trees, she was in the game. "I'll probably meet a girl tonight."

"You'll win Avery back." Lei-Ling brightened. "She still loves you, and you'll tell her how you feel, and she'll come back."

Lei-Ling: the unwounded Inner Child, her face like a little moon lit with love and happiness and optimism. Merritt wanted to tell Iliana to wrap Lei-Ling up in Bubble Wrap and protect her for as long as she possibly could.

"No," Merritt said. "That's not our story."

Chapter 35

Merritt did not dress for the Nostalgia-rom. There was too much to do, and there was no one to impress. She half expected Lei-Ling to protest that she just *had* to dress up because her next true love might be there, and it would be best if her next true love met her in a retro 1980s prom dress. But Lei-Ling didn't say anything. As the dance started, Merritt stood at the edge of the dance floor watching the space fill with people. Sporty, young butches flirted with femmes, and femmes took selfies with the cherry blossoms. A boy with purple hair waltzed with a man in a three-piece suit.

The Pride House kids had decided to simplify human interaction with color-coded, glow-stick bracelets. Green was for single. Dark blue was dating. Unfortunately, they had more designations than colors in their Dollar Store glow-stick packs, so they had complicated the symbolism like a New York subway map. Orange was polyamorous. But double orange was *prefers not to answer.* And double purple meant *questioning but leaning toward gay.* Everyone was ringed in neon.

It looked magic; Merritt could see it even if she couldn't feel it. If there were a magic wardrobe to another world, it would be here. But there wasn't. She knew because she'd swept every inch of the shop. She'd cataloged every chifforobe. She'd priced every lamp, and eventually she would sell every piece.

* * *

Near midnight, the DJ cut in with a few more words about the Pride House and the promise of more dancing. Merritt leaned against a Veltar woodstove, fiddling with her phone. A few months ago she would have picked up one of the girls on the opposite wall. Now she couldn't even tell which ones were pretty. They all were. She didn't care.

From across the room, Lei-Ling exclaimed, "Oh!" She stood on tiptoes peering out one of the rainy windows.

Merritt glanced up from her phone. The mood of the crowd had changed. People were only half dancing. A collective whisper traveled around the room. Everyone was looking at the door. Merritt wasn't interested in whatever drag-queen finale the Pride House kids had arranged. She turned back to her phone, scanning a website of antique chandeliers without really looking at anything.

From across the room, Lei-Ling called out, "Merritt, look."

It had to be a mistake, a trick of the light, an illusion to cut Merritt one more time. Avery was standing on the other side of the dance floor. Merritt gasped. It was her! Merritt felt too many emotions swirl through her: love, hope, tenderness, shame. Avery had always made Merritt feel too much. Merritt's heart was full of crows sitting on power lines, and crows and power lines worked for her, except that when she looked at Avery, she was a little girl on the deck of her stepfather's yacht again. She was a teenager contemplating another Thanksgiving alone. She was thirty-three, and her best friend had gotten married, and she wanted her own sweetheart to come home to, and she wanted it to be Avery.

The vintage dress Merritt had bought for Avery all those years ago still fit her perfectly. She looked like a ghost. A bride from 1890. The girl Merritt had expected at the Vale Academy prom.

One of the interns followed behind Avery with an armload of glowing bracelets. The boy was trying to explain the color system, holding up a variety of options that might have meant *pansexual, atheist vegetarian,* or *single libertarian seeking nonsmoker.* Avery waved him away gently.

When she reached Merritt, she said something. But Merritt could not hear her because she had stopped breathing. The locket hung at Avery's neck. Did it mean what Merritt wanted it to mean? Avery was going to open up her chest like an antique birdcage, reach inside, take out her heart, and drop it on the floor. Then she would leave. Again. It was too much. The sleepless nights. The yearning in her body that was so at odds with the cool detachment she wanted to feel. The jangle of Avery's voice mail. The hope she had felt as she'd mailed the locket. Then the stretching disappointment when she'd heard nothing back. The knowledge that a woman who wouldn't return her calls would not fall for a silver-plated trinket. The silence had been so expected and so crushing. Tears pressed at the back of Merritt's eyes. She tried to blink them back, but they weren't blinking tears. She couldn't hold her breath to stop them.

"I love you," Avery said.

"I called you," Merritt whispered. "That's the dress. That's the locket." She reached out and touched the tip of one finger to the cool metal. "I sent you the locket and you didn't say anything."

"I didn't know," Avery said. "TKO just took over. I knew Venner and my mom were monitoring my calls, watching out for publicity offers and stalkers. But I didn't know... I think they deleted half the messages. They owned my phones, my mail, my life. They did until today."

"You got married."

"I didn't."

"I saw it on Twitter."

"That's not real."

"Are you?" Merritt whispered.

Avery was very close. Merritt could smell her sweet, familiar perfume.

"If you come back and then you want to leave..." Merritt managed. "I wanted to belong to someone. I wanted a home. I wanted to matter. If this isn't real, you can't ask. Please don't ask me."

"Ask what?"

Merritt turned her back to Avery and the crowd with

their cell phones raised, eager to capture every moment of this fabulous celebrity spectacle. Merritt had said it too loud. Someone would hear. It would be on the Internet like a wildfire.

"They'll see you," Merritt said.

"Ask what, sweetheart?" Avery turned Merritt gently, her hands on Merritt's shoulders.

Merritt felt tears spill unbidden down her cheeks. "If you ask me to go home with you," Merritt said as quietly as she could, "I'll go. I won't be able to say no. But if you leave again, I won't make it, Avery. I'm not strong. I was wrong to push you away, and I want you so much..."

The part of Merritt that was still cognizant of the thirty or forty people watching her tried to suck back her tears and return her face to its usual cool. But her composure was a can of ball bearings spilled across the floor. She sobbed. She was a thirty-three-year-old woman crying *at her prom*. And Merritt did the only thing sad girls at prom can do. She ran. She didn't need to see to flee. She had memorized every crack in the floor and every piece of hardware. Hellenic Hardware was as familiar as a lover. For years she had thought Hellenic Hardware was the only love that would last. After all these years of loneliness and longing, the thought that it might be Avery was too wonderful to hope for. It was like looking into the sun.

She knelt down and fumbled blindly for the lever that raised the garage doors. It would be a dramatic exit. She couldn't help it. But she didn't make it out either. Somehow Avery was in front of her, kneeling on the floor, taking Merritt's hand off the lever. Then Avery's arms were around her.

"I won't leave. That's why I'm here. To tell you. I won't leave again. I just got the locket today. Sweetheart, I left the second I got it. It was rerouted through our PR firm. I left the wedding. DX landed a helicopter in your parking lot, and there is no show."

"If you lose the show, you'll hate me," Merritt said, but she was already giving in to Avery's embrace. It felt so good. She buried her face in Avery's hair.

"The show is over." Avery held her close. "I don't hate you. I gave it up. I quit. I wanted to. And I didn't give it up just for you. I love you so much that I would have, but I want my own life too. I want my own face and my own hair and my own phone. I don't want to be managed. I want to be out, and I want you."

Avery's words sank in slowly. Merritt pulled away. It took her a moment to recognize the expression on Avery's face. It was fear. Avery looked stricken. Her lips trembled. Her cheeks were pale.

"Please say yes, Merritt," she said. "I know I'm late. I'm so, so late." Avery clutched the back of Merritt's head, holding their faces close enough to kiss. "Please don't let me be too late. Please, Merritt. I know I don't get another second chance. Give me one anyway."

Slowly Merritt stood up and drew Avery up with her.

"I love you," Avery said.

"I love you," Merritt echoed.

"Do you love me enough?" Avery whispered.

Merritt wiped her eyes. "Enough for what?"

"To forgive me."

Merritt kissed her, her lips still wet with their shared tears. Their kiss deepened. *She's here!* Merritt thought.

"If you had only picked up your own phone, I would have told you that I'd be your trainer." Merritt couldn't help but laugh. At herself. At her life. At the crowd of Portlanders starting to wrestle with the desire to post the whole scene online and the desire to preserve *safe space*. "I would have been your cousin, your florist, your personal shopper."

"But I want you to be my girl," Avery said.

Merritt took Avery's hand. They looked at each other. Avery laughed too.

"I'm a mess," Avery said.

"Maybe we're just right." With that, Merritt turned to the crowd. She lifted Avery's hand. "Please welcome the lovely Avery Crown."

The crowd cheered.

"Old friends," Merritt said.

Avery turned and rested her head on Merritt's chest. "Old friends," she said.

"You gave up the show," Merritt said incredulously.

"You engraved the locket." Avery touched her throat. "And those decorations. They're so pink. They're so bright."

"I haven't slept since you left," Merritt said. "I didn't know what to do."

Avery squeezed Merritt tighter. "So you crafted."

"I welded," Merritt said with mock indignation. "Those trees are pure steel."

* * *

That night Merritt took Avery to the apartment in the Elysium.

"You didn't take down any of the decorations," Avery said, looking around.

"Of course not. They reminded me of you."

Merritt led Avery down the long lawn carpet into the bedroom. She touched the switch that turned the curtains into the northern lights. Looking at the crazy decor, she knew the truth. "I would have waited forever because I love you."

"I love you," Avery whispered.

"They're not bad," Merritt added. "These curtains. The lamps. I feel like I'm somewhere special. I am."

Slowly, Merritt turned Avery around and unbuttoned the back of Avery's dress with the care of an antiques dealer.

"How many buttons does the dress have?" Avery asked as Merritt slipped it off Avery's hips.

"I don't know. Twenty maybe." She turned Avery back to her and kissed her. "Why?"

"Alistair cut me out of a Delicata Vagrant wedding dress. I think that's a felony in California."

"Was he mad that you quit?"

"He understood."

Merritt kissed Avery's forehead, then her neck, then the curve of her shoulder. And as much as she needed Avery's skin on hers, she couldn't rush. This was her lover, her friend. Hers and not hers. Merritt unhooked Avery's bra and eased her lace underwear down to the floor. Then Avery undid each button on Merritt's shirt, and with each button Merritt felt her desire grow. And when Avery unhooked the button on her slacks and the zipper, touching her more than undressing required, Merritt wanted to pick Avery up and press her against the wall. She wanted to pull Avery down onto the green carpet. She wanted to hear Avery beg. At the same time, she felt shy. She wanted to be claimed, loved, handled. She wanted Avery to lead her to pleasure. Merritt leaned forward, her forehead resting against Avery's shoulder, frozen in place by a flood of feelings.

"Come here," Avery said.

The bed sparkled with heart-shaped sequins. Avery turned down the covers. It felt different kissing Avery now that she was out. Their kiss felt deeper. Avery's body felt closer. Her desire felt more urgent and more patient at the same time.

"I'll never leave," Avery whispered as she kissed her way down Merritt's chest. Avery lingered on both her breasts, kissing Merritt's nipples until Merritt arched to meet her. Then she kissed down Merritt's stomach, parted Merritt's legs, and stroked her open with her fingers. Merritt held her breath as Avery pursed her lips, holding Merritt's clit in velvet softness, encompassing her completely in the most intimate embrace. Avery stayed like that for a few seconds longer than Merritt thought she could bear; then Avery sucked, pulling a cry from deep within Merritt's chest. Avery circled that bright swelling with her tongue, and Merritt felt breathless and dreamy at the same time.

A jumble of memories filled Merritt's mind: the Vale cafeteria, Avery's first car, the deck of the yacht, Uncle Oli waving from his balcony. Then Avery's kisses grew more forceful, and Merritt could not think of anything besides pleasure. Avery penetrated Merritt with her tongue and drew Merritt's whole sex into her mouth. The feeling was irresistible. And it wasn't just the physical pleasure. Avery kissed Merritt as though she were guided by Merritt's racing heart. Merritt didn't have to resist, and Avery nursed every pulse of Merritt's orgasm and then held her, kissing her temple, her forehead, and her hair. When Merritt had relaxed completely, Avery nuzzled her neck and said, "Was that really so hard, my love, to just give in?" Avery traced a heart on Merritt's chest. "If you have glaciers and power lines, I love them all. I love all of you."

Then Merritt was ready to take the lead again, not because it was easier to hide her heart on top, but because Avery's chest was flushed with desire. And Merritt knew exactly how to comfort that need and to stoke it. She knew Avery, and she loved her. This beautiful woman. Her lover. Her future. Her oldest friend.

Epilogue

$\mathbf{M}$erritt Lessing stood behind the camera watching Avery on a small screen. Avery stood near a window in the old factory building, staring out over the river.

"It's been worth it," she said, "because we're here, because we made it."

Avery was playing Faith Cohen, a homeless woman trying to make her way back to her mother in Baltimore. She'd arrived, and in a devastating tribute to the plight of the homeless and the destruction of inner cities, she had found her childhood home replaced by a burned-out warehouse. Even the crew had teared up at Avery's performance. Avery's silent-movie-star beauty played perfectly in the bleak landscape.

Portland's infant film scene was growing up. The director had already had one hit that had broken out of the indie film scene into the mainstream. This one was slated for the Oscars.

"Cut," the director called. "That's—" He scrolled back

through the last seconds of footage, listening with three fingers pressed to his headset. "It's perfect. That's a wrap, folks. Well done!"

The crowd of actors and crew members cheered. A safe distance away from the equipment, someone popped a champagne cork. Some of Avery's costars rushed over and hugged her.

A moment later Avery flew into Merritt's arms. "How was it?" she asked breathlessly.

"You are incredible!" Merritt said.

Avery planted a kiss on Merritt's lips. "I thought you were working today."

"And miss the wrap?"

"I told you it would be another day before we finished the warehouse scenes."

"And I knew you'd be fabulous and finish early. Anyway, I have a surprise for you," Merritt said.

It had all worked out perfectly, although she had been so eager to see Avery's delight she had almost spilled the secret a dozen times. Merritt glanced up at the concrete balcony that overhung the warehouse floor.

Alistair leaned on the railing, his golden hair smoothed perfectly over his forehead.

"You were amazing, my dear," he called down.

"Alistair!" Avery beamed. "How...?" She looked at Merritt. "Alistair, you're supposed to be eating oysters in Boise or pigs' feet in Santa Cruz."

"Oysters in Santa Cruz and pigs' feet in Kansas City."

Alistair had launched the top-grossing food show, *Food*

Cart Fool. And with Alistair's promise that she'd never have to be away from Iliana for more than twenty days at a time, Lei-Ling had joined him. They were perfect. Tiny, adventuresome Lei-Ling popping sea urchins in her mouth like Cheetos. Alistair, the mining-town boy who wanted to live on See's chocolates and King Cobra, squeezing his eyes shut as he placed garlic-roasted crickets on his tongue.

Alistair jogged down a flight of apocalyptic-looking stairs and hugged them both.

"You two," he said. "Look at you. You're disgustingly cute."

* * *

The wrap party for Silver Eye Productions was hosted in Merritt and Avery's new home. After Avery had returned, Merritt and Avery had lived in the Elysium for a few months. Merritt had teased Avery that she had too many shoes to live in an apartment, but when Merritt was being serious, she said she thought Iliana was right. It was time for her to start anew, to let the chi move through her, to rent Oli's apartment to someone who would make new memories there. Lei-Ling and Iliana—or rather Mrs. and Mrs. Koslov-Wu—seemed like the perfect people for the job.

Avery and Merritt had bought a craftsman-style bungalow at the foot of Mount Tabor, near the path. Together they had installed Portland keepsakes and antique chandeliers. Merritt had installed a mantel from a Columbia River steamboat. Avery had bought glowing lamps in the shape of mushrooms—

for the nature—and strung the houseplants with twinkling lights. They both loved it.

Now the backyard was lit with garlands of iridescent glass grapes. More antique chandeliers hung from tree branches. (The Land of Lamps had a never-ending supply.) Merritt had adorned the chandeliers with LED candles that flickered like the candles of yesteryear...only without the fire hazard. Platters of food and bottles of wine and Sadfire whiskey were passed up and down long tables set under an enormous willow tree. Behind the smell of salmon, barbecue, and vegan mushroom cassoulet, Merritt thought she smelled a hint of fall in the air. It was September again, this time a beautiful one. The air was warm and the river was slow. Dry leaves were starting to crunch underfoot. There was cool dew on the morning grass. The rains would start soon, but for the first time in her life, autumn did not make Merritt sad.

"No Global Body Biscuits?" Alistair asked as he raised a drink. "And no crickets. Thank, God!"

Lei-Ling and Iliana sat a few seats down the long table. Lei-Ling regaled a cameraman from the Portland production company with her visions for the next *Food Cart Fool* episode. He laughed as she described the exotic delicacies she would spring on Alistair. Iliana talked to one of the stunt doubles from Avery's film. She tapped a finger thoughtfully against her lips.

Merritt heard her ask, "So how does someone get into stunt doubling?"

"You're too old," Merritt called out.

"I practice," Iliana called back cheerfully. "Unlike some people. If you practice, you're never too old."

Avery leaned against Merritt, taking her hand beneath the table and laying her head on Merritt's shoulder. The band struck up. It was not DX but a local Portland band: six men with their hair tied up in topknots and very well-trimmed beards. That was probably for the best. Nothing would get set on fire. Anyway, Avery and Merritt were going on vacation with DX and Tony in Taha'a, but not without a stop at the oldest brick house in America.

"So what's next?" Merritt asked quietly.

"You," Avery said. "In our bed."

"I mean what film?" Merritt kissed Avery's nose. "You nailed your auditions. Which one will you take?"

"I don't know." Avery gazed up at the twilight sky. "I always worried about *what next.* What if *King and Crown* went off the air? What if I never got another audition? I'm not worried anymore. You're my next."

Merritt pulled her closer. "You're my always," she whispered into Avery's hair.

Their friends said they were corny. The word *unbearable* got thrown around, but Merritt didn't care. Plus, most of her single friends had told her that she and Avery gave them hope. *You two,* Vita had said. *If you two could sort it out after fifteen years, maybe we'll all make it in the end.*

Us? Merritt had protested. *Iliana and Lei-Ling aren't enough to give you hope?*

But she knew what Vita meant. Fifteen years. She did not feel like they had been dating for just over a year. She felt like they had been together since they were sixteen. They had just lost each other in the confusion of growing up, and now they had found each other again. For good. For always. Each day sweeter than the last.

"Hey, what's going on with Hellenic Hardware?" Alistair asked, clinking his glass against Merritt's to get her attention.

"It's still going strong," Merritt said. "But I'm thinking of doing a little rebranding. A little more theater, a little more staging... Avery's helping me."

Merritt had started by keeping the Nostalgia-rom trees. It had just felt right. Everyone kept a little bit of their prom with them. What they hoped for. What they loved. What they lost. Where they went next, and how it all worked out in a way they could never have guessed at eighteen.

Please see the next page
for an excerpt from Karelia Stetz-Waters's
Something True.

Chapter 1

It was late June, the kind of warm summer evening when hopeless romantics make bad choices about beautiful women. The twilight was all watery, yellow-blue brightness, and Portland glowed with the promise of warm pavement and cool moonlight. It was, as it turned out, a dangerous mix for Tate Grafton, who stood at the till of Out in Portland Coffee trying to make out what her boss had done to the change drawer.

"How is it possible," she called without looking up, "that you are eight dollars over, but it's all in nickels?"

Just then the wind chime on the door tinkled. It was because of that evening light that came from nowhere and everywhere at the same time and filled the city with a sense of possibility that Tate did not say, "Sorry, we're closed."

The woman who had just walked in wore her hair pulled back in a low ponytail and had the kind of sleek magazine blondness that Tate was required, as a feminist, to say she did not like. And she did not like it in magazines. But in real life, and in the dangerous twilight that filtered through the front window, the woman was very pretty. She did not carry anything. No laptop. No purse. Not even a wallet and cell phone clutched in one hand. Nor did she have room in the pockets of her tight jeans for more than a credit card. Tate noticed.

The woman stood in the doorway surveying the coffee shop, from the exposed pipes, to the performance space, to the mural of Gertrude Stein. Right down to the cracked linoleum floor. Then she strode up to the counter and asked for a skinny, tall latte with Sweet'N Low.

"I'll, um..." Tate ran her hand through her hair, as if to push it off her face, although the clippers had already done that for her. "I'll have to warm up the machines. It'll be a minute."

"I'll just take what's in the airpot," the woman said, still surveying the shop.

Tate filled a paper cup and squeezed a biodegradable corn-plastic lid on it. The woman drew a bill from the pocket of her crisp, white shirt. Tate shook her head.

"On the house. It's probably stale."

She was about to go back to counting the till when the woman asked, "How long has this been a coffee shop?"

Tate considered. "It opened as a bookstore in 1979. Then it closed for a few years in the early eighties, opened back up as a coffee shop in 1988, and it's been running since then. I think. I've been here for nine years."

Too long.

" 'Out in Portland Coffee.' " The woman read the side of her cup.

"Out Coffee," Tate said. "That's what everyone calls it."

"Any other businesses in the area?"

"There's Ron's Reptiles, the AM/PM, the Oregon Adult Theater."

Across the street, the theater's yellow letter board advertised HD FILM! STRIPPER SPANK-A-THON WEDNESDAYS!

From the back room, Maggie, the boss, called out, "They're all perverts."

The woman nodded and turned as if to leave. Then she seemed to reconsider.

"Are there any women's bars in the area?" She glanced around the shop again, her eyes sliding past Tate's, resting everywhere but in Tate's direction.

"There's the Mirage." Tate gave her directions.

"Is it safe to walk?"

"As safe as anywhere in the city."

As soon as the woman left, twenty-year-old Krystal—Maggie's surrogate daughter or pet project, depending on who you asked—popped out of the back room, where she had ostensibly been studying.

"I heard that," she said. "As safe as anywhere in the city." She hopped up onto the counter next to Tate.

"Get off the counter." Tate ruffled Krystal's short pink hair.

"Is my butt a health code violation?"

"Yes."

"Well, anyway," Krystal said, swinging her legs and kicking the cupboard behind her, "I heard that. She practically asked you to walk her. *Is it safe?*" Krystal imitated a woman's soprano with an added whine. *"Hold me in your big, strong arms, you sexy butch."*

"Ugh." Tate rolled her eyes. "Why is she still here?" she called to Maggie in the back room.

"She's part of our family, Tate!"

Kindhearted Maggie; something had happened in utero, and she had been born without the ability to understand sarcasm.

"Some family," Tate said, winking at Krystal and pulling her into a hug.

"Did you like her?" Krystal asked, pulling away from Tate.

"Who?"

"The woman who was just here."

"No." Tate turned back to the cash register and rolled a stack of nickels into a paper sleeve.

"Why didn't you go after her, like in the movies? She probably thought you were cute."

Like in the movies. That was always Krystal's question: Why isn't it like the movies?

"I'm *working*," Tate said with feigned annoyance. "She just wanted a coffee. Anyway, I just got dumped, remember?"

"So?"

In the quiet minutes between customers, Tate had been reading *The Sociology of Lesbian Sexual Experience.* Now Krystal pulled the book from behind the counter and flipped it open.

"'The Alpha Butch,'" she read. "'In this paradigm'"—she pronounced it par-i-di-gum—"'the femme lesbian is looking for a strong, masculine—but not manly—woman who can protect her against the perceived threat of straight society.' That's you!" Krystal sounded like a shopper who had just found the perfect accessory. "I bet that's why she came in here. She saw you through the window and she was like, 'I've got to meet this woman.'" Krystal closed the book and examined the woman on the cover. "You're way cuter than this girl."

It wasn't hard; the woman on the cover looked like a haggard truck driver from 1950.

"Aren't you supposed to be studying for the GED?" Tate asked.

"My dad taught me most of that stuff already, when I was, like, a little kid."

"Then take the test and go to college," Tate said.

"I don't need to, 'cause my dad and I are going to start a club, and I don't need a degree for that."

"Right."

"She was pretty," Krystal said. "Like Hillary Clinton if Hillary Clinton was, like, a million years younger."

Tate took the book from Krystal's hands and pretended to swat her with it. "I am not 'Alpha Butch.'"

Nonetheless, Tate did steal a glance at her face in the bathroom mirror before leaving the coffee shop. The woman's perfect good looks made her aware of her own dark eyebrows and her nose, which jutted out and then took a hook-like dive. She looked older than her thirty-five years. She looked tired after the long shift. And she did not feel alpha anything, even with her steel-toed Red Wings and her leather jacket.

She did not even feel beta, or whatever letter came next in Krystal's alphabet.

Still, a spring spent rebuilding the network of railroad-tie stair steps in the Mount Tabor Community Garden had defined the muscles beneath her labrys tattoo. She was tanned from the work. Her head was freshly shaved. And it was summer, one of those perfect summer nights that Portlanders live for, so warm, so unambiguously beautiful it made up for ten months of steady rain.

When Tate sidled up to the bar at the Mirage, her friend Vita, the bartender, leaned over.

"She's here," Vita said.

For a second Tate thought of the woman.

"Who?" she asked.

Vita shot her a look that said, *Don't pretend not to know when you've asked me about her every day for six months.*

Abigail. Tate could see her legs wrapped around the body of the cello, her hips splayed, her black concert skirt riding up, her orange hair falling over the cello's orange wood.

Vita plunked a shot in front of Tate. "On the house. She's with someone."

Tate knocked the shot back, nearly choking as her brain registered the taste a split second after it hit the back of her throat.

"What the hell was that?" She wiped her mouth.

"Frat Boy's Revenge. Jägermeister and grape vodka. I made one too many for the baby dykes in the corner."

Tate grimaced and cleared her mouth with a swig of beer. Then she noticed something: that indefinable feeling of being watched. She turned. At a table by the door, the woman from Out Coffee sat, one hand resting on the base of a martini glass, as though she feared it might fly away. She caught Tate's eye for a second, smiled, and then looked away with a shake of her head. When she looked up again, Tate raised her beer with a slight smile.

"God, you have it so easy!" Vita said, punching Tate on the arm.

Tate turned back to the bar. "She's not interested in me. Look at her."

"*You* look at her," Vita said, raising both eyebrows.

In the mirror behind the bar, Tate saw the woman picking her way through the tables, hesitating, looking from side to side as though puzzling her way through a maze.

"She's cute. Don't blow it," Vita said in a whisper the whole bar could hear.

"Hello." The woman took the stool next to Tate's. She sat on the very edge, as though ready to flee.

Vita leaned in. She looked predatory. Her hair was teased into a rocker bouffant, and she had on more leopard print than Tate thought was appropriate work attire, even at a bar.

"Will you be buying this lady a drink?" Vita asked Tate.

"I'm fine," the woman said. "I was just leaving."

At that moment Abigail appeared. Tate took in the sight: Abigail on the arm of Duke Bryce, drag king extraordinaire. Duke grinned, a big toothy grin, like an Elvis impersonator on steroids. Abigail clung to Duke's arm, a romance heroine hanging off the lesbian Fabio.

"Someone you know?" the woman asked.

"Knew."

A moment later Abigail released her lover and came over, an apologetic look on her face.

"I'm sorry. I didn't think I'd see you here. I mean, I was going to tell you about me and Duke, you know, earlier."

Tate shrugged. The music had dropped a decibel, and a few of the other patrons turned to listen.

"I mean, I know you're still really upset about the breakup. About us. Really, I wasn't looking for anything. I just saw Duke one day and presto!" Abigail's giggle made it sound like she had suddenly been transported back to seventh grade. "I thought I wanted someone who understood my music."

That had been the explanation when Abigail cheated on Tate with the oboist.

"But then I met Duke, and she's just so . . . brava."

Duke was an alpha butch, Tate thought. She could take a picture and show Krystal.

"I just know it all happened for a reason, Tate."

Tate was trying to think of a response to this when she was startled by a touch. The woman from the coffee shop had touched the back of her head. She ran her hand across Tate's cropped hair, then slid her fingertips down the back of Tate's neck. Then she withdrew her hand quickly.

"Who is she?" The woman's voice was much softer than it had been in the coffee shop, almost frightened.

Tate was still concentrating on the woman's touch, which seemed to linger on her skin. It had been six months since Abigail officially dumped her, but much longer since she had been touched like that. Abigail had never caressed her.

Abigail seduced her cello, everyone in the orchestra agreed, but she had squeezed Tate. Tate had always come away from their lovemaking feeling rather like rising bread dough: kneaded and punched down.

Now Tate stumbled over her words. "This is...this is Abby. She's a cellist."

The woman leaned closer to Tate, and Tate could smell a sweet perfume, like citrus blossoms, rising from her hair.

"What seat?" the woman asked Abigail.

This had been an important distinction that had always been lost on Tate.

"Third," Abigail answered defensively.

"Oh. Only third." The woman turned and, with a gesture even more fleeting than her fingers on Tate's neck, she pressed her lips to Tate's cheek.

Abigail mumbled something Tate did not catch and walked away, disappearing down the hallway that led from the bar to the dance floor. The woman straightened and crossed her legs.

"I'm sorry," the woman said. She took a large sip of her drink. "I don't do things like that. I just don't like all those freckles."

"Freckles?"

Tate had loved the beige-on-white-lace of Abigail's freckles. Plus, one couldn't hold someone's freckles against them. Or maybe, if one looked like this woman, one could.

"She reminds me of my sister." The woman spoke quickly. "The freckles and that whole 'I'm going to be nice to you, but I'm actually sticking the fork in' thing. 'You can't tell me to piss off because that would make you look like a jerk, even though I'm the one who's ruined your life.' I know that routine." The woman finished the rest of her martini in one sip.

Tate was still trying to figure out what to do with the feeling that suffused her body. The woman's touch, offered unexpectedly after months of abstinence and then just as quickly withdrawn, left her dizzy. She felt like she had just swallowed a bowl of warm moonlight. But she recovered her manners and held out her hand.

"My name is—"

The woman cut her off. "I don't want to know."

Tate withdrew her hand, the moonlight cooling. But as soon as she withdrew her hand, the woman grabbed it, holding on as though she were going to shake hands but lingering much longer than any handshake.

"I didn't mean it like that," she said.

She leaned forward, her perfect good looks furrowed by worry.

Behind the woman's head, Vita flicked her tongue between the V of her two raised fingers.

Tate widened her eyes, the only nonverbal cue she could flash Vita. *Embarrass me, and I will strangle you*, her eyes said. But she wasn't sure Vita was listening.

"It's not that I don't want to know you." The woman still held Tate's hand, now stroking the back of Tate's knuckles with her thumb. "It's just...I don't live here. I live a thousand miles away." The woman raised Tate's knuckles to her lips and kissed them. "Right now I don't want to be me."

"You're straight," Tate said.

Behind the woman's head, Vita mouthed, *So?!*

The woman said nothing.

"You've got a husband and two kids at home." Tate extracted her hand. "A husband with a shotgun and two kids who will spend thousands of dollars on therapy when they realize you weren't going to the PTA meetings at all."

The woman bowed her head and laughed. Tate could only see her dimples, suddenly apparent in the smooth face. *All right*, Tate thought. *I'll take it.* It was the first time in months that she had sat at the Mirage and not thought about Abigail. She hadn't even looked up to see if Abigail had come back in the room.

"I don't have any kids," the woman said. "I can promise you that. I was married once, but we divorced years ago, and I'm not straight. I just wanted one night where I'm not what I do or where I work or who I know, but that's silly, isn't it?"

Tate thought about Out Coffee. About Maggie, Krystal, Vita, and the Mount Tabor Community Garden Association. About her studio apartment off northeast Firline and the old Hungarian couple who lived in the unit below hers. She thought about Portland, with its mossy side streets and its glorious summers.

"If you're not who you know, where you work, where you live, who are you?" she asked.

"I'm this," the woman said, and took Tate's face in her hands and kissed her.

At first it was just a soft kiss, lip to lip. Then Tate felt the woman's hands tremble against her cheeks. Their lips parted. Her tongue found Tate's. Beneath the bar, their knees touched, and Tate felt the woman's legs shake as though she had run a great distance.

A second later Tate pulled away, but only because she wanted the woman, and she felt herself going down in the annals of barroom legend. She could already hear Vita's rendition of the story: *Tate just reached over and grabbed the girl, practically swallowed her. It was like she unhinged her jaw, and the girl's head was in her mouth. Bang! Like a boa constrictor.* Friends and customers would listen attentively, waving away Tate's protests. Who wanted a story about a lonely barista longing for summer romance when they could have Vita's tale about Tate Grafton, Python Lover?

"Would you like to play a game of pool?" Tate said, to get out from under Vita's grin and to give herself a moment to think.

She was not the kind of woman who picked up girls at the bar. Vita picked up girls. Vita had picked up so many women she remembered them by taglines like "The Groaner" or "Wooly Bicycle Legs." She often told Tate that Tate could do the same, if she would only "put out some effort." According to Vita, half the girls at the Mirage were in love with Tate. But Tate did not believe her, nor did she want an assortment of half-remembered encounters.

But she wanted this woman.

They moved toward the side of the bar where two pool tables stood on a raised platform under low-hanging lights.

"Are you any good?" she asked.

"I'm all right," Tate said.

The woman rolled her pool cue on the table to see if it was true.

"None of them are straight," Tate said.

"I suppose not." The woman glanced toward the door. "Not here."

Tate laughed.

"You break, then," the woman said.

Tate cracked the balls apart, sinking two solids and following with a third.

"So, if you won't tell me your name," Tate began. "Or where you live or what you do, what are we going to talk about?"

"We could talk about you."

The woman sank a high ball but missed her next shot. Her hand was unsteady, and she looked around the bar more than she looked at the table. She looked at *Tate* more than she looked around the bar—but only out of the corner of her eye.

"I already know where you work," she said, casting that glance at Tate and then looking down. "And I know that, prior to right now, you've had bad taste in women. So...what's your name? How long have you worked at the coffee shop?"

Tate took another shot and sank a ball.

"No," she said slowly. "I'll tell you what you tell me."

"Okay." The woman leaned over the pool table and her hair draped in a curtain over one side of her face. She took her shot but missed. "I learned to play pool in college with three girls who I thought would be my friends for life. We played at a sports bar called the Gator Club. And I don't know any of them now. They could be dead. They could be professional pool sharks." She leaned against the wall and surveyed the table. "How about you?"

"I learned to play here the summer I turned twenty-one," Tate said. She sank another ball and shot a smile in the woman's direction. "The table is off. It slopes. It's not fair, you being from out of town and all. I should give you a handicap."

"Tell me how it slopes and give me two out of three."

Tate had never been the kind of person who made bets or the kind of person who sidled up to beautiful women, looked down at them lustfully, and said things like, *What will you give me when I win?*

But apparently that was the kind of woman she was. Tonight. In the summer.

"What will you give me if I win?"

The woman did not step away. Or laugh. She rested one hand on Tate's chest, right over Tate's racing heart.

"I'll answer one question," she said. "About anything. I'll tell you one true thing. And if I win—it's that corner, right?—I want you to take me someplace."

"Where?"

"Someplace special. You've been playing pool here since you were twenty-one. You must know someplace no one goes. Someplace I wouldn't see otherwise. Something I'll remember."

"Okay."

They played in silence, standing closer than necessary, touching more than necessary. The woman seemed to relax, and her game got better. Tate won the first game but only just barely. The woman won the second, masterfully compensating for the uneven table. Tate was in line to win the third game but scratched on the eight ball. The woman laughed a sweet, musical laugh tinged with victory.

"Take me somewhere," the woman said.

At the bar, Vita pointed and mouthed, *You rock.* At a table near the door, Abigail leaned against Duke's leather vest and scowled. But Tate did not see them. She slipped her hand through the woman's arm and stepped out into the moon-light.

Acknowledgments

I used to think that writing was a solitary activity, ideally done in a tower by candlelight. Now I know that writing a book, like all worthwhile pursuits, takes a village, and the most important people in that village are the readers. Thank you, readers! Thank you for your e-mails, letters, and posts. Thank you for telling me how my books touched you. Thank you for reading. You're why I write!

Thank you to my writing partners, Alison Clement and Susan Rodgers, for your critique, encouragement, friendship, and community. Thank you to Bill and the Interzone for providing us with a place to meet. If I ever run out of quirky characters, I'll just take my eyes of the screen and look around.

Thank you to Anna Burke for reading my work and letting me fan-girl all over your novels. I'm kind of jealous that you're that young and that talented, but I'll let it slide if you keep writing.

Thank you to all my friends and colleagues at Linn-Benton Community College and to all the friends, near and far, who make my life rich. Thank you to the singers—LP, the

Revivalists, the Decemberists, Tegan and Sara, and so many more—whose music inspired me as I worked. Thank you to Sam Guy for help with social media, publicity, and generally keeping me up-to-date with the 21st Century.

Thank you to Portland—Stumptown, Bridgetown, P-Town, PDX, the Rose City, my urban love—for being just as curious and delightful as in the book. (Don't forget to visit the Peculiarium, folks! Thank you to Old Portland Hardware & Architectural for being the model for Hellenic Hardware, although Hippo Hardware played a role too. That's where the Land of Lamps comes from.

Thank you to director Dean Devlin and his crew for letting me hang out on set and learn just enough about film production to get the details wrong. Sorry, guys! I'm sure *King & Crown* is using the wrong cameras (but it's romance; we're in it for the feels. Thank you to John Friendlander for telling me to wear a vest with lots of pockets when I went on set, so I looked like the crew. I think it worked.

Thank you to Lambda Literary the Golden Crown Literary Society for all you do to support the lesbian writing community.

Thank you to Jane Dystel and her agency for being my friends in the wide world of publishing. Thank you to Madeleine Colavita and the staff at Forever Yours for making this book the best it could possibly be.

Thank you to my parents, Elin and Albert Stetz, for providing a beautiful model for happily ever after. And as always, thank you to my wife, Fay; when I heard my first love story, I started looking for you.

About the Author

Karelia publishes in several genres, but romance is her favorite. She is passionate about providing happy endings and a vision of redemptive love for readers of all orientations. Her novels include *For Good*, *Something True*, *The Admirer*, *The Purveyor*, and Lambda Literary Award and Golden Crown Literary Society finalist *Forgive Me If I've Told You This Before*.

She and her wife live in Oregon and have been together for nineteen years. Karelia has a BA in comparative literature from Smith College and an MA in English literature from the University of Oregon, and she currently teaches English at Linn-Benton Community College. Karelia loves to hear from readers, and you can find her at KareliaStetzWaters.com.

CPSIA information can be obtained
at www.ICGtesting.com.
Printed in the USA
FSHW012255041218
54236FS

9 781538 727034